LORENZO

THE UNSEEN UNDERGROUND

BERETTA

ABIGAIL DAVIES

Editing: Jennifer Roberts-Hall

Proofreading: Judy's Proofreading

Cover Design: Pink Elephant Designs

Formatting: Pink Elephant Designs

PROLOGUE

AIDA

My stomach rolled for what felt like the thousandth time that morning. Outwardly I was calm and collected, but inside I was a complete mess of emotions. I couldn't pinpoint which one was strongest. Regret? Sadness?

Maybe a mixture of both.

I placed my palm on my stomach to quell my nerves and stared at myself in the mirror. I shouldn't have agreed to this. I should have changed my mind.

But did I really have a choice?

From the time the first words were uttered, I knew my life had taken a turn—a turn I'd never expected. A turn I never wanted. But I was raised to confront challenges head-on—to never give in. So why did it feel like I was about to give away my entire life? Why did it feel like today would be the last day of the life I'd always dreamed of?

I inhaled a breath and gazed down at my shaking hands while trying to ignore the buzz of women around me. As soon as I'd opened my eyes this morning, everything had been a whirlwind of activity. The time ticked by, bringing me closer and closer to my final destination. It haunted me, promising that nothing would ever be the same again.

My finger smoothed over a bead on my white dress, causing a smirk to pull at my lips. The symbol of this dress was ironic. I wondered if the people around me truly believed I was a virgin? I may have been raised in an Italian family, but that didn't mean I'd saved myself for marriage.

Marriage.

Holy shit. I was about to get married.

My eyes widened, and the long fake lashes one of the women had applied to me poked me in the eye.

"Fuck," I murmured. Gasps echoed around me, but I didn't care. I was doing this for the family.

My family.

His family.

I ground my teeth together and stepped closer to the mirror. My face was made up to within an inch of its life, and I could have sworn I had cracks in my makeup where it was layered on so thick. "No." I shook my head and sidestepped the woman trying to push a veil into my hair. "No," I said, louder this time. "Out," I gasped, feeling the world starting to tilt beneath my feet. "Everybody but Noemi…get out."

I spun around, waiting for them to exit the room we were holed up in at the back of the church. Apparently, it was tradition in *his* family, but at this point, I didn't give a flying fuck.

"Aida——"

I held my hand up. "I mean it. Everybody out."

There was a pause and then, "You heard her." My big sister stepped closer to me. "Get out."

It was only seconds until the room was empty, leaving just me and Noemi, and it was in that second, I knew I'd made a mistake. Maybe I could run away and forget all of this ever happened? Maybe I could dye my hair and move to another country? Maybe I could——

No. I couldn't.

My family would be left behind, and I couldn't bear to think about what would happen to them if I left *him* standing at the altar. I was fucked either way.

"I hate my life," I groaned, turning back to the mirror and pulling off the fake lashes that weighed heavy on my eyes. I finally felt like I could actually open them properly. "I hate this dress. I hate this makeup." I threw my hands in the air. "I hate it all."

I knew I was acting like a teenager and not the twenty-year-old woman I was. *Twenty.* I scoffed. In a matter of hours, I'd be married off and have to live the rest of my life known as *his* wife. I was getting married to a man I barely knew. Sure, I knew *of* him, which also meant I knew exactly *who* and *what* he was. A dangerous man. A man who got every-thing he wanted.

Including me.

"I can't do this," I whispered.

"Aida." Noemi rushed forward and planted her hands on my shoulders. She was always the impul-sive one of the two of us. I was level-headed and planned things to a T. I even knew what college I'd be attending when I was nine years old. And yet, it had been *me* thrown into this situation. I didn't do well with change, and my entire life was about to be turned upside down.

"You can do this." She bent at her knees, so our eyes were level. "Think about what this will do for Mom and Dad. It'll change everything." *That was what I was afraid of.*

"But—"

"You can do it, Aida." She nodded, almost as if she was trying to do it for me. "I have an idea." She smiled, the kind of smile that told me she was about to go rogue, but at this point, I couldn't bring myself to care. My skin itched from the layers of material I was wearing, and the pins in my hair pulled on my scalp every time I moved. "Sit." She led me over to the chair I'd sat in for hours as people had transformed me into someone I didn't recognize.

"We don't have time," I huffed out as Noemi rushed across the room and came back with her bag. "It starts in ten minutes—"

"I only need five." She stood between me and the mirror as she pulled a wipe from the packet. "If he wants to marry you, then he needs to see the real you, not the you they all think he wants." She swiped the wipe over my cheeks and eyes, and I finally felt like I could move without cracking. I closed my eyes and let Noemi work her magic. She started with my face, then moved to my hair and pulled every pin out of my head. "There. All done."

I opened my eyes and stared in the mirror, only this time I actually recognized the woman staring back at me. A light layer of foundation along with a swipe of mascara and lip gloss was all I ever wore, and Noemi had stripped me right back to that. My wavy dark-brown hair came to the middle of my back, covering most of the lace on the huge dress.

Loud knocking rang on the door, followed by, "Aida, they're ready for you."

"One minute, Dad!" Noemi shouted. She pulled me up and dragged me to the screen I'd dressed behind. "Mom got you this the day we went dress

5

shopping," Noemi whispered. She pulled a box from under the chair and placed it on top. "Today isn't just about what he wants." She put her hands on either side of my face. "Make it about you too, baby sis. Don't let him decide the rest of your life." I heard her words loud and clear.

"Get changed." She undid the buttons on the back of my dress, winked, then stepped backward. "I'll see you out there."

The door clicked shut a couple of seconds later, and I reached down to open the box. My stomach rolled in excitement when I saw the simple dress I'd fallen in love with at the bridal shop. It only took me a minute to get out of the dress I hated and into the one I loved—a simple A-line with no sleeves, and intricate lace from my collarbone working down into the off-white material. It was a statement, one that I knew most of the people sitting in the church wouldn't appreciate, but it was me. It was my style.

"Aida?" Dad called again.

"Coming!" I took one final look at myself in the mirror, pushed the comb of the veil into my hair, then stepped toward the door.

I worked on autopilot as we walked to the big, ornate doors of the church. This was it. This was the moment everything would change.

"You're doing great," Dad murmured from next to me. He was dressed in a perfectly pressed suit, something that I'd never seen him wear before. I was used to his usual T-shirt and jeans while he worked in the food store he owned. Even on Sundays, when we all came to church, he only wore a shirt with his jeans. But that wouldn't suffice for today. Today I was getting married. I was about to promise vows to a man I barely knew. What the hell was I doing?

"I don't think I can do this," I whispered, glancing around to see if anyone heard. A few people were still milling about, but as soon as they went through the side door to the main part of the church, it was just my dad and me.

"Baby girl." He turned to face me fully and clasped my shoulders. His brown-eyed gaze met mine, but I looked away, concentrating on his graying mustache that was perfectly combed and trimmed. I wasn't sure what he was thinking, but as soon as I stared him in the eyes, I knew I wouldn't have a choice. This wasn't just about me. This was about all of us. With this one sacrifice, it would mean my dad wouldn't have to work eighteen hours a day like he had for most of his life.

"If you don't want to do this, we can walk out of here right now." He squeezed a little and nodded. "You'll always be my baby girl, and I'll always protect you."

I'd have been lying if I said I wasn't tempted to take him up on his offer. No one was making me do this, at least not physically, but I knew what the fallout would be if I didn't do it. My family would suffer. The family who had supported me every step of the way. The family who fought to make sure Noemi and I had a better life than they did. I couldn't walk away because, if I did, I'd be turning my back on them all.

"No," I croaked out. "It's just nerves." I tried to smile behind the veil and spun around to face the doors.

"If you're sure…"

"I'm sure."

I wasn't sure, but it didn't matter now. The doors swung open, the music started to play, and I took a step forward with my dad next to me. My legs felt like Jell-O, my breaths becoming pants, but I kept moving one foot in front of the other.

The pews were full to the brim, and there were even a few people standing at the edge of the church to witness this event. An event that meant more than just two people creating an unbreakable union. That was what I'd been told. I was making history. I was making a difference. I was helping *The Family*.

But at what cost? What was the price that I was going to have to pay? My freedom? My choices? What would happen after this? I was two steps away from the man waiting at the altar.

Two steps away from my life no longer being mine.

FOUR

WEEKS

EARLIER

CHAPTER

1

LORENZO

I closed my eyes and leaned my head back as she took as much of me in her mouth as she could. It wasn't the best blow job I'd ever had, but it would be enough to erase the tension in my body—tension that had been building up from the moment my dad told me I had to attend this function with him. I fuckin' hated these things. I despised being surrounded by rich assholes who thought they were better than everyone else.

As the oldest child, it was my job to set an example, to show a united front with the Beretta family. From a young age, I'd known what my role would be, and I was okay with that, but it didn't mean I hadn't envied my brother and sister, who had lived completely different lives than me.

My younger brother didn't have to answer to our father in the same way I did. He didn't have to learn the ins and outs of the business—both legal and illegal. He didn't have to train in several martial arts, and he didn't have to have the perfect aim while shooting a gun. But it was nothing compared to my sister and the protection from all the bad things surrounding us.

They'd lived a childhood that I hadn't.

They hadn't witnessed what was behind the curtain.

I had. I was shown exactly what our family was at a young age. I'd watched my father torture a man for lying to him. I'd been seven, and the screams of pain had woken me up. That was the first time I'd listened to someone begging for their life. Somewhere along the way I'd lost count, and the person causing the pain had turned from my father to me. I'd become his project, his work of art that he'd molded into shape.

I gritted my teeth as her tongue lapped around the head of my cock, and I tried to push all of my thoughts aside. I needed this, even if it was subpar. So, I took control. I weaved my hand into her hair, opened my eyes, and forced my cock down her throat as far as it would go. Shock flashed across her face as her gag reflex kicked in, but I didn't care. This wasn't about her—it was never about the women. It was about *me*.

"Fuck." My muscles tensed as I exploded into her mouth, and as soon as I was done, I pushed her off, then zipped up my slacks.

"That was so…"

I blocked the rest of her sentence out, not wanting to listen to her grating voice. It was too high for my liking—too sickly sweet. I inhaled a deep breath, getting a lungful of her cheap perfume, and snarled at the smell. I didn't want her around me. She'd served her purpose, so as soon as we pulled up outside the art museum, where the function was being held, I told her, "You can go now."

"What? Lorenzo, I thought I was attending with you?"

I pushed out of the limousine and adjusted my suit jacket and tie. "You thought wrong." I didn't turn back to look at her as I strode over to the steps lined with red material. A smirk lifted on my lips at the color. It was appropriate for the Beretta family.

People milled outside with clipboards and headsets, but I didn't look at any of them. I was here for my father, nothing else. If I had my way, I'd never attend another one of these fuckin' things again. But Father said it was to keep the connection with the world everyone could see. Protection for the underground business only a select few people knew about.

Sure, they knew we were Mafia, but that didn't mean they knew *exactly* what we did. The feds had tried to take us down countless times. Once, they even tried to frame my father for a crime he didn't commit, but they were unsuccessful, and it would remain that way as long as we kept the peace.

"Good evening, Mr. Beretta," a soft voice said from beside me. I raised a brow and moved my gaze to the woman in a slinky black dress with a headset placed over her perfectly straight hair. "I'll escort you to your table."

I didn't grace her with a response, not that I needed to. Her arm brushed against mine as she led me into the vast entrance full of drapes covering most of the artwork. I scoffed. What was the point in using an art museum for a function if you were then going to cover up the art?

The woman pointed. "Your father is just over there."

I tilted my head at her in a half nod, then stalked toward my dad. He was sitting at the table next to my mom, and they both looked perfectly put together. I could never remember a time when they didn't. Outwardly they always presented the perfect picture, but those closest to them knew how much my mom hated this life and how much my dad loved it. He lived for the blood soaked onto his hands.

"Lorenzo." Ma's voice was a mere sigh of relief. She knew how much I didn't want to come to these things. Sometimes I bailed to try and show that I couldn't be controlled, but the older I got, the more I realized I needed to be here.

"Hey, Ma." I dipped down and placed a kiss on her cheek. "You look beautiful, as always."

She rolled her eyes, but you couldn't misinterpret the smile pulling at her lips. "And you look handsome, my son." She smoothed out the lapel of my jacket and indicated the seat next to my father. It was a silent command, one I listened to without any thought.

I undid the button on my jacket and lowered into the seat, not disturbing my dad, who was talking to someone on the opposite side of the table. Respect for my elders had been drummed into me from a young age, and I knew exactly how to present myself in the right way—in public at least.

A glass with a finger of whisky was placed in front of me—no ice—and although all I wanted to do was take the shot in one, I sipped on it, trying to look as refined as possible.

The string quartet playing and the eyes burning into the side of my face didn't go unnoticed. "Lorenzo," a voice to my left said. It was low and deep, a distinct tone that couldn't be mistaken for anyone but my father.

I turned to face him, my gaze flashing over his strong nose and cut jawline. He may have been sixty-five, but he didn't look a day over fifty.

"Father." I sat up a little straighter when his deep brown gaze didn't move off my face.

"How did it go?"

"Good." My nostrils flared, knowing that when we were home, he'd want to know every single word said in the meeting I'd attended that afternoon—the same meeting I'd been in charge of for two years, and a deal that had only taken place because of me. Yet, my father liked to believe it was because of him that we were currently the only people dealing on this side of the state. But whatever. I wasn't one who wanted praise. I did my job, and I did it well, no questions asked. I didn't need praise from my father in the same way my brother, Dante, did.

"As always," I tacked on to the end.

His brow rose at my comment, but I ignored it, just like I did with most things he did lately.

"Luca," Ma whispered. "Dance with me." Dad didn't look away from me for several seconds, not until he thought whatever he was trying to silently say sunk in, but it didn't make an inch of difference. He may have been the boss as well as my father, but that didn't mean I had to be treated like a child. I hadn't been a child since the first time I'd gotten another person's blood on my hands.

"Luca," Ma repeated, only this time she placed her hand over his.

Dad turned to face her, his gaze skimming two of his bodyguards. They weren't the only two in the room, but they were the only two visible. When you were the Mafia boss, you had enemies in places you didn't even realize, and Dad had been targeted too many times to count by both the bad guys and the good guys. "Of course, Rosa." Dad's lips quirked at the corner, giving Ma the smile that he only ever graced her with.

I looked away and searched the room for something to take my mind off the meeting this afternoon. My contact had tried to skim product off the top of our usual order, and it meant I'd had to take it into my own hands. I sent him and everyone else in his organization a message by cutting off his hand. Criminals in the underground would know who had done it because it was my trademark. Dad had always taught me to create my own path. I smirked as I remembered the screams of pain echoing throughout the warehouse where we'd met. They ricocheted off the walls as I'd sliced at the bone with the knife I always carried. I never knew when I would have to assert my authority, and this afternoon was just another example of that.

"Luca!" Ma screamed, and I jumped out of my seat. "Luca!" she shouted again, and my heart jumped into my throat.

"Ma!" I lunged around the table and to the dance floor where a crowd was gathering, blocking my view. "Move," I ground out, pushing the members of high society out of the way. They stumbled to the left, making a space for me to slip through.

"Someone help him!" Mom screeched in a tone I'd never heard from her before, and as soon as I looked down at the floor, I understood why. "Call nine one one!"

"Dad." I fell to my knees, my hands hovering over his body and his pale, sweaty face. He clutched at his chest, his mouth open, but he couldn't form any words, couldn't say a single thing. His hand reached for me, his body slow and languid. "Dad." I tried to keep my emotions at bay, but I had no idea what to do, what to say, or what was happening.

"I'm a doctor," a voice shouted through the crowd of people. "Let me through."

"Son," Dad finally managed to whisper. I leaned closer to his face, trying to make out what he was saying. "Yours," he stuttered. He groaned in pain as someone slid down next to him, feeling his chest and taking hold of his arm. "It's all yours now."

"He's having a heart attack," the man who told us he was a doctor said. "Sir, look at me."

Dad's gaze attached to mine, refusing to let go. "Rosa," he whispered, so low only I could hear him.

"Ma," I called out. "Ma, come here."

Her sobs mixed in with the words the doctor was saying, but I couldn't concentrate on any of them because I knew deep down this was it. This was the moment everything would change. This was the moment my life would take a turn I wasn't sure I was ready for.

This was the moment that would define the rest of my life.

———

AIDA

I bounced my foot up and down on the floor as I stared at the clock on the wall, wishing the seconds would tick by faster. Friday was always my busiest day of the week because I had three classes and a six-hour shift at the family store. The problem was I had exactly four minutes to make it from my last lecture of the day to the bus stop. The days I didn't get there in time meant I had to run home to make it to my shift. *Those* were the days I hated.

"Assignments are due in two weeks. All reference material needs to be inputted correctly and cited on the final page."

My gaze flicked down to the lecturer for my psych lesson—my least favorite class. There was only one thing I wanted to study at college—music —but apparently, you couldn't get a degree based on electives, which was why I'd left this class until my second year here.

I sighed and let my head drop back. I wished I'd taken it as a freshman. At least then it would have been out of the way, and I could concentrate on what I loved most. But I'd been too eager my first year of college, too excited that I was even here on a part-scholarship, along with some help from my parents. The workload hadn't bothered me then, but the longer I attended, the more I felt like it was piling on top of me.

"You may all go," Mrs. Potts said, waving her hand in the air, then pushing her papers into her quilted tote bag. "Email me if you need any help," she finished off, and I knew I'd be doing just that. I didn't want to half-ass anything, which meant I had to fully understand the subject I was doing. Too bad I didn't understand even a tiny bit of all the theory Mrs. Potts spoke about every week.

Some students rushed out of their seats, ready to get their Friday night started, and others took their time because they had nowhere they needed to be. But I did. I had to make it all the way across town and to the store I'd been working in since before I could remember. A store my ma and dad owned.

When they'd first opened it, it was full of items imported from Italy; things you couldn't get anywhere else. And although more stores had opened over the years and tried to emulate Ma and Pa, none succeeded in the way they did.

"Excuse me," I huffed at a group of students gathered in front of the lecture hall door. No one moved, and my nostrils flared. I was on a time crunch. Ma had gone to the wholesalers, and Dad was out on his usual deliveries taking food to the people who couldn't get out of their homes. And, of course, the few people who *could* get to the store but didn't want to be seen on our side of town—*the poor side*.

"You coming to the party tonight?" a deep voice from behind me asked someone.

"Hello?" I waved my arm in the air and in front of one of the students' faces. "Can I get by, please?" I was acting nice, but inside I wanted to yell at them to move the hell out of the way. I tried to tamp down the frustration building, knowing it wouldn't make an inch of difference to the mellow students in front of me, but I couldn't help muttering, "Maybe I should talk to the wall? Then I might be able to get a goddamn answer."

Someone chuckled, and several of the students blocking my way snapped their heads around. Their wide eyes settled on something behind me, and I took their lull in conversation to push through the middle of them. Every damn week they congregated around the door, blocking the way.

As soon as I was out in the hallway, I pulled both straps of my backpack on my shoulders and speed-walked to the main entrance. Once I was outside, I'd run as fast as I could to the bus stop.

"Hey, Aida?" A hand wrapped around my bicep when I was inches away from the door, and I recognized the voice as the one from the lecture hall who asked someone if they were going to the party.

I frowned as I spun on my feet and stared up at the huge guy in front of me. "I...huh?"

"I asked if you were coming to the party tonight." Brad—captain of the lacrosse team— pushed his hand through his highlighted hair and gave me what the other girls would have called a panty-dropping smile. But my panties were firmly attached to my body.

Wait...had he been asking *me* if I was going to the party?

"Erm..." My gaze batted to the door, then back to him. "I need to get my bus." I omitted his question, not sure whether I should have answered it or not. People like him didn't ask students like me to parties. In fact, the last party I'd gone to was during my senior year of high school, and that was only because Noemi had dragged me there, demanding I experience at least one high school party in my lifetime.

Brad's lips quirked on one side as he stepped closer to me, his almost overpowering cologne too much for my nostrils to handle. I dipped my head back to keep eye contact with him, my gaze scanning his face and realizing he was the typical all-American guy. "I'm not letting you go until you answer my question, Aida." He was trying to be flirty, and while I appreciated it, I had—

I glanced at the time on my cell. "Fuck," I growled. "I missed my bus."

"I can give you a lift home," Brad said, his voice silky smooth. The mantra Ma had embedded into my mind blasted through me, but at this point, I didn't have the energy to run across town so I could make it there in time. "You'll be safe. Promise." He finally let go of my arm and made a cross motion on his chest. "Come on, you can answer my question on the way."

I looked around us as he opened up the doors, seeing if anyone was watching, but there wasn't. A couple of students milled about, but other than that, we were alone. "I...I'm not sure..." I bit down on my bottom lip, fully aware that it was now me who was blocking a doorway. Brad didn't say anything as I stared at him. He just kept his gaze fixated on my face, letting me make the decision. It was his silence that had me caving because I really didn't have another choice. "Okay," I whispered, opening my cell and shooting off a quick message to my sister, just in case.

Neither of us spoke as we walked across the quad to one of the parking lots. His keys jangled as he pulled them out of the front pocket of his light denim jeans, and then lights flashed on a bright red truck.

Brad walked over to the passenger side, opened the door for me, then closed it once I was inside. It smelled like cologne and…sweat. I scrunched up my nose. Was this what all athletes' cars smelled like? I tried not to let my disgust show on my face as he got into the truck and backed out of the spot, but as soon as we were pulling out of the college grounds, I opened the window a little.

"Where am I heading?" he asked, tapping his fingers on the steering wheel.

"Do you know *Ricci Italy*?"

"I've heard of it," Brad said, taking a right onto the main road.

"There."

He nodded, not saying anything else until we were pulling up outside my family store. The windows to our apartment above the store were wide open, the curtains flapping out onto the outside wall from the wind. "So…" He kept the engine running and turned to face me. "Are you going to the party tonight?"

I shook my head and undid my belt. "Can't." I pointed at the store. "I gotta work." I probably could have just told him that when he'd first asked, but my brain had been trying to figure out what was going on and why he was asking *me*.

"Oh." His face dropped, and I wasn't sure what to do. I never was good in situations like this. I was awkward, and not the cute, endearing kind of awkward, just the plain *awkward* awkward. "Maybe another time?" I continued, feeling like it was the right thing to say.

"Next Friday?" he blurted out but immediately shook his head. "No, I have a game that day. Friday after? Two weeks from today?"

"I—"

"I'll take you out somewhere nice. Maybe for Italian or something?"

I chuckled. "No one cooks Italian food the way Ma does."

He laughed with me, his easy smile coming back onto his handsome face. A face I was beginning to enjoy staring at. "I'll take you somewhere nice."

"Like a…" I glanced over to the front of the store, catching sight of my niece's little eyes watching me. "A date?"

"A date," Brad confirmed, and my stomach dipped in response. "What do you say?"

"Erm…" I looked back at him and inhaled a deep breath. "I guess? Sure, why not." He grinned and opened his mouth, but I knew I had to leave now, not just because my shift would be starting any minute, but because I had to quit while I was ahead and not embarrass myself. "I have to go."

"Yeah, yeah, sure." His lips pulled wider. "I'll see you in two weeks if not before that."

"Okay." I smiled, then pushed out of his truck, not looking back once as I scooped up Vida on the way into the store and held her to my chest.

"Who was that, Auntie Aida?" her sweet little voice asked.

"No one," I sang, boosting her on my hip and walking toward the cash register that Noemi stood behind. "You look extra pretty today, Vida."

She giggled, her body giving way to the motion, and I couldn't help but tickle her side, causing the laughter to get louder and her dark-brown hair to whip at my face. "Auntie!" she shouted, her body trying to squirm away from me.

Once I was satisfied that I'd successfully distracted her, I halted and placed her on the counter between Noemi and me. I should have known better than to use Vida as a shield against Noemi's verbal attack because it was only seconds until Noemi demanded, "Who's the guy?"

"No one," I repeated, not veering away from the line I'd given Vida. I placed my hands on either side of Vida, the cool metal of the counter seeping into my palms. Noemi raised her perfectly shaped brow, silently telling me that I wasn't fooling her. "Fine." I rolled my eyes, feeling every bit like the teenager I was only a few years ago. I may have been about to turn twenty and Noemi twenty-six, but that didn't matter when it came to our relationship. At heart, we'd always be the angsty teens fighting over who got to stay up later—which was always Noemi because she was the oldest. "He's captain of the lacrosse team."

"What's lacrosse?" Vida asked as she twirled my hair around her finger. She'd been trying to learn how to braid, but all she'd managed so far was a twisted version that left behind an epic number of knots.

"It's a rich guy's game," Noemi spluttered, unable to keep a straight face as she said it. "So, he brought you home, huh?"

"Yep." I pulled Vida off the counter and hoisted my backpack on my shoulder, itching to get away from this interrogation. I stepped around the back, so I was closer to Noemi and the door that led to the stairs of our small apartment. "He also asked me if I wanted to go out." I darted away, knowing what would come next, but I didn't have time to talk it to death with Noemi. Partly because I still didn't understand it. I'd never spoken to Brad. During high school, I'd learned to keep to myself, and I'd perfected it by the time I'd gotten to college.

"What?" Noemi's voice got louder as I ran up the stairs, and as I turned at the top, I saw her at the bottom, staring up at me with wide eyes. "You're going on a date with him?"

I shrugged. I'd told him I would, but I wasn't sure. I didn't know Brad, but wasn't getting to know the other person the whole point of a date? "Sure," I whispered to Noemi, then spun around, getting as far away from her as I could so I didn't have to think about it any longer.

CHAPTER

2

LORENZO

Everyone was dressed in black, a sign of mourning but also respect for the head of the Beretta family. We stood in a line; first me, then Ma, followed by my little brother, Dante, then my little sister, Sofia. People shook our hands, apologizing for our loss, but none of it sunk in, not until my father was buried six feet under the ground.

It was tradition to have people at the house after a funeral, but all I wanted was silence and space, neither of which I would get today—or what felt like ever again. As soon as we pulled up to the Beretta mansion we'd all grown up in, my body worked on automatic. I walked through the double wooden doors, carved with an elaborate B and gilded with gold. The double-sided staircase led to the upstairs wings, but it wasn't there that I moved toward. Instead, I headed down the hallway and toward the second door on the left, past the living room that no one ever sat in, and into my dad's office.

The door squeaked as I opened it, and part of me wondered if I would see my father sitting behind his desk, just like he'd always been. But he wasn't. The room was empty of life—empty of him. A glass of half-drunk whisky sat on the middle of his desk with a couple of papers next to it.

I walked past the two matching leather sofas and toward the drink cart in the corner adorned with all kinds of spirits. It was my father's favorite whisky that I picked up, not bothering with a glass. Today wasn't the day to hide how I felt, no matter how much I should have. Dad dying didn't just mean he wasn't in my life anymore. Our entire family hung in the balance, and the pressure of what was about to come pushed down on my shoulders, threatening to knock me off-kilter.

"You gonna share that?" a deep voice asked, but I didn't have the energy to turn and face him. I knew who it was.

"Nope." I strode toward my dad's desk and sat on his old, leather chair. "Get your own bottle."

"Nah," he replied, and I finally looked up at

him—Christian Gallo, my best friend since before I could remember. He pushed his hand through his short inky black hair. "Think I'll stay sober for now."

I snorted. There was no way I could face what would happen today. As if this morning wasn't enough, I had to prepare for a meeting with The Enterprise. Ma said it couldn't wait, that it had to be done asap, but all I wanted was *one* goddamn day so I could bury my father and not have to worry about the family.

I leaned back in the chair and took a swig of the thousand-dollar liquid, loving the burn at the back of my throat. "Are they all out there?" I asked, already knowing the answer.

"Yep." Christian leaned on the arm of one of the sofas, his hands in his slacks pockets. "They sent me in to see if you're ready."

Inhaling a breath and closing my eyes to gain clarity, I replied, "I'm ready." It was a lie, and I had a feeling Christian knew that, but there was nothing either of us could have done about it.

Christian didn't say another word as he walked across the office and opened the door, letting everyone in. Ma was the first to step inside, her emotions carefully put aside for the moment. She'd been the perfect wife to the head of this family, and I wondered if she'd miss it now. She wasn't just mourning for the loss of her husband, but also the place in the family she'd held for so long. Uncle Alonzo and Uncle Antonio followed behind, and bringing up the rear was my brother, Dante. He shut the door behind them all, and I knew then that this would be the meeting *before* the official meeting.

No one said a word as Ma and my uncles sat on the sofas. Christian and Dante stood to the side, watching and listening for what was about to happen. The words were coming, I knew they were, and as soon as they were spoken, nothing would be the same. It wouldn't be my dad everyone looked to for answers, but me.

My heart hammered in my chest, and I wasn't sure which of them to look at while I waited for everything to change.

"We have a problem," Ma started.

I whipped my attention to her. *Those weren't the words I'd expected to hear.*

Ma looked to Uncle Alonzo, and once he nodded, she continued, "Your dad wanted you to take over the...business." I blinked. I'd known this since I was a little kid. It wasn't like the prospect of me being head of the Beretta Mafia was new to me. I'd been taking on more responsibility lately, almost as if my father knew something nobody else did. "But...there are rules."

"Rules?" I snorted, not expecting that word. "What kind of rules?"

"Rules for you to become boss," Uncle Alonzo said, his deep voice gaining my attention. His dark-brown hair was peppered with gray, and even though he was sixty-one years old, he didn't look a day over forty.

"What the fuck you talkin' about?" I stood, the bottle of whisky held tightly in my hand. "Dad died, and I'm the oldest son. That's all anyone needs to understand." I stormed from around the desk and toward the door. I wasn't going to sit here and listen to this. I'd buried my dad hours ago, and now they were telling me I had to follow some fuckin' rules I'd never even heard of? Fuck that. *I* was the new boss of the Beretta family, whether people liked it or not. It was my birthright. I'd been a captain of my own soldiers for years, I was used to dictating what would happen around me, and I wasn't about to change that now.

"Wait," Ma shouted, her tone frantic. "Wait, Lorenzo." I halted, my gaze focused on the office door. I couldn't turn around, not with how I felt at that moment. I needed time to process everything that had happened over the last few days. And I needed to drink this entire bottle of alcohol, and possibly another one just to numb all of my swirling thoughts.

Rules? Fuckin' rules?

"Lorenzo," Dante said, his voice so much like mine. "Listen to what they have to say." Dante had always been the calm brother, the one who took it easy, but that was because he didn't have to do what I did. Things weren't expected of him, the second son. He hadn't seen what I had, but now Dad was gone, and he wouldn't have a choice but to do more, just like I hadn't for my entire life.

"Three rules," Uncle Antonio said. He was the stricter uncle. The one who didn't take an ounce of shit. He was also married to the gentlest woman I'd ever known, my auntie Vivianna. Both of my uncles weren't blood-related but were married to my dad's sisters. They'd come up in the business and knew it inside out, but they were also in here, trying to steer me in a direction I had no idea existed.

I took a breath, trying to sort through my scattered thoughts. I took another gulp of the burning alcohol, winced, then turned to face them.

"*The Enterprise* needs to agree to you becoming boss," Uncle Antonio continued, standing. He brushed off the lapels of his jacket, his lips spread into a thin line. He looked stern now, but I knew how quickly that sternness could turn to terrifying anger. I'd watched him torture a man for twenty hours straight without a flicker of emotion. "They have all agreed, as we knew they would." I nodded, trying to take it all in. I'd known *The Enterprise* had to be unanimous because my father had already told me that. *The Enterprise* consisted of five bosses of differing organizations, each working in tandem with each other.

"Okay," I ventured, stepping toward everyone. "What else?"

Uncle Antonio kept his gaze locked on to mine. "You need to be thirty to take over as boss."

"What?" I sneered. "Why?"

"Have you heard of the 1924 massacre?" Uncle Alonzo asked, and I frowned. Dad had told me about it once upon a time. The Mafia boss who killed his wife and two young kids. He'd said the pressure of being boss at twenty-four was too much, right before he pulled the trigger and killed himself, leaving behind a bloody mess that authorities couldn't explain, at least not publicly.

"Yeah. Dad told me about it." My shoulders drooped. It made sense, but…

"I don't turn thirty for another three weeks."

"It'll give us the time we need," Uncle Alonzo said, a small smile on his face.

"Time for what?" Everyone was suspiciously silent, their gazes flickering everywhere but at me. They'd said that there were three rules, but they'd only told me two, which meant they knew I wouldn't like the final rule. A rule I had no choice but to follow if I wanted to continue my father's legacy. "Tell me," I demanded, using the tone that I knew would get me answers.

"You have to get married," Ma blurted out. I blinked. "To an Italian girl."

"What?" I wasn't asking her to repeat what she'd said, but she did anyway. I couldn't believe what she was saying. "Bullshit," I growled. "That's fuckin' bullshit."

"Doesn't change the rule whether you think it's right or not," Uncle Antonio said, his voice easygoing for the first time. It sounded so unlike him. "Arranged marriage. It's the old rules."

"Wait." I laughed and stepped toward them. "You're saying that it has to be *arranged*?"

"Well, I'm guessing you don't have anyone ready to marry you, son," Uncle Alonzo said, wincing at the last word. He'd always used that name with me, but it held more right now—more on this day, more when my father dying meant I had to get married to a good fuckin' Italian girl.

I didn't want to be weighed down by a woman at home, waiting to see if I survived the violence I faced every day. I didn't need her to be in the back of my mind as I was dishing out punishments to men who tried to break our rules.

Fuck.

Rules. It shouldn't have surprised me what was happening right now, not when we were surrounded by rules and hierarchy.

"Fine." My nostrils flared as I agreed to it all. "Bring me options, and I'll get married on my goddamn birthday. Then we can get on with business." I paused, realizing that until I turned thirty, I couldn't be boss. "Who's gonna take over until then?"

"Me," Uncle Alonzo said, and it made sense. He was my dad's right-hand man, he had been for more years than I'd been alive, and most importantly, he was the underboss. You couldn't jump ranks in the business, so he was the only one who could be acting boss. "You keep doing what you normally do, and I'll just act as boss until you can take over."

"Good." I stared at each person in the room. My younger brother, whose life would change more than it ever had. My mother, who had lost the love of her life. My uncles, who were determined not to let the business get into someone else's hands. And finally, my best friend, the man who had been by my side every step of the way. But right now, I didn't want to look at any of them.

I needed to be alone.

I needed to drown my goddamn sorrows.

I spun around, leaving them in the office that would be mine in three weeks.

LORENZO

The roar of the engine vibrated through me as I pulled through the open, vast, metal gates and into the property that was now my home—again. I looked around, trying to see if the truck delivering all of my things from my penthouse had turned up yet, but from the looks of things, it hadn't.

The mansion we'd all grown up in was now officially mine, but if I was honest, I didn't want to be here. I wanted to be back in my own living room, looking out at the entire city with my floor-to-ceiling windows. Ma's words echoed in my mind: *You need a house with protection.* The penthouse apartment I'd lived in since I was eighteen wasn't good enough, apparently. No. I needed a mansion now to house the staff, security detail, family, and of course, my new wife.

So, here I was, back in the same place I grew up, only now things were different. I was the boss—well, nearly. *Thirteen days.* I only had thirteen days to get married and turn thirty. *Then* I would become the boss. The head of the family.

Christian's car pulled up behind mine, and I stared in the rearview mirror as he got out, but I didn't make a move. Instead, I just stared at him as he waited patiently for me. He'd done that all morning while I took my frustration out on a soldier who'd tried to double-cross us. He'd thought that my father's death would allow him to jump on opportunities presented to him from other organizations. He was wrong. And he'd learned that lesson slowly and painfully.

I'd left the underground bunker near Uncle Antonio's house feeling some of the pressure lifting off my shoulders, but as I stared at Christian, it all came tumbling back, almost taking my breath away.

My morning may have been full of relief, but my afternoon was going to be full of yet more prospective women brought my way. I groaned, already fed up with today and it wasn't even lunchtime yet. For the last eight days, I'd been presented sixty-two women—sixty-two prospective wives—and not one of them was right. I needed someone who didn't want attention and wouldn't use the family name for her own agenda. It was a delicate balance, one that was proving more difficult than I ever would have thought.

The most important thing was that she would be in name only. I had no intention of being a loving husband to a good Italian woman. She'd want things I wasn't capable of giving. Like babies, a family, a life where we held hands and I bought her flowers.

I wasn't that person. I'd never be that person.

Closing my eyes, I took a deep breath, schooled my features into the mask everyone expected of me, then pushed out of my car. I didn't take one look at

Christian, knowing he would follow me inside while also watching my back.

The large double doors opened as I came within a few feet, and there, in the circular entryway, were four women, lined up, ready for me to see.

"No," I said, flicking my hand in the air in a shooing motion. It took me two seconds to look in their eyes and know whether they were right or not. And none of these were right, not for me anyway.

"You're too damn picky," Christian groaned as several sets of heels clicked on the tiled floor and outside. Not one of them said a word as they were ushered out. They knew better than that.

"None of them are right," I told Christian simply as I turned around to face him. "Whoever it is is gonna be around for years. She's gotta be the right person."

"You have thirteen days left," Christian reminded me, his brow raised. "You may be Lorenzo Beretta, but that don't mean shit if you turn thirty and you don't have a bride for the wedding your ma is already planning."

I growled, frustrated at the whole situation. I hadn't committed to anyone for a goddamn reason, but now, in one fell swoop, I was going to become *the boss* and a husband. Fuck. I couldn't deal with this shit, not right now. The high from this morning had well and truly dissipated into nothing.

"I need a drink."

"Lorenzo," Christian snapped, but I ignored him and made a beeline for the kitchen at the back of the house. I hadn't been in my dad's office since the day of his funeral, and that was where the good stuff was. Right now, alcohol was alcohol, and I knew exactly where I could find some.

The side door to the kitchen was open, but I didn't take any notice of it as I headed for the top shelf of the secret cabinet Ma kept. She thought no one knew about it, but we all knew that was where she kept her favorite drinks. They weren't the same kind of expensive alcohol that was in my dad's office, but even a weird-flavored vodka was better than nothing right now.

I huffed out a breath. Christian was right. I'd never find a wife, not with the people they kept bringing to me. Maybe I just needed to settle with one of the women and call it a done deal. Maybe I *was* being too picky.

I sneered at the light-purple color of the vodka, twisted the top off, and took a swig. "Fuck." I slammed the bottle down. "That's disgusting." I darted for the sink, slammed the faucet on, and filled a glass with water, hoping that would take the awful flowery aftertaste away.

"I think you're meant to mix that *with* something else," a soft, lyrical voice said from behind me. "Like, you know, a *mixer*."

My back straightened, my nerves on edge. I was

always aware of what was around me, and yet I hadn't even noticed someone coming into the room. Slowly, I turned, wondering if another prospective woman had been sent my way. I was about to open my mouth, to ask her what she was doing in a part of the house she wasn't allowed in, when Mr. Ricci halted behind her.

"Oh, hello, Mr. Beretta." He gulped, his wide eyes veering from me to the woman who I now realized was holding a box filled with groceries. "I'm bringing your mother's delivery for the week." He shuffled from side to side, unease clearly spreading through him. "I apologize if my daughter disturbed you."

The woman turned to face Mr. Ricci. *His daughter.* I tilted my head to the side as I watched her. Her gaze lowered but remained focused on her dad. I could sense she didn't like him apologizing for her, but she wasn't going to say anything in front of me to him. She had respect for the people around her. *Interesting.*

"It's okay. Don't let me get in your way." I leaned against the counter, crossed one leg at the ankle, and clasped the counter behind me. My attention didn't move off the woman as she entered and placed the box of groceries on the kitchen table. She stared at me out of the side of her eyes, a frown appearing on her face as she spotted me staring. Again though, she didn't say anything.

Mr. Ricci exited, probably going to get more of the delivery. I expected the woman to scamper after him, but she didn't. She unpacked the box and sauntered around the kitchen, placing the items in what I was assuming were the correct place.

"You do this often?" I asked her, feeling like my voice was too loud for the room and her ears. I was to the point, but maybe she wasn't used to that. My wheels were turning, and for some reason, I didn't want to scare her off. She was the first woman I'd seen over the last week that had me wondering what else there was to her. The problem was that she wasn't brought *to* me. Instead, she'd stumbled upon me. Accident? Fate? Coincidence?

"Who? Me?" The woman opened another cabinet but paused to look at me.

"Yeah. You." I raised a brow, waiting for some kind of comeback, but there wasn't one. Her gaze veered down to my white shirt, and her eyes widened slightly, just enough for me to know she could see the blood splatter on the material. I wasn't sure how I was expecting her to react. Maybe she'd clam up and get out of here as fast as she could, or maybe she'd—

"Mrs. Beretta likes her things put away properly."

I blinked, and she shrugged as if that was enough of an explanation for me. She didn't mention the blood or acknowledge who I was. It intrigued me. *She* intrigued me.

She closed the cabinet, swiped her hand down her jean-covered thighs, and for the first time, I got a good look at her body. She was short, but I didn't mind it on her. The curve of her hips was begging for my hands, and the dip in her waist called for my arm to wrap...

Huh.

I blinked several times. Maybe she *could* become an option.

"That was the last one," Mr. Ricci announced, standing in the doorway to the side of the kitchen. It led out into the driveway that nobody knew was there, a secret spot used for deliveries. He blinked rapidly. He'd clearly seen the blood on my clothes and didn't want to get any closer. Where his daughter was as cool as a cucumber, I could practically see his hands shaking from here.

"Let's go, Aida."

Aida. Her name was Aida.

She lifted her hand in a wave, and without saying another word, she exited, her dad following. I couldn't help my feet moving toward the open door. My gaze refused to move from her, my brain wanting to know more.

Her ass swayed as she walked toward Mr. Ricci's truck, but it wasn't something that she put on. It was natural, just like her. And fuck if it didn't draw me to her even more.

"What are you looking at?" Christian asked, his footsteps nearing as Mr. Ricci started the engine. I crossed my arms over my chest as Mr. Ricci pulled away and slowly made his way down the driveway. The farther they moved away, the more I knew. She was it. She was the answer to my problem. "Lorenzo?" Christian asked again.

I turned to face him, lifted my lips on one side, and simply stated, "My future wife."

CHAPTER

3

AIDA

My stomach dipped, my nerves running rampant the closer to the restaurant we got. I couldn't remember the last time I'd gone on a date. Maybe that was why I was so nervous? Brad hadn't told me where we were going, so I'd had a stressful few hours deciding what to wear. In the end, I let Vida choose. At least that way, I'd look pretty enough.

She'd paired my high-waisted, wide-legged pants with a simple white sleeveless top. To finish the look, I'd gone with a pair of heels, then shoved some flats into my bag. I was prepared for any situation—that was what I kept telling myself anyway. The reality was, I wasn't ready for this. I wasn't ready to be alone with Brad when I felt like I barely knew him.

He pulled to a stop outside a steakhouse, and I didn't wait for him as I got out. I was on edge—more on edge than usual—and I wasn't sure if it was the good kind or the bad kind. There was something in the back of my mind telling me to be aware of everything going on around me, but I didn't know why. It was probably because this was the first date I'd been on in so long, or maybe my spidey sense had kicked in and was trying to warn me. Either way, when Brad took my hand to lead me inside the restaurant, I jumped out of my skin.

"Sorry." I laughed, trying to sound easy, but I knew I was anything but that.

"No worries," Brad said, his lips pulled up on one side in that smile I'd seen him use so often. It was the kind that I knew people melted at, but for me, it made me even more nervous.

What would happen after this? Would he expect anything of me? I wasn't a virgin by any stretch of the imagination, but I also didn't do this kind of thing often. I hadn't had a man hold my hand since…well, damn, I couldn't even remember since when.

Had it really been that long?

I rolled my shoulders back and tried to give myself a pep talk as we were shown to our table. It wasn't long until our orders were taken, and then Brad started talking about himself. I listened intently, not wanting to miss any of what he was saying, and as soon as he paused, I opened my mouth, about to volunteer something about me, but before I even got the chance, he was back to talking about himself and what his plans for the future were.

By the time we'd finished eating, and the bill was placed on the table, I knew his entire life story, but he knew absolutely *nothing* about me. I bet he didn't even know what my last name was. In some ways, I was glad he'd done all the talking because that prickly feeling I'd had since I got out of his truck hadn't gone away, but I also knew there was no way I could go on another date with him.

Brad was all about himself, the typical high school jock who hadn't changed one bit even though he'd been in college for a couple of years. I smiled at him as he stood and offered his hand, and this time I took it, knowing there was no reason to be nervous around him because I wouldn't be going out with him again.

He pulled me closer to him as we made it to his truck, and once we were both inside, he asked, "Wanna go somewhere else and continue this?" *Did he not realize how bad this date had gone?*

My face reddened as I stared at him, wondering how to politely say no. Just as I opened my mouth, my cell beeped, saving me. I pulled it out of my purse, unbelievably grateful for the interruption.

Noemi: You need to get home right now.

I frowned at the message and typed a reply.

Aida: Why? Is everything okay?

I waited several seconds, staring at my screen as I bit down on my bottom lip, but when the *read* signal didn't show up, I turned to face Brad. "My sister said I need to get home." I showed him my phone, trying to prove that she had messaged me and that this wasn't some kind of ploy to get away from him. *I was glad I'd be getting away from him, though.*

"Okay." He smiled, but this time it didn't quite reach his eyes, not like it had throughout the night. My stomach dropped, and I winced. I hated letting people down, and I wouldn't be able to think of anything else but how I'd technically bailed on our night. Although a quick look at the time said it was already 10:30 p.m., so I hadn't *really* bailed. Right?

The truck was silent save for the low singing on the radio. He'd talked nonstop, and now he wasn't saying a word. I wasn't sure which one I liked less... no, I did—definitely the silence. I couldn't stand when there was no noise. It made me want to fill it with useless chatter and information, but more than that, it made my ears ring, almost as if the silence was so loud it was deafening me.

Brad pulled the truck to a stop a couple of cars

down from the store, and relief flowed through me. It would only be seconds until I was out of the truck. I grabbed my purse off my lap and looked ahead. *What the…*

Two blacked-out SUVs took up the spaces directly in front of the store. It wouldn't have bothered me if the store was open, but it was nearly 11 p.m. now, so why were they parked there?

I stared up at the apartment, seeing all of the lights on. Had they waited up for me? Were they watching me right now? My eyes widened. Had something bad happened? Noemi said I needed to get home right now, but my brain hadn't computed that something seriously wrong could have transpired.

"I had a great time," Brad said, his voice low. I felt his hand whisper over my knee, and I jumped in response—yet again.

"Sorry." I laughed it off, trying to be easy breezy, but the lights being on in the apartment had taken over my brain, and all I could think about was my ma looking out of the window and seeing what I was doing. At that thought, I flung the passenger door open and shuffled out of Brad's car. "Thanks for tonight," I stumbled out. "Erm…" I hooked my thumb over my shoulder, signaling the store. "I better head inside."

Brad opened his mouth, but before he could say anything, I slammed the door shut and twirled around. I didn't turn back to face him as I walked past the SUVs, and it wasn't until I was at the side door that led straight up to our apartment that I realized a man was standing in front of it—a man I didn't recognize.

"Aida?" he asked. His face was a weird mixture of rough and smooth and his hair was in a crew cut, as if he didn't have the patience to style it.

"Y-es." He nodded, opened the door, and waved for me to go inside. "Who are you?" I asked, unable to keep my curiosity in any longer.

He winked. "You'll find out soon enough."

I frowned, not understanding what he meant, but walked by him anyway. My heels clicked on each stair as I made it up to the apartment door at the top. As soon as I opened it, Noemi's face appeared. Her wide eyes told me something was going down, and when voices from the living room echoed toward us, she yanked me into the bathroom.

"Noemi!" I whisper-shouted. "What are you doing?"

"Shhhhh." She placed her hand over my mouth, and every bone in my body wanted to fight her off, but several sets of footsteps getting closer had me freezing.

I couldn't make out anything they were saying, but we both stayed silent as the footsteps disappeared, a door closed, then engines turned on.

Several seconds ticked by, but neither of us moved from our position.

"You can come out now, girls," Ma said from the other side of the door.

Noemi let go of me, pushed the door open, and dragged me out with her. "What the hell was that?" she asked. "Why was he here?"

Ma's gaze veered to me, then to my dad, who stood a couple of feet to the side. "Let's go sit down."

"Why?" I asked, following them because Noemi wasn't giving me a choice with the strong grip she had on my arm.

"We need to talk," my dad replied, his voice somber but also shaky.

Neither of them said another word as they sat on one of the sofas and signaled for me and Noemi to sit opposite them. We did as we were told, but when I pulled in a deep breath, the distinct smell of cologne overtook me—a cologne I recognized but couldn't quite put my finger on where I knew it from.

Ma and Dad looked at each other, and with a nod of Dad's head, he turned to face us. "You both know of the Beretta family, correct?" Noemi and I nodded because we did—*everybody* did. "Well, Luca Beretta died recently." I blinked, trying to figure out where this was going. Why was this so important that Noemi had messaged me to come home right away? "Which means his son, Lorenzo, will be taking over."

"Okay." I shuffled to the edge of my seat and leaned my forearms on my thighs. The atmosphere was intense, promising something that I wasn't sure I was ready for. "What does that have to do with us?"

"Well." Ma cleared her throat. Her brows pulled down in concern—or was that fear? "Mr. Beretta— Lorenzo—needs several things before he can become boss." Ma paused, and I stared at her, waiting for her to continue, but when she turned to face Dad, so did I.

"You remember him, right, Aida?" My gaze flicked around the room, trying to place who he was talking about, but I was still occupied with why the tension was so thick around us, and why this meant I had to come home, and why there were people in our apartment.

"Erm…"

"We made the delivery the other day. He was standing in the kitchen."

My eyes widened, and I shuffled even farther onto the edge of my seat. "I…I remember him." I inhaled another breath, smelling the distinctive cologne, and it was all I needed to remember standing in the kitchen across from the man covered in spatters of blood. "That was Lorenzo Beretta?"

"You've met him?" Noemi asked, her voice sounding far away.

"Yeah." I stared at Ma, then Dad. "Why are you telling us this?"

"He…" Ma cleared her throat and shuffled on the seat. "He needs a wife before he can take over as boss."

I blinked.

"And he wants you," Dad finished for her.

At first, I wasn't sure who he was talking to, but somewhere outside of my body, I knew he was looking at me. His dark eyes bore into mine, saying a thousand things silently.

"Me?" I pointed at my chest as I stood. My legs were wobbly. I felt like a baby giraffe trying to gain its footing, only I didn't fall over on my first try. "He wants *me* to be his *wife*?" I laughed—the lose-control-of-your-body type of laugh. They were joking. They had to be.

I turned to face Noemi, expecting the same reaction from her, but it wasn't there. She was staring down at the floor, her hair covering half of her face.

"Aida," Ma said, standing up, and my laughs waned into somber gasps. "You don't have to say yes. You have a choice." She stepped toward me, but I moved to the side.

"A choice?" I raised my brows, my emotions all over the place. I wasn't sure whether I was feeling anger or sadness or full-on rage, but whatever it was, it was taking over quickly and I didn't know how to handle any of it. "Was he here?" Dad stood, so I moved my attention to him. "Was that who was here just now? The two SUVs outside?"

"Yes," Dad said, his face not giving anything away now. He'd carefully schooled his features into an expression I hadn't seen before. "If you say yes, the wedding will be in ten days."

"I…I don't believe this." I threw my hands up in the air, trying to make sense of all of this. Ten days? He wanted me to become his wife in ten days? "He came here to ask if I'd be his wife and didn't even have the decency to ask *me*?"

"It's tradition to ask the family." Ma stepped closer to me, only this time I didn't move. I couldn't process everything that was happening. I'd gone out on a date with Brad and come home to someone wanting me to be his wife. "As I said," Ma continued, "you don't have to say yes. You can—"

"What happens if I say no?" I waited, wondering what they would say. I wasn't sheltered from the workings of the world. I knew we paid the Beretta family each month for protection of the store. There wasn't a street in this city that wasn't controlled by an organization, so where would we be if I said no?

I took several steps away from them, and by the time my back hit the doorframe, all three of them were standing, watching me with wide eyes. "I…I can't deal with this." I felt behind me and held on to the wall, feeling like if I didn't, I'd fall down in front of them. "I have an assignment to do."

I didn't say another word as I spun around and darted to the room I shared with Noemi and Vida.

I hadn't lied. I did have an assignment, but there was no way I would be able to concentrate. We'd all grown up listening to the horror stories of the Beretta family, and there was one rule we all lived by: *don't cross them.*

Would me saying no be crossing them?

Ma said I had a choice, but I knew I didn't.

———

LORENZO

I grabbed the back of her neck, needing something to hold on to for traction as I pounded into her, unrelenting in my rhythm. She squealed but soon followed it up with a groan. They were all the same—the women who sated my needs. They didn't think twice about what I was going to do, and once I was done with them, they knew to leave. I wasn't going to entertain them. I wasn't going to give them hope. I knew who I was, and so did they.

I ground my teeth together and thrust deep

inside her again, feeling my anger building with each movement of my hips.

Two days.

It had been two days since I'd gone to the other side of town and met with Aida's parents, and I hadn't heard a thing from them since. Why was it taking so long? What did they have to think about so seriously?

I'd made them an offer they couldn't refuse. Not only would their daughter be taken care of financially, but they'd have even more protection by being part of the family. Oh, and of course, a big payout would come their way too.

So, the question remained: what the fuck was taking so long?

"Lorenzo," the woman moaned, and I snarled. I hated when they used my name.

"Shut up," I ground out, thrusting a couple more times before finishing inside the condom I always wore. There was no way in hell there were going to be any accidents on my watch. My dad had schooled me on that from the time I'd turned ten. *Always have protection: a condom and a gun.* It was two things I lived by, and neither had ever failed me.

I yanked myself out of her, pulled the condom off, then tied it at the end. "You can go," I told her, staring down at her naked ass. She didn't make a move, staying in the same position over the arm of the sofa in my bedroom.

Closing my eyes, I took a breath. I didn't have time for this today. I had business to attend to and a thumping behind my eyes that promised an unbearable headache. By the time I'd opened up my eyes and zipped up my slacks, she was standing.

Veev was one of my favorites, had been since I was twenty-two, and I was sure she thought she could get away with things the other women couldn't. Sometimes I let her think that because it was easier, but I knew things would have to change once I was a married man. I'd have to be more discreet—or maybe I wouldn't. Maybe continuing like this would be best. At least that way, my future wife wouldn't get any ideas.

I snorted at the thought and spun on my heels. How much longer was I going to have to wait for an answer? I had eight days left—*eight goddamn days.*

"Want me to stay for a while?" Veev asked.

"I've got work to do," I grunted, throwing the condom in the trash, then washing my hands. The bathroom attached to my bedroom had been refitted recently. In fact, my whole bedroom had. It was the same room I'd slept in every night as a kid, but now it was twice the size with brand-new furniture. Ma said that Dad had commissioned it to be redone a year ago, yet no one else knew about it.

It made me wonder if he knew he wouldn't be around much longer. In fact, the more I looked into things within the business, the more I knew that was true. He'd put clauses in contracts for when he was gone. He'd transferred money to offshore accounts. He'd detailed the inner workings that no one else knew about in a ledger kept in his safe that only he had the combination to. The only reason I'd gotten inside of it was because of a letter one of his lawyers had hand-delivered.

It all seemed too…smooth.

I splashed my face with some water and stared at myself in the mirror, trying to make sense of everything going on. It was too much to think about all at once. I had to focus on what was right in front of me.

I wasn't boss yet. I had two things to complete before I could be, and that was all I needed to worry about at the moment.

Veev's footsteps came closer to the bathroom. "We could take a shower together," she said, her voice deceptively soft.

"No." I swiped a towel over my face and side-stepped her. "You can shower." I paused in the doorway, staring at her naked body. She wasn't as curvy as Aida was, and she was taller by at least a foot. This was my usual type, yet Aida had intrigued me. She'd wormed her way inside my mind without even realizing it. My nostrils flared, and I spun around, not wanting to look at Veev any longer. "Then you can leave."

I didn't wait to hear what else she had to say, so

I grabbed my jacket and headed straight out of my bedroom door, where Mateo, one of the soldiers, waited patiently. "Make sure she's gone within thirty minutes," I demanded. He nodded in response and shuffled closer to the door.

I walked past the stairs that led into the main foyer and headed toward the secret door at the end of the hallway. Only a handful of people knew the door existed—a secret passage built for extra security.

Voices from downstairs drifted up to me as I pulled it open, but I didn't take any notice of them. There was always something going on in the house, especially with both my brother and sister still living here. To add to that, other family members seemed to be hanging around, checking on Ma after Dad's passing. I knew they were trying to help, but she hated being fussed over. She hated being the center of attention.

The stairs were illuminated by two sconces attached to the wall, giving off just enough light so you could see. It turned, winding down two levels. On the lower level was the basement, where we kept anything we didn't want to be found. It had always been locked up tight, but now that Dad was gone, I was the only one who could get in there, and I intended to keep it that way. It was the first level's door that I headed toward, the one that led into my dad's office—no, it was my office now. I shook my head as I stepped into the room, not sure I'd ever get used to it. Not a single item in there had been touched. A new boss hadn't been officially appointed yet, and until then, everything had to stay the same, which was why I hardly came in here.

The click of the door shutting sounded like a bomb exploding in the otherwise silent office. Each wall had been soundproofed, and I wasn't sure whether that was a good thing or not. Dad said he needed the quiet to work, but I knew it was so that he could do anything inside this room and not be heard.

I kept my back to the wall, staring at the furniture, unable to imagine what it would be like when it was all removed. How was I meant to make this space my own when my dad's ghost haunted it? I stared at the decanter of whisky and stepped toward it, needing the burn of alcohol to tamp down all of my thoughts. But I'd only made it halfway there when the office door that led into the main part of the house flung open.

"What the fuck—"

"Language," a deep, Italian-accented voice said. "Is that any way to talk to your uncle?"

I blinked, keeping my expression neutral as I stared at my uncle Paolo—my dad's brother. "Uncle," I greeted, pushing my hands into the pockets of my slacks and trying not to act surprised at seeing him. It was a move I knew he noticed as his gaze flicked down, then back up to my face. "What are you doing here?" What I really wanted to ask was why he was here now and not weeks ago. He'd missed his own brother's funeral, so why was he here, barging into what would be my office.

He tilted his head, his inky black hair moving as he did, and sauntered toward the desk. "I came to see my family." He tsked as if me asking was a stupid question, but both he and I knew it wasn't. I hadn't seen him since I was a little boy, and even then, my dad had kept us as far apart as he could. "Such sad news about my brother." He pushed aside some papers on the desk, trying to read them. "And now you're left with no leadership."

I narrowed my eyes on him, taking in his wrinkled, tan face and his pristine gray suit. He'd dressed for business. "We have leadership." I stepped toward the desk, clenching my hands in my pockets.

"Do you?" He raised a brow, staring at me like I was an annoying fly buzzing around him. "Who?"

"Me."

He laughed, and it took everything in me not to make a dart toward him. "Are you forgetting the rules, nephew?" I knew the rules. I knew them too fuckin' well. "I don't see a ring on your finger." He lifted the cane he held in his left hand and signaled to my pockets. "Or was I mistaken when I first walked in here?"

My chest heaved. "It's under control."

"Hmmm." He walked around the desk, stopping several feet in front of me. "You only have eight days until you turn thirty." He tapped the designer watch on his wrist. "Time is ticking, nephew."

He smiled, the kind of smile that was fake as fuck. "It was nice to see you." My muscles locked in place as he tapped my shoulder, then spun around. Each of his steps was measured, but I wasn't sure whether it was him trying to invoke some kind of stature or whether it was because he was nearly seventy years old.

My guard was well and truly up now that he was in the country. My instincts told me whatever he was here for didn't bode well for me.

"Oh." He halted at the door and faced me. "Don't forget, if you can't meet the requirements by your thirtieth birthday, you forfeit your position…" I opened my mouth, about to tell him I was aware of that, but he continued before I could even say anything. "To me."

I ground my teeth together, my body taking an involuntary step toward him. "That'll never happen."

"We'll see," he sang. His Italian accent made him sound like he was being polite, but I heard the veiled threat. He was here to take the business.

He was here to steal what wasn't his.

My father had been given permission to move from Italy to America when he was eighteen so he could expand the business. And he'd done just that, making it ten times more profitable than the Italian arm of the operation. The Italian arm that Uncle Paolo was the boss of.

I wasn't going to let him take anything from us. He'd destroy my father's legacy.

Fuck. But he wasn't wrong. If I didn't meet the requirements, he could take it without a fight from a single person.

I yanked my cell out of my pocket and clicked call on Christian's name. Two rings, and he answered, "Lorenzo."

"I need an answer from the Ricci girl," I gritted out, walking toward the office door and staring down the hallway, watching my uncle make his way out of the house with his two personal guards. Who the hell had let him in in the first place? "Now."

CHAPTER

4

AIDA

"Aida?" Noemi called as she walked into our bedroom. "There's a package for you." She stared down at the box in her hands. "It's from Lorenzo Beretta." Her gaze focused on me, an expectant look in her eyes.

I'd tried to push everything to the back of my mind since my date with Brad, but it felt impossible when everyone in my family would stare at me, waiting for me to give them an answer. Every day there'd be something to remind me I hadn't answered yet. Yesterday, a guy called Christian had come to see if I needed any more information—which I didn't—and now I'd been sent a package.

I just wanted to be a normal twenty-year-old:

attend college and get drunk at random parties. But I couldn't be that—I'd never been that.

"Open it," I said with a wave of my hand, turning back to my open laptop. I had another assignment due in two days. I didn't have time to think about anything else until it was finished. I didn't have the capacity in my brain to think about the proposition.

No. That wasn't true. I was lying to myself. All I'd been able to think about was the offer made to my parents. A wife. He needed a wife, and he'd chosen me.

Why? That was always the first question that popped into my mind, closely followed by how much would everything change? What about college? There was no way I was giving that up, not if I said yes. If I had one stipulation to this ridiculous thing, that would be it. I winced. Maybe I should have told Christian that yesterday.

I sighed. There were only four days until the wedding took place. Four days until I could be standing at the altar, giving up my entire life.

"Aida?" Noemi sat next to me on my bed. "Would it really be that bad if you said yes?"

I blinked. "I don't know." I huffed out a breath and closed my laptop, knowing I wouldn't be able to concentrate. "What if he wants me to give up college?"

"Tell him you won't." She shrugged as if it was

that easy. And maybe it was. Maybe I was over-thinking the whole situation.

"But..." I threw my head back, staring up at the off-white ceiling. "What if it doesn't work out?"

"What if it does?" Noemi replied, raising her brows. "What if you end up having an amazing life because you said yes? What if it meant you could achieve all of your dreams?" She paused. "Plus, Ma said she'd help me pay for my own apartment."

I laughed. "Only you would think like that."

"I'm only saying the truth." She chuckled, but I could see the hope in her eyes. She wanted her own freedom. A place where Vida could have her own room. "Open it." She thrust the box at me. "I want to know what he sent."

"Fine." I rolled my eyes and tore open the box to reveal another box. This one was smaller with the signature blue of the designer jewelry shop. My shaky fingers reached for it. "I'm scared to open it," I confessed to Noemi.

The grin on her face spread wider. "Just open it already!"

Slowly, I flicked the clasp on the front of the box and pulled the top up. "Holy shit." My breath left me in a whoosh, my eyes not quite believing what was right in front of me.

"Dayuuuuum." Noemi pushed closer to me. "That's one huge-ass ring."

She wasn't wrong. The dark-blue, shiny stone

wasn't anything I'd ever seen before, and surrounding it were more stones—what I was guessing were diamonds. I'd only ever seen rings like this in the movies or worn by obnoxiously rich people.

"There's a note in here," Noemi said, pulling a card out of the original box.

I placed the open ring box on the bed in front of us, unable to stop staring at it as I opened up the card. The front was plain, nothing to indicate what it was going to say inside. "I can't believe he sent me a ring," I whispered.

"Maybe he's trying to buy your attention," Noemi said, snickering. "He clearly doesn't know you."

Clearly, he didn't. Because if he did, he would have known things like that didn't impress me. If anything, they scared me away. We'd never spent money on things like that. Everything we had was what we needed, not wanted. We were frugal, not wasting a cent of our hard-earned money, but that was because we didn't have access to the kind of money the Berettas did. We lived opposite lives at totally different ends of the spectrum.

"What does the card say?"

I bit down on my bottom lip as I opened it up, seeing what I assumed was Lorenzo's scrawl on it, and read each word out loud. "Aida." I paused, trying not to let my gaze read ahead. "I know you haven't decided yet, but I wanted to send you something blue to wear on the day if you *do* say yes."

"Well…" Noemi cleared her throat. "I'm not sure he gets the concept of something blue."

"Yeah, me neither." I closed the card and caught sight of something on the back of it. "He's given me his number." My breaths came faster as I said his number in my head. "Does that mean he wants me to call him?"

"Do it," Noemi said, plucking my cell from next to my laptop. "Call him. Maybe it'll make it easier to make the decision." She handed me my cell. "It's not like you have a lot of time left."

She wasn't wrong. The church had been booked by Lorenzo's mom four days from now. And if I said yes, I'd have to go and buy a dress. Shit. I hadn't even thought about a dress. I'd blocked it all out, but now it was becoming all the more real. It wasn't just about me agreeing to become his wife. It was the production of the day. And then what about after? How would it all work?

I groaned and rubbed at my temples. "My brain is in overdrive."

"Call him," Noemi repeated as she stood.

"I—"

"Call him." She nodded, keeping her attention on me for several seconds, then spun around and walked out of the room, leaving me with the huge ring and my cell.

I stared at it for way too long, hoping the numbers would disappear so I wouldn't be able to call. But they didn't. They stayed scrawled onto the back of the card, willing me to dial them. So, I did. I bit the bullet, put the numbers into a new contact, then clicked call.

My stomach rolled with nerves as it rang out, and after several clicks, a deep voice answered, "This is Lorenzo."

"Lorenzo," I whispered, holding the open ring box in my hand. "This is erm…" I cleared my throat. "It's Aida." Silence greeted me, and I wondered if maybe he hadn't wanted me to call him. What if I'd jumped the gun? Crap. I turned the card over to see if there was a message with the numbers, but there wasn't. "I…I got your package."

"Do you like it?" he asked, his deep voice vibrating through the speaker.

"Well…" I bit down on my bottom lip, not sure whether I should be honest with him or tell him the truth. "It's very big." I heard a snicker from outside of my bedroom and narrowed my eyes on the half-closed door. Of course, Noemi was listening.

"But do you like it?" he repeated. *Did* I like it? I wasn't sure. In another world, maybe I would have been ecstatic with the ring, but in the land I lived in, I couldn't see myself ever wearing it. But that wasn't what he'd asked. He'd asked if I liked it, and the truth was, I did. It was pretty.

"Have you tried it on?" he asked, his voice lower now.

"Not yet."

"Try it on, Aida."

I swallowed at the sound of him saying my name. It sounded so different coming from his mouth. "Okay." I slowly reached for the ring, plucking it from the velvet pillow it was wedged in, then slipped it onto my left ring finger. "It fits." It was so big it extended up to my knuckle. "I…" I closed my eyes, trying to make myself invisible as I asked, "Why me?"

"Why you?" I heard the creak of a chair, and I imagined him sitting up.

"Yeah, why me?" I opened my eyes and stared at the ring. "Why do you want to marry me?"

He cleared his throat, and I wondered if he was processing what to say. He didn't come across as someone who thought before he spoke, but then I didn't know him. Which was the whole point. Why would he choose to ask me to marry him when I was sure he had a line full of women ready to take this ring.

"Because my gut told me to." I opened my mouth, not sure what to say, but he continued, "I don't overthink things, Aida. When my gut tells me to do something, I do it."

He made sense, but that didn't mean I fully understood him.

"What is your gut telling you, Aida?"

I wasn't sure I could take much more of him saying my name. The way the letters rolled off his tongue had warmth spreading through me and a deep need in my stomach to hear it over and over again.

"I…I'm not sure what it's saying." I huffed out a breath and leaned my head in my hand. "I just… there's too much to think about."

"Aida."

"Yeah."

"I'm going to ask you a question. Don't think about it. Don't pause. Just answer it with your gut."

I pulled in a deep breath. "Okay."

"Okay." There was a pause and then, "Will you marry me?"

I didn't think. I didn't process the question and think about all of the what-ifs. I let my gut answer for me. "Yes." I slammed my hand over my mouth, shocked at the single word that had come out. I'd been fretting over this entire situation from the moment Ma and Dad had told me, and all it had taken was one conversation with Lorenzo for me to finally come to a decision.

"I'll see you at the altar, Aida."

Holy shit.

I was getting married.

To Lorenzo Beretta.

I was going to be the wife of a Mafia boss.

———

LORENZO

The church was packed with people who had come from all over the world to see the next boss of the Beretta family get married. A mixture of old and new generations filled each of the pews, but still, there wasn't enough room for everyone. People lined the edges of the church, several of the families not mixing with one another, but they were here as witnesses.

Witnesses to a new age.

An age of the modern reign.

A reign I intended to take full control of.

My gaze roved around the giant building, first landing on my ma's smiling face and then on my uncle, who sat next to her. He was becoming a permanent fixture in the house—a fixture I didn't like. He was trying to insert himself, offer advice that wasn't wanted. And all I could do was sit back and take it. Until I was married, I wasn't the boss. Only then could I tell him what I really thought.

Uncle Paolo's lips curved up into a smile. I tilted my head in greeting, not willing to give him more than that. He thought I didn't know who he was, but I did. My dad had prepared me for this day for what felt like my entire life, and that included detailed accounts of the Italian arm of the operation. Which included Uncle Paolo. I knew he wasn't here for the good of the family because, if he was, he would have come to my dad's funeral.

But he hadn't.

He'd only come stateside when he could gain something—or that was what he thought.

As soon as I had the ring on my finger and Aida as a wife by my side, I could take over. And my first order of business was to find out exactly what Uncle Paolo was doing here.

My nostrils flared the longer we stared at each other, neither of us willing to look away or back down. He may have been the senior person right now, but he wouldn't be for long. And as if I had willed it, the music started.

I snapped my attention away from Uncle Paolo and onto the aisle that ran through the center of the church. People stood, their gazes veering to the doors as they opened.

And then she walked in.

I couldn't help but quirk my lips at the simple off-white dress. The closer she got, the more I saw the lace detail, and I knew the women of the family wouldn't have approved this. Tradition was to get married in white, but she was bucking it. I reasoned that she should have had some control. After all, this wasn't a real marriage. It was a union made out of necessity, one she didn't really have a choice in. So, I didn't think too much about her breaking the tradition. I let it slip away, deciding I had bigger problems than the damn color of her dress.

She turned to face her dad when she was a couple of feet away, whispering something to him, and then she was standing opposite me, her small smile making me feel uneasy.

I had to do this. I had to marry her; otherwise, I wouldn't be the boss. I repeated those words over and over in my mind, needing them to solidify why we were doing this.

The priest started talking, but I didn't take in a single word, not when he spoke of the promises we would make each other, and not when he spoke to all the guests. It whizzed by in a flurry, and then he told me to repeat after him. My laser focus zoomed in on Aida. Her dark hair was curled, partly down and whispering on her shoulders. She was beautiful, that was undeniable, but she wasn't for me. She'd never be for me. It didn't stop me spewing the vows, promising her things I had no right to promise. Because I would break every single one of them. I knew that. People closest to me knew that. But I wondered if she did.

Did she truly know what she was getting herself into? Or had I depicted an image that would never be a reality?

It was too late now, though. Because as I slipped the black wedding ring onto her finger, and she to mine in return, the vows were sealed.

I was married. Married when I had no intention of seeing her as my wife.

Cheers rang out, and the priest told me I could kiss the bride. I leaned forward, taking in a deep lungful of air and letting her rose scent flow through me. It was delicate, not too overpowering, but not too subtle. It was there, enticing me, telling me to come closer.

"I can't believe we just did that," she whispered, her gaze capturing mine. I didn't answer her as I placed a soft kiss on her lips, then grasped her hand in mine. Now wasn't the time for words. It was time for putting on a show. Time to appear like this wasn't one big fuckin' lie.

Because that was what it was.

A lie.

A lie I was already beginning to regret, but a lie I couldn't go back on—not now. Not now that I had all the power of the underground. I'd just been crowned the king, but I'd also been deemed a husband.

Fuck.

I veered Aida down the aisle, trying to keep the smile on my face and act like I was happy. And I was. I was happy that all the uncertainty in the business was now gone. Happy that I could finally have the final fuckin' say.

"Lorenzo," Aida gasped. "Slow down. My legs aren't as long as yours."

I grunted as I gripped her hand harder, trying to silently tell her to hurry up. We had a party to get to, and then my work would get started. Why the hell did people have parties after weddings? The ceremony should have been enough to satisfy, but Ma wasn't hearing a single word about it.

So off we went, in the back of the SUV Christian drove, and to the mansion. The place I now called home. The place Aida would call home.

I slid over the back seat, trying to get as far from Aida as I could. If she noticed, she didn't say anything, and the thought sent a thrill through me. I'd made the right choice with her. She'd be a good Italian wife and keep her mouth shut, so I could handle the business I'd been trained to take over.

The drive was only a few minutes, and then we were pulling into the sprawling driveway. She gasped beside me; her face nearly pressed against the closed window. She'd been here before, but with quick clarity, I realized she'd probably only ever come through the delivery entrance and into the kitchen.

"This is where you live?" she asked, her voice small.

"Yeah." I typed off a quick message to one of the captains, then stowed my cell away. "You live here now too."

"With you."

"And Ma." I pulled the handle on the door. "As

well as Dante and Sofia." I pushed out of the back of the SUV and made my way around the back, staring up at the mansion and trying to imagine it through new eyes, but it was impossible because it was all I was used to.

A throat cleared, so I snapped my head toward it. "You forgetting something?" Christian asked, raising his brows. When I didn't answer, he pointed toward the back door of the SUV. "Your wife."

Fuck.

I sneered and darted toward her side of the car, then opened the door. "Thank you," she said, her gaze not quite meeting mine. I grunted in reply, not expecting anything else to come from her, so when she asked, "Who are Dante and Sofia?" I puffed out a breath.

"My brother and sister." I signaled my hand toward the house. "Shall we go in?"

"Okay." She stumbled a little on the stones lining the driveway, and Christian shot his hand out to help steady her. It was a move I should have done now that I was her husband, but I didn't want to give her the wrong idea, not this soon into our arrangement.

The doors opened as soon as we walked toward them, the housekeeper holding a tray of drinks in greeting. She spoke to Aida, but I had no intention of standing around and chatting. I had work to do, deals to make, and people to take care of. If I had it my way, none of this would be happening. I vowed to myself that it would be the last time someone told me what I had to do.

It didn't take long for the guests to spill inside the mansion, and I was forced to make small talk, to walk around introducing Aida to everyone. My practiced smile and good manners came in useful, that was until we made it to my family.

"Ma," I said, placing my hand on her elbow. "You've met Aida."

Ma gasped and spun around, her face lighting up in a way I hadn't seen since before my dad had died. "Oh, Aida." She kissed her cheeks. "You look so beautiful."

"Thank you, Mrs. Beretta."

"No." She clasped her shoulders. "You call me Ma from now on. Got it?"

Aida smiled, and I hated it. I hated how sweet and innocent it was. She wasn't like us. She was good, and I'd dragged her into this without a second thought.

"Thanks, Ma." She took Ma's hand in hers. "Your house is so amazing." Ma grinned, and I knew these two would make fast friends.

"Are you going to introduce me, nephew?" Uncle Paolo asked, and Ma froze, her gaze slipping to mine, a warning in her dark-brown eyes. She knew more than she let on, and I wondered how much Dad had confided in her. Did he confess everything to her each night? Or did he leave her in the dark, not wanting her to know what he did when his darkness took over?

"Yes." I placed my hand at the small of Aida's back and pulled her closer. "Uncle Paolo, this is Aida." I looked down at Aida, the top of her head coming level with my shoulders. She was too short, and I was guessing she had heels on—just another reason why she wasn't my type. "Aida, this is my uncle Paolo. He flew all the way from Italy to see us get married." I tried to silently communicate with her, but I wasn't sure if she got the message because she flashed him her innocent smile and held her hand out.

"Uncle Paolo." He took her hand, bringing it to his lips and planting a kiss on her knuckles. "It's so nice to meet you."

"You too, bella." He winked, his gaze instantly meeting mine. "Could I interest you in a dance?"

"I…" Aida glanced up at me, asking permission, and I gave it to her with a tilt of my head.

"You shouldn't have done that," Ma said, watching them move to the middle of the floor in the living room. "He's trying to—"

"Boss," a deep voice said from behind me, and I turned to it, seeing a stern-faced Christian. "There's been a problem."

I didn't hesitate to step away from Ma. It was my excuse to escape, and I took it with both hands. I didn't say a word to Ma as I moved away from her and toward Christian. "Not here," I told him, doing up the button on my suit jacket and making my way out of the room.

As soon as we were near the front door, he pointed to it. "Out there." I stepped outside, noting the two guards at the front doors and the SUV parked at an angle near the water feature. "We caught two soldiers in the warehouse." I snapped my gaze to him, already feeling my anger building at his words. "Stealing."

"Stealing what?" I asked, moving toward the SUV.

"The latest shipment of guns."

"Get them out." I signaled, halting a few feet from the SUV.

My blood thrummed through my veins, my heartbeat throbbing in my ears. I needed this. I needed to let out some of the frustration I felt at… everything. Nothing had been right since we'd buried Dad, and I wasn't sure anything ever would be again. But this? This would give me the relief I needed—for now, at least.

The doors swung open, and two figures were hauled outside. I recognized them from the streets, but more than that, from the family. Our own family had tried to steal from us, and on my wedding day of all days. I tutted and pushed my hands into the pockets of my slacks.

"Well…" I paced in front of them, the stones crunching under my shiny dress shoes. "I hear you've been stealing."

"No, please, sir," one of them begged, holding his hands up in front of him. "It was a mistake. We just—"

"Shut up!" the other one shouted at him.

"No." The beggar turned to the other one. "It was all your idea!"

"Snitch," he sneered, trying to get closer to him, but Christian held him back. It was only then I realized that Dante, my brother, was holding the other guy. His face was carefully neutral, not showing a single emotion.

I could hit two birds with one stone. I could get out my anger while also showing Dante what he would have to do now. He wasn't the favorite child any longer. He wouldn't be able to walk away from the violence, not when it would be *him* dishing it out. I'd been a kid the first time I'd watched my father torture a man, and now it was time for Dante to see a snippet of his future.

"Hands," I said simply, crouching down and retrieving my knife strapped to my leg. I never went anywhere without it.

"No! Please!" The first guy begged again as I unsheathed my blade. "Please, Mr. Beretta, please. I have a family, and a—"

"Shut the fuck up," Dante snapped. "Hold your hand out."

I raised my brow at Dante, not having expected that.

"You committed a crime against the family," I started, twirling the knife in my hand. "And on my wedding day of all days." I tutted again, shaking my head like I was disappointed when, in reality, I was glad I had something else to do but stand next to Aida and act like we were happy as shit.

"I'm sorry. I'm sorry."

The apology went right over my head. "Hand." I waited, but when he wasn't quick enough, I growled, "Your fuckin' hand. Now."

The beggar slowly held it out in front of him, and with one quick movement, I slammed the knife onto his wrist, chopping his hand clean off. Blood spurted out onto the stones, a spot landing on my shoe. He squealed in pain, collapsing to the ground as Dante let him go, but I didn't pay attention to him anymore. I'd only done half of the job, and the vibrations working through me *needed* me to finish the other half.

"You no longer have the protection of the family," I said, my voice sounding far away. I was in the zone, a zone I'd created when I was a kid. "This is your warning." I pointed the bloody knife at the other soldier who stood taller as I halted in front of him. "You don't get a second warning." I raised the knife and held eye contact with the man who would soon lose his hand too. "You'll simply be dead," I said lightly, acting as if I was talking about the weather. It was a threat I always followed through with, and they both knew this.

Maybe they'd thought they could get away with it today.

They'd been wrong.

I lifted my arm, whooshed it through the air, and slashed right through his wrist. He'd done a good job so far of keeping quiet and showing a brave face, but even this low-level soldier couldn't keep his screams of pain inside. He went limp, his body collapsing on the ground, his face as pale as a ghost.

"Clean this up," I told Christian and Dante as I pulled my pocket square out of my top pocket. I dragged the expensive material over the sharp blade, sheathed it in its carrier, then attached it back to my calf.

"You got it, boss," Christian replied, and with that, I spun around, making my way back toward the front doors of the mansion, but what I saw there had me pausing.

Aida stared at me, her off-white dress looking more like pure white in the dimming light. Her gaze veered behind me as her shaky hand pushed away some hair that had obscured her face. She opened her mouth, a small gasp of air escaping.

She didn't know what to say, but at least she wasn't running and screaming.

I stepped toward her, demanding her attention as I got closer. She involuntarily backed up a step, and I smirked at the move. She didn't know what to think—what to feel.

She blinked several times as I stopped next to her. I grinned down at her, waiting to see if she would do or say something. I wasn't sure how much she'd seen, but it was clear as day what I'd just done. When she stayed carefully silent, I winked.

"Welcome to the family."

CHAPTER

5

AIDA

Welcome to the family.

I couldn't get the four words out of my head. Not after I followed him back inside, and not after we mingled with more guests. A spot of blood stained his hand, and I wasn't sure whether he wasn't aware or just didn't care. It was more likely the latter.

I'd known exactly who Lorenzo was. I'd heard the horror stories. I'd seen the papers and articles written about the Berettas. I'd listened to the gossip that always flowed in the city. But I'd never seen it firsthand. Not like that.

My gaze veered down to his leg as we walked Ma, Dad, Noemi, and Vida to the mansion doors. It had been a couple of hours since I'd witnessed the violence Lorenzo so easily displayed, and I was afraid the aftermath of what he'd done would still be there.

But as the doors opened, the driveway was clear, all of the evidence gone as if it never happened. I thought I'd known what I was getting myself in to, but the more time that ticked by, the more I understood I had *no* idea.

"Thank you for coming," Lorenzo said smoothly with his hand on my back again. At first, I hadn't minded it, but since I'd watched him outside, all I could think about was what that hand had done earlier tonight. Was that normal for him? Had he done worse? I inwardly rolled my eyes at myself. Of course, he had.

"It was a great day," Ma said, her lips pulled into a smile, but only those who knew her most could see that it was fake. She was trying to put on a facade, but I could spot the worry in her eyes as she looked at me. "You'll be okay, Aida?" She cleared her throat, probably realizing how her words could have come across to the most powerful man in the state. "I mean, you have everything you need?"

I nodded, too afraid to say any actual words. What if I blurted out what I'd seen? What if I begged them to take me with them? I couldn't do either of those things, so I stayed silent.

"I'll miss you tonight, Auntie Aida," Vida said,

her little arms wrapping around my legs as tightly as they could.

"I'll miss you too." I knelt down, trying to stay on balance with the heels I was wearing, and took her face in my hands. "Don't frown. Your face will get stuck like it." She giggled, a failsafe to have me forget about everything else around me. "I'll always be here." I moved my hand to her chest, placing my palm over her heart. "And here." I tapped the side of her head. "And if that fails, you can steal Mama's cell and call me."

Her bottom lip popped out. "But what about morning cuddles?"

I blinked, not sure what to say to that. Every morning I held my arms open when she woke up, and we spent at least twenty minutes talking about nothing and everything all at the same time.

"Auntie will have morning cuddles from Uncle Lorenzo now," Noemi said, her voice sickly sweet.

"You will?" Vida stared up at me, her eyes wide and innocent, and I had no idea what to say to her. "Uncle Lorenzo?" Her attention moved higher; her brows raised. "Will you make sure Auntie Aida gets her morning cuddles?"

"I…" He cleared his throat, his hand landing on my shoulder. "I'll make sure." His fingers squeezed, and I didn't think he was aware he was doing it, not consciously anyway.

"Okay, then." Vida stepped back and lifted her

hand in a wave. "Love you, Auntie Aida." She paused and grinned wide, showcasing her missing front tooth. "Love you, Uncle Lorenzo."

"Love you too, sweetie," I whispered. I felt a lump build in my throat as I stood, watching my family get into a car that would take them home. The tears burned the back of my eyes, and all I wanted was to get into the car with them, to go home where I knew what would happen in the morning. I didn't even know where I was sleeping tonight, and if I didn't get this damn dress off soon, I was going to go out of my mind.

"Shall we?" Lorenzo said, but I didn't look up at him as we both turned around. The doors shut behind us thanks to the house staff, and it was now too quiet. Only Lorenzo and I were left in the grand foyer of the mansion. "I can show you upstairs," Lorenzo continued. He made it sound like a question, but he was already walking toward the staircase, so I followed. At least it would mean I could get out of this dress.

The double-sided staircase was grand, just like everything else in the house, and I wondered if it had been built the same time as the mansion or whether it had been added later. Elaborate Bs were carved into the wood, gilded with gold just like in the mansion's front doors.

"This side is where everyone else sleeps," Lorenzo said as we got to the top of the stairs, pointing toward the left. He turned right and started to walk down the wide hallway. My heels sunk into the plush burgundy carpet, and my eyes widened. Should I have taken my shoes off up here? *Crap.*

"This is our wing." *We had a wing?* He halted in front of the first door on the right. "This is an extra bathroom." He pointed to the door opposite. "Guest room," he continued, pointing to the next two doors. "Guest rooms." Then he stopped in front of the next set of doors. "This is us." He pushed open the door on the right and waved me inside.

"Wow," I whispered. In the middle of the room sat the largest bed I'd ever seen. The crisp white bedsheets begged me to get inside them. "This is... amazing." It was just as elaborate as the rest of the mansion. A doorway to the left led into a dressing room and a closet as big as my bedroom and Ma and Dad's bedroom put together. Then, through that, was a bathroom with a shower, a single sink, and a toilet.

"You have everything you need?" I heard Lorenzo ask, and it was only then that I realized he hadn't followed me inside.

I frowned as I moved back into the main part of the bedroom, swiping my fingers across a dresser that had my toiletry bag on top of it. "Are you not coming inside?"

"No." Lorenzo's stern gaze met mine. "I'm

across the hall if you need anything." He took another step backward. "I'll see you at breakfast."

I blinked, not sure what to say, but before I got anything out, he disappeared through the door opposite my room. *My* room. I had my own room. I didn't know why I was surprised by it. I didn't know why I couldn't hold back the tears that had been burning the back of my eyes from the moment my family had left.

My family. They weren't my family now, though. *He* was my family. And I already hated him.

———

LORENZO

"Morning, brother," a soft voice greeted.

I glanced up from my cell screen to see Sofia pulling out her usual chair. "Morning."

"I see it didn't take you long." She pointed to the seat I was in—a seat I'd hesitated to take. For all of our lives, we'd had our set places at the table. My dad at the head, my ma at his right, and me at his left. Dante sat next to Ma and Sofia next to me.

But all that changed the moment I said my vows. The second I became the boss.

Now it was me sitting at the head of the table.

"It's my rightful place," I told Sofia and set down my cell on the table. I had a meeting in ten minutes, and she was the only one who had come down for breakfast so far.

Sofia shrugged, her highlighted hair drifting over her shoulder at the move. "It is. I just…I hadn't expected it so soon." She paused, her gaze meeting mine as her usual breakfast was placed in front of her. "It's just different, I suppose."

I knew what she meant, and if I was honest with myself, I agreed. It was different. *Everything* was different now.

"You'll get used to it," a voice said, and my lips immediately lifted at the corners. Ma always knew exactly what to say. Where Dad had struggled with the emotional stuff, Ma had excelled. She tapped my shoulder twice and placed a kiss on my cheek. "Morning."

"Morning, Ma." I tracked her movements as she pulled out her usual chair.

"Wait." She halted, her eyes widening. "This isn't my seat anymore."

"What?" I frowned over at her. "Of course, it is."

"It's not." Her gaze moved behind me, and my back straightened. I could feel *her* before I'd seen her. And although I knew I should have turned around and greeted her, I couldn't. I needed to set out as I meant to go on. She wasn't here to be my partner. She was here to be my wife in name only.

"Sit down, Ma."

Ma cut her eyes at me, not needing to say a single word for me to know she wasn't happy with what I had said. It was on the tip of my tongue to tell her I was the one who decided where everyone would sit, but I knew my limits. Respect was a two-way street, and she was still my ma.

"Aida, come and sit here." Ma pointed at the seat she'd half pulled out. "Your place is by Loren-zo's side." I hated the words she'd spoken. I didn't want anyone by my side. If I had it my way, I would have stayed as free as a bird and put all of my energy and focus into the business. But rules were made for a reason, and not even I could break them —not yet anyway.

I heard the shuffling of feet, the waft of Aida's rose scent, and then she was sitting next to me. I gritted my teeth, trying to tell myself to act in a certain way, but it was hard when all my head was focused on was a stranger sitting at the table. I didn't know her—I didn't *want* to know her.

"What would you like for breakfast, Mrs. Beretta?" the housekeeper, Mrs. Larson, asked, her gaze downcast. She'd been working here for twenty years, and I could count on one hand the number of times she'd actually looked any of us in the eyes.

"Erm…" My nostrils flared at the sound of Aida's voice. "I don't usually eat breakfast."

"It's the most important meal of the day," Sofia supplied, her tone mocking. I stared at her, willing her with my eyes to look my way, but she was too focused on Aida. "Right, Ma?"

"Oh. Well." Aida cleared her throat. "We don't usually sit and eat breakfast together as a family. It's more of a grab-and-go type situation."

"You don't eat together?" Sofia asked, bringing a spoonful of oatmeal to her lips. "That's…weird." Her eyes widened. "I don't mean it's bad. Just… something we don't do. I'm sorry—"

"Don't be silly." Aida laughed. "I get it." My gaze drifted to her, but my head stayed in exactly the same position. "We're all just so busy at home." Her eyes lit up and her lips lifted into a smile I hadn't seen on her face before. "Dad is normally out on deliveries, and Ma is working in the shop. Noemi is at her second job, which just leaves Vida and me."

"Vida?" Ma asked, engrossed in what Aida was saying. Part of me wished she'd sat down silently like I'd wanted her to do, but the other part of me was intrigued.

"She's my niece." Aida leaned forward, her hands planted on the solid oak table. "She was here yesterday."

"Oh! Yes." Ma laughed. "I remember her. Such a little beauty."

"She is." Aida sighed. "So yeah, it's normally just us two. I help Noemi out by taking her to school some mornings if she's not back from her job in time. If I'm not doing that, then I'm heading to college."

"College?" Ma asked. "I didn't realize you were in college."

"Yeah. I'm in my second year. I'm there on scholarship."

"That's amazing," Sofia said, her tone wistful. "I always wanted to go to college, but school just wasn't my strength."

"It's not for everyone," Aida said, winning over Sofia in a single sentence. "I'm sure you have other awesome talents."

"I do." Sofia leaned forward, fully into the conversation now. "I love to draw. And paint. Anything artsy. I have part of my bedroom converted into an art studio upstairs. Maybe you can come and—"

I pushed my chair back and stared at my half-finished breakfast sitting on the table. "I have a meeting." All conversation stopped at my words, but I didn't look at any of them. I needed to get out of here. I needed to get away. I needed to not be reminded of what I'd done yesterday—what I'd committed to.

"I'll see you later, Ma." I spun on my heels, not acknowledging anyone else, and headed straight for my office.

I hadn't been in there since it was officially mine. For weeks I'd waited to make it my own, haunted by the memories inside the four walls. But now, I was able to do whatever I wanted to it, and I had the perfect person in mind who could help.

Grinning, I pulled my cell out and shot off an email to Veev. She'd not only get the job done, but she'd be able to distract me from everything else.

The perfect combination.

———

AIDA

"You don't understand," I groaned. "It's like I'm constantly walking on eggshells."

Noemi laughed as she rang up another customer, clicking the numbers on the screen with her fake nails. "*I* don't understand?" She raised her brow and turned her head so she could make eye contact with me. "You're right, Aida. I don't understand. I don't understand what it's like to live in a freaking *mansion*."

She turned back to the customer. "Fifteen dollars and fifty-eight cents." The guy placed a twenty in her palm, and I watched as my sister grabbed his change from the drawer and handed it to him.

"It's not about the mansion," I snapped as soon as the bell over the door rang, signaling there was no one in the store but Noemi and me. "It's been four days, and he hasn't said a single word to me."

"He's adjusting."

"Or maybe he's just an asshole." I ground my teeth together and sloped forward. "Why did I agree to this?"

"Because you wanted to live in a fancy mansion?" Noemi asked, laughing so loud it ricocheted off the walls. "Listen"—she put her hand on my shoulder—"it's been four days, give it some time." She shrugged. "Get to know each other. Find out what he likes and what he doesn't like. Cook him dinner. Just get to know him."

I let out a breath, knowing she was right. Lorenzo and I didn't know each other, not really. "Fine." I stood and glanced around the store. "I suppose I could take the ingredients to make Ma's spaghetti."

Noemi moaned and rubbed her stomach. "Yes. There's no way he'd turn down spaghetti." She wagged her finger in my face. "The way to a man's heart is through his stomach."

I laughed at her words, but I agreed with her. We needed to get to know each other. We needed to not be strangers living in the same home. So instead of sitting here for another two hours moaning about how much Lorenzo was ignoring me, I decided to do something about it. It wasn't as if he was going to come to me, so that meant I had to go to him.

It was already nearing five, and I knew the housekeeper would have dinner ready for seven, so if I got a taxi back to the mansion, I could make it there in time to cook.

I gathered everything I needed, told Noemi to put it on Lorenzo's tab, and hightailed it out of there. Luck was on my side because as soon as I held my hand out for a taxi, one pulled over. It was almost as if destiny was trying to work her magic because not one red light stopped us from the store to the mansion.

"Thanks!" I handed the taxi driver some cash and pushed out of the back, then headed toward the gates. I'd already managed to forget the code to get inside, so I pressed the buzzer, waiting for someone to answer, but after a couple of minutes of silence, I started to get antsy.

Standing outside the Beretta family mansion on my own was asking for someone to put a target on my back. I'd been warned by Lorenzo's ma to always watch my back and to be aware of everything going on around me, so the more I waited out here, the more on edge I became.

"Trying to get in?" a deep, gravelly voice asked.

I squealed, my heart jumping into my throat. "Fuck." I slammed my hand onto my chest, my eyes widening as a tall man sauntered toward me, but the closer he got, the more I recognized him as Dante, Lorenzo's brother. *Thank God for that.*

"I forgot the code," I said sheepishly, trying to balance the bag of groceries and my backpack. I wasn't sure which one was heavier—the backpack. Definitely the backpack. "I should have memorized it or—"

"I've been living here all my life, and I still don't remember it," Dante said, swiping his hand through his hair. Where Lorenzo was all harsh lines and broodiness, Dante was easygoing and smooth. They were complete opposites, but he still had the telltale Beretta stare, and no doubt the same violence ran through his veins. I shivered, trying to shake the memory of the blood from my wedding night, and focused back on Dante. There was something about him that put me at ease. Something less intense.

He leaned past me, his arm touching mine, and pressed the buzzer. Only he didn't let go after a couple of seconds. He just kept his thumb planted on it, smiling into the dome above it.

"Does that really—" The gates opened up, and I blinked. "Work?"

"Yep." He stood to his full height, at least as tall as Lorenzo, definitely over six feet, and took the bag from my arms. "What's all this?"

I blinked, not overthinking it as I walked by his side through the now open gates. "I wanted to cook...for Lorenzo."

"Yeah?" Dante grinned. "Do I get to taste it too?"

"If you want." I hauled my backpack higher on my shoulder. "I always make enough to feed ten thousand anyway." I laughed, feeling like the tension that had been a permanent fixture in my body was starting to ease. "Lorenzo likes pasta, right?"

"Of course." Dante's gaze flicked to the area opposite the mansion doors, and I knew he was remembering what happened in that spot. He'd been there, witnessing it all, and I wondered whether that was what happened on the regular. These weren't normal men. No, these were Mafia men who grew up with their fate pinned to their backs. They knew they'd be nothing other than part of the family. And for the first time, I wondered if that was what Lorenzo actually wanted.

He hadn't had a choice in marrying me either. He couldn't walk away from this. He couldn't say no, not unless he didn't want to take over. Maybe I'd misjudged him? Maybe we were more similar than I realized. We were both stuck in this situation, so we may as well make the most of it. Right?

The doors swung open as we got closer, and the action pulled both Dante and me out of our own heads. "You need this taken into the kitchen?" Dante asked.

"Please." I smiled over at him, trying not to show that it was forced. He headed toward the kitchen at the back of the mansion, and as soon as I stepped inside the bustling room, my shoulders slumped. I felt at home back here. It was familiar, like this was where I was meant to be. Not on the other side, having someone cook for me.

"Mrs. Beretta," the housekeeper said, her tone shocked. "Do you need something?"

I shook my head and placed my backpack on one of the chairs. "Just your permission to cook tonight."

The housekeeper's eyes widened. "You don't need my permission." She lunged away from the stovetop. "It's all yours."

I laughed as Dante placed my bag of ingredients down. "Only for tonight," I told her, trying to make it seem like I wasn't taking over. "I just wanted to cook something special for Lorenzo." My tone got more and more unsure the more I spoke, but as Dante slipped past me and grinned, I felt a little more confident in what I was doing. I mean, what was the worst that could happen?

CHAPTER

6

LORENZO

I sniffed, my stomach rumbling at the smell wafting through the house from the kitchen. I had no idea what Mrs. Larson was cooking, but it was unlike anything else I'd ever smelled.

"So, we're agreed?" Uncle Antonio asked, sitting in one of the chairs on the other side of my new black marble desk. Veev had gone to work right away on the office decor, and although it wasn't exactly my taste, it would be good enough for now. Just until I felt like I wasn't walking in my dad's shadow.

"Yeah." I leaned back in my chair and clicked the top of my pen over and over again. It was hard to think clearly when all I could smell was what promised to be a tasty meal. "What about the guns?"

"What about them?" Uncle Alonzo asked.

"Can we expand?" I asked, trying to get back on track. I had big ideas moving forward, but I knew it couldn't be done all at once. I had to tread lightly to make sure that when we made our move, it wouldn't be temporary. We needed new ways of working, new connections, and I'd been working on those connections for a long fuckin' time.

"To where?"

"Out of state." I tilted my head. "I have some contacts."

Uncle Alonzo groaned. "Not the bikers." I grinned at him. "Your father didn't want to get mixed up with—"

"I'm not my father," I snapped, throwing the pen onto my desk and trying not to wince at the loud clang. "Things are changing, Uncle. Nothing is like it used to be. Dad was stuck in the old ways, but the feds have worked it out. If we want to sustain the lives that we have—or make them better—then we need to look at new places and get into business with people that no one thinks we would." I rapped my knuckles on the desk and stood. "We need to make surprises at every turn." I walked around the desk and pushed my hands into my slacks pockets. "It's the future."

Uncle Alonzo looked skeptical, but the curve of the corner of Uncle Antonio's lips told me he approved. Not that I was looking for approval, but it was nice to see either way.

"You're the boss," Uncle Alonzo finally said.

"I am." I glanced around the room at the men inside it—the men I trusted most. Uncle Alonzo, Uncle Antonio, Christian, and Dante. Dante was still learning the inner workings, but I knew it wouldn't take him long. Beretta blood ran through his veins, and there was nothing stronger than that. "Tomorrow we need to discuss the Paolo situation—"

A knock at the door interrupted me, and I narrowed my eyes at it. Everybody knew not to disturb the room when the door was closed.

"Dinner is ready!" a sweet voice sang. I clenched my hands at the sound, trying to shoot daggers through the door.

"Why the hell is she—"

"She cooked for you," Dante said, and I growled at being interrupted a second time. He acted like he didn't hear my frustration loud and clear as he grinned at me. "She's trying to be a good Italian woman." He winked. "That's what you wanted, right?" He laughed, walking past me and skimming his shoulder against my arm. "Come on now, Lorenzo. Your wife has summoned you."

"Fuck you," I ground out. "I don't get fuckin' summoned."

"So that's not your stomach rumbling at the smell of her food, then?" My stomach rumbled as if on cue, and Dante let out an obnoxiously loud laugh.

I stepped toward him. "You better fuckin' run, little brother."

"Or what?" He backed away, holding his hands in the air. "You gonna chop my hands off too?"

"Only if you steal what's mine," I gritted out, advancing toward him.

"That a promise?" Dante asked as he turned the door handle and pulled the door open just enough for him to slip through it.

"Yeah, it is." I followed him out of the office, not taking my attention off him for a second as he backed all the way up to the dining room door. Only when it hit his back did he spin around and dart inside.

I pushed my shoulders back and smirked. He knew better than to put his back to me. No one ever turned their back on me, not if they knew what was good for them. I'd spent my entire twenties building a reputation in the city—in the state. A reputation I knew I'd need if I was to take over as boss.

"Oh. I didn't realize we had guests." I halted at the sound of her voice again, feeling a shiver roll up my spine. How the hell did she keep appearing out of nowhere? "I made extra, so there's enough for everyone." Of course, she did. Not only was she sweet, but she'd also made sure there was enough food to go around. Why the hell had she done that? Why was she grating on me so much? And why the hell couldn't my stomach get the memo and stop fuckin' grumbling.

"We're not staying," Uncle Antonio grunted. "My wife will shoot me if I'm late for dinner again this week." Inside, I wanted to laugh because there was no way my aunt Vivianna would do anything to hurt him. She was the sweetest, most kindest damn woman I knew.

"Okay, then." I turned my head to see Aida standing there, holding a hot dish with several towels. "What about you, Uncle Alonzo?" she asked.

"I've got to head off too." He smiled down at her. "Maybe next time?"

She nodded, her cheeks lifting as her smile widened. "I'll hold you to that."

"I have no doubt," he replied, then walked away with Uncle Antonio at his side. I should have made them stay. At least then I would have had an extra buffer at the dinner table.

"And you, Christian?"

Christian shrugged, glancing at me and then

back to Aida. "Sure." He stepped toward her. "Want me to take that?"

"Nope." She kept her smile in place, and I sneered at it. I was getting real damn sick of her smile, but more than that, I was getting frustrated with myself for wanting to see it more. Four days. It had taken four days for her to take me off guard. "I got it." She drifted past me, turned at the last second so she was only inches from me, then pushed the door open with her back.

"Damn," I muttered under my breath. I scraped my palm down my face, trying to make sense of everything around me.

"Damn is right," Christian murmured, following her into the dining room.

I stood there, staring at the door, wondering if I should just turn around. Going in there would only give her more fuel. *Right?* I gritted my teeth and closed my eyes. I was trapped. Damned if I didn't and damned if I did.

My stomach grumbled, making the decision for me, so I pushed open the door, taking in everyone's faces and the way they were watching Aida standing and dishing up the food onto plates. The first one she placed at my seat, and then she went around the table, serving herself last.

"This smells so good," Sofia moaned, bringing her face closer to the pasta.

"It tastes even better," Aida said, placing her

hands in her lap. "My ma taught me how to make it when I was a little girl."

Ma made a noise in the back of her throat. "Sofia would never get in the kitchen with me." She narrowed her eyes at Sofia and pointed her fork in the air. "No matter what bribery I tried."

Aida laughed, the sound a soft tinkle that caused my body to lean forward. I was standing on the periphery, watching them like I wasn't even here as they shoveled food into their mouths. Everyone but Aida, that was. She was waiting—waiting for me.

"Do you like to cook, Ma?" Aida asked, giving Ma her full attention. And as her head was turned, I took my opportunity to sit. I didn't want her looking my way, not when I was fighting in my own head. From the moment she'd arrived at the house, I'd been on edge. Maybe it was because I had all the responsibility on my shoulders now, or maybe it was because I hadn't been able to get the relief I apparently needed.

I picked up my fork, trying to block out their conversations, and twirled the bright red sauce-covered goodness on my fork.

"I do. Though I get to do it very little now." Ma's lips turned down into a frown.

"We could cook together," Aida offered, and I stopped midway to my mouth. I couldn't sit here and listen to this. She was becoming part of the family, and I would be damned if that was going to happen. She was here to fulfill the need for me to become boss, not become a permanent fixture.

"No," I ground out, cutting my eyes to Aida. "Your place isn't in the kitchen. We have staff for that."

She blinked several times. "Erm…but I like to cook sometimes. And I—"

"I said *no*." I opened my mouth and put the food inside, trying not to give an ounce of reaction at the taste. It was good. No, better than good. It was the best damn food I'd ever tasted. But I wouldn't admit that. Not now. Not in front of her.

"Lorenzo," Ma whispered, but I didn't look at her. I kept my gaze fixated on Aida, not giving in even a little. She needed to learn her place. And fast.

Aida glanced down at her untouched plate of food, her head moving just enough to tell me she understood my words.

All conversation stopped, the atmosphere dropping to ice-cold levels, and for the first time since I'd stepped into the room, I felt at ease. I was back in control.

LORENZO

I rubbed at my temples, trying to keep the inevitable headache at bay, but it was no use. It was coming thick and fast, the stress of the last week building up to an impossible level. I'd been boss for two weeks, but that wasn't what had me losing my damn mind. No, it was the new woman living in my home—my wife—that was driving me insane.

She was always there, at the dining table, walking around the house, talking to the staff like they were her damn friends. I was sick and tired of hearing her voice, but there was nothing I could do about it. Not only that, but I had more important things to worry about than Aida.

My uncle Paolo was still hanging around, turning up at the house whenever he felt like it. Add to that the new meeting I had scheduled for next week, I was stressed to the max. And I needed a good fucking.

I glanced around the room, seeing the finished office, and knew who would be perfect for relieving how I was feeling—Veev. She hadn't been here for anything but decorating since before the wedding. Maybe that was the problem? I needed to focus on something other than work and my wife.

A knock sounded on my office door, but I didn't answer right away. I needed to get myself situated first. So, I stood, sauntered over to the new bar cart with mirrored shelves, and poured myself a finger of whisky. "Come in," I called, keeping my back to the door. It was a conscious move, one I knew he would take notice of.

His footsteps echoed from the wooden flooring, then silenced as they met the carpet in my office. I waited, taking a sip of the amber liquid, then turned, capturing his gaze right away. "Uncle," I greeted, pushing one hand in my pocket.

"Nephew," he replied, his tone to the point. "You requested my presence." Uncle Paolo raised a brow, his lips in a straight line, and I knew he wasn't happy about it. I'd kept tabs on him from the moment I knew he was in the country, which meant I knew exactly what he'd been doing—and who he'd been having meetings with.

"I did." I dipped my head to the side, not making another move closer. "It's time you left."

He laughed, his wrinkles around his eyes becoming more prominent. "I just got here." He leaned on his cane, getting comfortable. "Why ask me to come here just to tell me to leave?" He knew exactly what I was saying, but acted as though he didn't, and it made me want to pull my gun out and fire off a clip right into him.

Fuck.

I clenched my hand in my pocket, trying not to let my anger show.

"You've been interfering with business."

"Have I?" He blinked.

"Yes, you have." I swayed toward him but pulled myself back at the last second. He was an expert at acting like nothing affected him, and if there was one thing I was going to learn from him, it would be that. "You have no jurisdiction here." I raised my glass toward him. "It's time you went home."

"And if I don't?" He paced toward the sofa, trailing his finger over the brown leather. "What if I want to stay stateside, hmm?" His gaze connected with mine—a clear warning displayed in his eyes. "The Beretta estate is rightfully mine. Your father died, and therefore, it is mine."

"No." I pulled my hand out of my pocket and stepped toward him. The time for being nice had left the building. "This is *my* birthright. Not yours."

He narrowed his eyes at me. "I've spoken to The Enterprise." My heart rate sped up. I knew he'd spoken to them because they'd called me afterward, filling me in on everything he'd told them.

"I know," I said, feeling like I had one up on him now. "They told me you tried to get their votes to take over." I grinned, loving the way his face turned red from anger. "They wouldn't give them to you." He opened his mouth, but I held my finger in the air to stop whatever bullshit he was going to say. "And even if you *had* gotten their votes, it wouldn't have made a difference. We're part of The Enterprise by choice. Now that I'm boss, if I want to break away from them, I can."

"You wouldn't—"

"I would." I moved over to my desk, leaning on the front of it and crossing my legs at the ankles. "To stop you getting your hands on the business? I'd do it over and fuckin' over again."

"You have no respect!" he shouted, advancing toward me with his cane in the air.

I was lightning quick, reaching for my gun in the holster strapped to my chest. I held it in the air, pointing it directly at his face. "Any closer, and I'll empty my clip into your head," I warned. My hand was steady, my attention laser-focused. "And I won't blink twice doing it."

His chest heaved, his face now turning purple. "You think you can hold a gun at me and get away with it?" He pushed his shoulders back, trying to make himself bigger, but it did nothing to deter me.

"Yeah, I do." I pushed up off my desk and took two steps toward him. The muzzle touched his forehead, the sweet feel of it against his skin begging me to squeeze the trigger and be rid of him. Deep down, I knew I couldn't do that. He was still boss of the Italian operation.

"My dad told me all about you," I said slowly. "He told me what you did to get ahead, the massacres you approved to make it to the top." I pushed the gun into his face, knowing it would leave a mark. "My dad taught me more than you will ever know." I paused. "He taught me not to hesitate. Not to hold back. But more importantly, he taught me patience." Slowly, I lowered the gun but kept it firmly in my grip. "Which is why I give a warning."

I grinned as I thought about my signature move. The warning was a loss of a limb or extremity. It was usually enough to put people back in their places. There was strength in showing some kind of compassion, but I wasn't to be taken for a fool. And he was going to find that out. "I give everyone the opportunity to have a second chance."

"Weak," he spat. "You're weak."

I shrugged, not giving a flying fuck what he thought. "That's your opinion." I waved the gun toward my half-open office door. "Leave. Leave my house. Leave my country." I stood to my full height, towering over him. "And don't come back unless you're invited."

He didn't make a move. He just stared at me, trying to search for something in my gaze, but he wouldn't find anything. I'd allowed him to stay this long out of respect, but now I was done. I was done listening to my captains and soldiers tell me who he'd been meeting. I was done finding out he'd tried to undercut my deals.

I. Was. Done.

Uncle Paolo's shoulders slumped, his gaze finally leaving mine. I smirked as the fight left his body, but

I knew better than to let my guard down with him. He'd been the boss in Italy for longer than I'd been alive, and I had no doubt that this wouldn't be the last I heard from him.

But as he walked out of my office without saying another word, it felt like my first victory. A victory I knew I had to celebrate.

CHAPTER

7

LORENZO

I pulled up my zipper as Veev pushed her feet into her ridiculously high heels, half watching her and half watching the time on my Rolex attached to my wrist.

I was cutting it close to Aida being home, but I couldn't bring myself to care. She may have been living in this house and taken my last name, but she was a means to an end, the one thing I needed to get what I wanted.

"Same time next week?" Veev asked, doing up the buttons on her red silk blouse. She left the top two undone, her cleavage peeking out at me. To any other man, it would have been alluring, but they did nothing for me. Veev was yet another means to an end. She sated a need I had—nothing more, nothing less.

"I'll let you know," I said, moving around to my desk and sitting on the leather chair. I had work to do, especially now that Uncle Paolo was gone. The legacy I intended to build would take time, money, but most of all, connections. Connections that I'd worked on for years, and now it was time to cash them in.

"Okay." She grinned, knowing that she'd be back next week. There was no doubt that she was becoming another fixture in my life, only she was easier to get rid of than my wife. I flared my nostrils as Veev flitted out of my office, her heels clicking on the floor as she made her way out of the house. She'd only been in the mansion a handful of times since I'd moved back in here, but it didn't seem to faze her—the extra guards or the possibility of running into my ma.

"You're playing with fire," a new voice said. I looked up, my gaze meeting Christian's.

I raised a brow at him. "I'm always playing with fire." I spread my arms wide, grinning. "It's what I do."

His eyes didn't move off of me as he stepped fully into my office and shut the door behind him. The door only ever got shut when something important needed discussing, so I straightened, preparing myself for what he was about to tell me. We'd been changing up how we did things—how we distributed our goods—and so far, it had all gone to plan. "You're gonna push her away before you've even gotten started."

I laughed, shaking my head as I leaned back in my seat. "Got started on what?" I tapped the arm of my chair with my fingertip. "What the hell are you talking about?"

Christian sighed, a sound unlike him. "Aida."

I screwed up my face, already tired of this conversation. "I married her to take my rightful place, Christian, nothing more than that."

"I know you did." He paused, his eyes narrowing. "But that don't mean you have to push her away." He leaned forward, his voice dropping. "People are noticing."

"And?" I shrugged, not liking where this conversation was going. My personal life was personal for a reason, and I didn't like the fact that Christian was in here schooling me about it. "If I wanna fuck Veev, then I'll fuck her." I ground my teeth together, trying to keep my emotions at bay. "Aida doesn't get a goddamn say."

"Never said she did," Christian murmured. "Everyone knows why you got married, but that doesn't mean that you need to flaunt it in their faces." His brows rose, waiting for me to say something, but when I didn't, he continued, "You have enemies, ones that are waiting for a chance to pounce on one of your mistakes."

I blew out a breath, understanding what he was saying. My enemies were closer than anyone knew, enemies who I kept close—like The Enterprise. All they needed was something for them to jump on, and right then, I couldn't afford for that to happen. I needed to build the family up, not destroy it before I'd even gotten started.

"What the hell do you suggest I do, then?" I tilted my head to the side, my nostrils flaring.

"People aren't seeing you out with her. You haven't even been to church since you got married."

"Then I'll go to church." I could hear my voice getting higher, my frustration over everything that had happened since my dad died boiling over. "Fuck's sake. I never wanted any of this."

Christian stood. His face was carefully neutral as he said, "Neither did she." He blinked. "Don't forget that."

"Are you serious?" I stood, unable to tamp anything down any longer. "I paid her fuckin' parents so I could marry her. I'm the reason her dad has been able to employ someone new and isn't working every waking hour." I pounded on my chest. "I set her sister and niece up in their own fuckin' apartment." I heaved a breath. "I provide for her, and I don't ask her for anything other than to be my wife to the outside world."

The silence stretched in the room, and Christian's eyes darkened. He'd always been my best friend, but now that I was boss, there was a line he wouldn't cross. But that hadn't stopped him when I was his captain. He was the only person around me who didn't placate me, and right then, I wished he would have. I didn't need him pointing out all of the flaws in my life, not when I had a ton of things on my plate.

"You asked her to give up her life." I opened my mouth, but he didn't stop. "The night you went to see her parents, you know where she was?"

I frowned, wondering where he was going with this. "The fuck do I care?"

Christian chuckled. "She was on a date."

My muscles froze, my brain short-circuited. She was on a date? Why hadn't I been told? Why had he left it until now to inform me? I narrowed my eyes on him and clenched my hands at my sides. I didn't want to admit the thought of Aida on a date with another guy angered me, but it did. She may not have been mine in all the ways a traditional wife was, but she held my family name. She was part of this home, whether I liked it or not.

"It doesn't matter," I lied. It did matter. It mattered a fuckin' lot. Was she still seeing this guy? He would have told me sooner if she was, right?

"If you're not careful," Christian said, moving toward the office door. "She'll give up on you and turn to whatever guy who gives her the attention that she needs." He halted at the door, his last parting words: "Then where will you be?"

I stared at the door as he left, leaving behind a shitstorm in my head. He was right, but so was I. I didn't want to let Aida think that there was more going on between us than there actually was, but I needed to keep her close. I needed her to be close enough so there was still hope within her. It was a balancing act, one I was afraid I wouldn't pull off.

———

AIDA

I closed my bedroom door behind me, my head down as I searched through my purse, making sure I had everything I needed to attend church. Church on Sundays was a sacred tradition to all of the Italian families I knew. I'd been attending every week for my entire life, not missing a single service. And today was no different.

The Beretta family went too, only they sat at the front of the church, their own pew kept open just for them. I hadn't grown up that way. Us Riccis usually sat at the back, merging with the other families that lived in the city. We didn't like to be seen, but it was different now—everything was different.

My heels sunk into the carpet as I made my way

to the stairs, glancing up at the last second when I'd made sure everything was in my purse. I wasn't really looking anywhere in particular, so it wasn't until I made it halfway down the stairs that I spotted Lorenzo standing in the main foyer on his own, his gray suit fitting him like a glove.

He looked my way, his eyes narrowing for the barest of seconds, and I wondered if he didn't like what I was wearing. The lilac dress hit just below my knees, hugging my hips and flaring the tiniest bit over my thighs. It was the embroidered bodice of the dress that had me falling in love with it, though. I didn't care that I'd found it in a thrift shop because it was perfect to wear to church.

"Lorenzo," I greeted as I got to the bottom of the stairs, feeling a little wobbly on my three-inch heels. "I didn't realize you were coming today." It was a reasonable sentence because he hadn't attended church with us once since we'd been married. In fact, I'd barely seen him other than at breakfast and dinner. Part of me wondered if he was avoiding me, but his ma had told me he was just busy with work. I understood that, but it meant he was just as much a stranger to me now as he was the day I'd walked down the aisle.

"It's Sunday," he said simply as if that should have answered me. "Everyone else has left already."

"Oh." I felt my cheeks heat as he kept his broody stare focused on me. It made me feel uneasy, but also lit a fire within me—a fire I had no idea was even there. "So, it's just me and you, then?" I asked, feeling my voice crack. He'd waited for me, and although I didn't want to overthink it, he could have easily left with the rest of the family.

"Service starts in ten," he told me, spinning around and walking toward the main doors. I blinked, not sure how to react, but followed him anyway.

An SUV waited outside, Mateo—one of the soldiers who was always in the house—stood beside the open back door. He greeted Lorenzo with a nod and smiled at me as I slipped in beside Lorenzo. My stomach rolled as we drove down the driveway and away from the house, the air in the SUV feeling like it was running out the longer we were in the enclosed space.

I hadn't been in a car with Lorenzo since we got married, and that was almost three weeks ago. How had I been married to him for this long yet not even had a real conversation with him? My mind immediately thought back to the last time I'd tried to get to know him—when I'd cooked. He'd shut me down quickly and left me reeling, wondering how to be and act around him. But nothing worth having came easy, right? So, maybe now was the perfect time to ask him something—anything.

I opened my mouth, keeping my focus on the back of the driver's seat, and asked, "How's your week been?" I felt him still next to me, then oh so slowly I turned to face him.

"Busy," he responded, his gaze focused on me again. "Yours?"

I shrugged. "I've been doing a lot of assignments." I bit down on my bottom lip, not sure whether I should keep talking or not. But I reasoned that if he didn't want to listen, he'd probably tell me to shut up anyway, so I continued, "I'm nearly caught up now, though. My one professor seems to hand them out nearly every week. I swear he does it just to torture us."

Lorenzo's lips curved at the corner, and I had a feeling he was thinking about a different kind of torture than what I was talking about. "I could make the professor stop handing out so many assignments," he said, raising his brows. "Or you could quit college altogether."

"No," I gasped. "No to both." I shook my head. "I was only venting to you. I wasn't asking you to resolve a problem."

Lorenzo was silent for several seconds, his gaze drifting away from me as we pulled into the street the church was on. "I know you weren't." He sighed as we stopped in front of the church. "You never ask for anything." He said it so low I was sure he didn't mean for me to hear, but I did. I heard him loud and clear, and I wondered what he meant by it. But before I got the chance to ask, he was pushing out of the SUV and walking around to my door. He opened it, offering his hand, and I took it without hesitation.

His large palm squeezed mine, and he didn't let go as we walked toward the church steps. People were milling about, their attention zooming in on us as we entered the church, and I understood then. He was putting on a show, making out like we were a normal couple.

I spotted Ma and Dad in our usual pew at the back and lifted my hand in a wave. Vida jumped up and down, mouthing something to me, but Noemi pulled her back down to sit before I could make out what she was saying.

Lorenzo greeted several people on the way to the front pew, and when we got there, two spaces were left open for us. "Ladies first," Lorenzo said, his tone different now. It was sweeter, a voice I'd never heard him use. I didn't like it. I didn't like it one bit. I'd take broody asshole Lorenzo over this version any day of the week. At least then I knew what I was getting—kind of.

"Hi," I whispered to Sofia as I slipped in next to her. She frowned at the sight of Lorenzo, probably thinking the same thing I was: Why had he come today?

Lorenzo settled in next to me, his face turned toward the front, and as soon as the doors at the back closed, the priest started talking. I wasn't sure what he was saying because I was too preoccupied with my own thoughts and the fact that Lorenzo was sitting only inches away from me.

I was hyperaware of each of his movements, so when his arm reached out, and his hand landed on my knee, I nearly jumped a foot in the air. I gaped at his long fingers as they covered my entire knee and part of my thigh. His fingertips grazed my bare skin, and I shivered. Why did he have to be such an asshole but also make my body go haywire? It wasn't fair. None of this was fair.

"Relax," Lorenzo whispered, low enough for only me to hear, but I didn't turn to face him. I acted like the only thing I was doing was listening to the priest, but in reality, my mind was racing at a mile a minute.

His hand squeezed, a move no one around us could see, and it hit me like a freight train. Outside he'd held my hand for show, but here in the front pew, no one else could see. What did that mean? What was he trying to say? What was he trying to achieve? I had no idea. And I wasn't sure I wanted to know, not when I felt this confused.

I squirmed as his hand moved a little higher, and I stared at it, seeing his wedding band on his finger. It looked so sexy on his tan hand, and I wondered if he thought the same about my wedding band. Did he like the way it looked? Or had he not even noticed?

I was in a world of my own, trying to make sense of everything, so when people started standing, signaling the end of service, I blinked, trying to break free from my own thoughts. Lorenzo's hand slid from my knee and to my hand as he helped me up.

He didn't let go as people drifted toward us. Normally at the end of service, I made a beeline for my family, but I couldn't escape the crowd of people surrounding us. And when I tried to let go of Lorenzo's hand, he held on tighter. "I'm sorry," he said to the man standing in front of us—a man I'd never seen in church before. "It was nice seeing you, but we need to go and see my wife's family." He tilted his head toward the back of the church, and my shoulders dropped in relief.

Lorenzo pushed us through the crowd, keeping his lips in a straight line as he did. He was polite but to the point, getting away from them as they asked him all kinds of things. Help with businesses, investments, and wanting to talk to the boss of the Beretta family. He was treated like royalty.

"Lorenzo," I whisper-shouted as he pulled me down the aisle. "Not so fast." I chuckled, but it was out of nerves. "These heels aren't easy to walk in."

He paused and turned back to me, his gaze trailing over my hips, down my legs, and to my heels. "They look good on you."

"I..." I cleared my throat. "Thank you." My

attention snapped to the pew my family sat in, trying to distract myself from him, but it was empty now. My stomach dropped. We'd missed them. Too many people had gotten in the way, and now I wouldn't be able to have my usual Sunday cuddles with Vida. "They're gone," I said lowly. "We missed them."

Lorenzo turned to face the doors, but he didn't give anything away as he pulled me down the rest of the aisle and outside. "You can see them next week." He didn't let go of me until we were standing next to the SUV, where Mateo waited patiently. "Or you can go after college one of these days." He pulled open the back door and waved his hand for me to get in. "You do that a lot anyway."

I frowned, wondering how he knew that, and for the first time since he'd put the ring on my finger, I felt a little bravery simmer up. "How do you know that?"

He laughed as he got in and slammed the door behind him. "I know everything, Aida." His gaze met mine, the darkness a clear warning. "No one makes a move in my city without me hearing about it." He leaned his arm on the door as Mateo sped away from the church. Was he trying to tell me something? Was he trying to warn me? I racked my brain, trying to figure out what he meant, but I was coming up empty.

"You should remember that," he finished, not

looking at me now. "And so should that guy you dated."

"What?" I screwed my face up. "What are you talking about?"

He didn't answer me. He stayed silent as if he didn't even hear me, but I knew he did. He heard me loud and clear, but he was choosing to ignore me. He blew hot and cold, and I had no idea what to expect next.

CHAPTER

8

LORENZO

Morning meetings with The Enterprise weren't a common thing, but today I had been the one to call it. Several of the heads of the families weren't happy about it, but I honestly didn't give a single fuck.

They were trying to block all of my deals that were in the works, too afraid of what message it would send to everyone else, and I wasn't having it. The Enterprise was there to protect us, not halt our businesses because of the opinions of other people.

I glanced at Mateo in the driver's seat and Christian in the passenger seat. They'd both be attending the meeting with me as my personal guards, but Christian was there for more than that. He'd been a captain in the few weeks that Uncle

Alonzo was acting boss, and now that I was in charge, he was underboss, but only until Dante took his rightful place. Dante had only ever been a soldier—he still was—so there was no doubt it would be years until he moved through the ranks to become my second-in-command.

"Sorry I'm late, Mateo," Aida shouted as she ran out of the front doors and across the gravel, trying not to drop her backpack. "I was up all night —" She cut herself off as she spotted me sitting in the back. "Oh…sorry, I…"

"No, do continue," I said slyly, tilting my head to the side. "Why were you up all night?" I could feel my anger building at her words, and I hated it. I hated how under my skin she was getting. Hated how I liked sitting next to her. Hated how she was becoming a fixture that I wanted in my home. I'd taken Christian's advice to keep her close, but it was backfiring, and I didn't like it one fuckin' bit.

"Erm…" She glanced at Mateo, but he couldn't help her. "No reason." She slid into the back and closed the door behind her.

I didn't take my gaze off her as she placed her backpack on her lap and pulled her laptop out. "Aida," I warned.

"What?" she asked, her focus on anything but me. She started typing away as Mateo pulled out of the gates, the clacking of the keys driving me insane. How the hell did she type that fast anyway?

"Why were you up all night?"

"Does it matter?" she asked, finally turning to face me.

My nostrils flared, my hands clenched, and I saw Christian shuffle in his seat in front of me. "Yes, it does fuckin' matter." I leaned closer to her. "I asked you a question. Answer it."

Her breath fanned over my face, her sweet goddamn scent driving me insane. It was too much. *She* was too much. All of this was too much. I couldn't take it, not anymore.

"Why do you care?" she asked, her brow rising. She was defying me, being evasive, and I hated it. I hated her. I hated this entire situation. She was pressing my buttons, something no one had ever been able to do, and she knew it. She could see it in my face; read it in my eyes. She was playing a dangerous game, one she wouldn't win. I'd make sure of that.

"Answer me," I ground out, trying to keep my voice low. "Now."

She rolled her eyes, a move a teenager would do, and groaned out, "I was finishing my assignment." She turned back to her laptop. "Which I still haven't finished, by the way. And you talking isn't helping." Aida pushed some hair behind her ear, her face getting redder the more she stared at the screen of her laptop. "And this piece-of-shit laptop keeps trying to update, so I'm losing hours at a time."

It was on the tip of my tongue to tell her to buy a new one, but I wasn't here to solve her problems. That was what a real husband did, and I needed to remind myself of that. I needed to remember that she didn't matter to me. So, I turned back to face the front of the SUV, keeping my attention focused on the road ahead of us and trying to ignore the clacking of her laptop keys.

I ground my teeth together, feeling like I was about to explode, when Mateo finally pulled to a stop outside of her college. She slammed her laptop closed, haphazardly pushed it into her backpack, then left without another word.

"What the fuck?" I whispered, staring at her as she rushed down the path and into one of the buildings. "Did that really just happen?"

"Yep," Christian answered. "That really just happened." He chuckled, and if he wasn't my best friend, I would have put a bullet in his arm. "I didn't think she had that in her."

Yeah, neither did I. She answered me back, had an attitude, and I fuckin' liked it.

Fuck.

"Drive," I barked out, slumping in my seat and needing something to distract me from the woman who was turning out to be more than I'd realized. She wasn't meant to be a handful. She wasn't meant to talk back to me. She wasn't meant to have me on edge.

"Call Veev," I told Mateo as he pulled up outside of the restaurant. "Tell her to be at the house by four."

I smirked as I did my suit jacket button up and ignored the burn of Christian's eyes on me as I slipped out of the back of the SUV. I'd teach Aida a lesson, but more than that, I'd remind myself what was most important: the business. I didn't have time or space in my brain to think about her. I didn't *want* to think about her, which was why, as I walked into the restaurant, I schooled my features, forgetting about the ride here and preparing for the meeting. I needed to be respectful, but I also needed to let them know that *I* was the boss of the Beretta family, the founding Mafia family in this state.

Aida didn't know who she was messing with, but they didn't either.

No one else was in the restaurant, just the waiting bosses sitting around a large table. All chairs were taken apart from one in the middle of one of the sides. I bypassed it, stopping next to the chair at the head, and staring down at Alessandro Roti. "You're in my seat," I told him, keeping my tone even.

He looked up at me, his lips quirked at the corner. "Is that so?"

"It *is* so," I snapped back, narrowing my eyes. "The head of the Beretta family sits at the head of The Enterprise." I glanced at the other three men around the table. They were all older than fifty, with Alessandro Roti being the youngest of them all.

"He's right," Neri Riva said, leaning forward. Neri was the oldest here. He'd been at the table when my dad had set this entire thing up, and I knew if there was one person on my side, it would be him. He'd been the one to fill me in on what Uncle Paolo had been up to. Neri's business was all about money. He dealt as a loan shark and also made most of his money through gambling, owning an array of casinos throughout the country. "His place is at the head."

"And what if I want to take a vote for a new head to be appointed?" Alessandro asked. He didn't make a single move to get up. Instead, he sat there, waiting for what everyone else was going to do. Alessandro knew he had power at the table, especially with the business he was in. He held several unions in the palm of his hand, but most importantly, the construction union.

"Fuck's sake," Stefano gritted out. "Just move, Alessandro." I raised a brow at Stefano, head of the Cerutti crime family. Their business flourished in washing money. He reminded me of Uncle Antonio, straight to the point and little patience.

Alessandro ignored Stefano and Neri, his eyes laser-focused on me. "Then vote," I ground out. "Do it now so we can get down to the real business."

"Patience," Alessandro tutted. "All those in favor

of Lorenzo Beretta being head of The Enterprise, raise your hands."

Neri's hand rose first, followed by Stefano, and finally, Piero. He'd been quiet, silently observing what was happening around him. Piero Pozzi was the head of the Pozzi family. His was the lowest crime family, making deals with politicians and growing as much marijuana as they could. They were trying to offset the balance between legal and illegal so they were seen as legitimate, and whatever he was doing was working.

"Looks like a clean sweep to me." I flicked my fingers in the air. "Now move." He grumbled in the back of his throat but didn't say another word as he slinked to a different seat.

"Now that that has been resolved," I started. "Let's get to the issue at hand." I stared at each of them in turn, knowing I would walk out of the restaurant getting exactly what I came for. They didn't have a choice in the matter, and deep down, they all knew that. I got what I wanted. I *always* got what I wanted.

AIDA

I slowly walked out of my last class of the day and down the hallway to the main doors. I had no reason to rush, not like I did before I became a married woman. I had nowhere to go but back to the mansion and nothing to do other than getting started on yet another assignment.

My college classes felt like they were getting harder—either that or I wasn't as focused. I'd darted to my class this morning to hand in my assignment on time, but I'd managed to get my schedule mixed up because it wasn't due for another two days. I was lost without my usual routine, trying to wade myself through unchartered territory, but I felt like I was failing epically.

Every day was the same, a repeat of the day before. I got home, had a shower, ate dinner in silence with the rest of the family, and then went to my room. It was boring, but more than that, it wasn't the life I wanted to have. I may have agreed to marry Lorenzo, but I hadn't signed my life away in the process.

But this morning had been different. Lorenzo had been in the car with me, and I'd...I'd snapped at him. I winced as I walked through the building doors and outside. I knew I needed to apologize, but something bubbling up told me I shouldn't. He'd spoken to me like crap over and over again, and not once had I bitten back. But this morning, with my lack of sleep, I'd lost my patience.

Dammit. I scrubbed my hand over my face. I had to apologize. So, as I got into the SUV, I knew I had to talk to him and explain the pressure I was under. Maybe if I explained how I felt, he'd ease up a little. I silently went over scenario after scenario in my head during the drive back, trying to prepare myself for any kind of reaction he would give me. But ultimately, I knew I wouldn't know how he would act until I'd said what I needed to say. And there was only one way to find out. When the SUV pulled through the gates and stopped in front of the mansion doors, I resolved to go straight to him. It was an unspoken rule not to go knocking on his door—I'd found that out the night I'd cooked—but right then, I didn't care. I needed to get this out. I needed to tell him that I couldn't live like this anymore.

The stones crunched under my feet, my breaths coming faster as the doors opened up. I didn't stop to greet anyone like I normally did. Instead, I beelined it for his office, hearing voices the closer I got.

It didn't register at first because I was going over and over in my mind what I was going to say and how I was going to say it. It was only when I got within a couple of feet and saw the door wide open that I realized Lorenzo wasn't alone.

I halted. Wondering if I should wait. Then a moan rang out.

What the…

I stepped closer, blinking several times, swearing

my eyes were deceiving me. But they weren't. I was seeing the truth. Seeing who Lorenzo really was.

A head full of long dark hair turned, a face appearing, and I gasped. Laid out on his desk was a naked woman, the one who had been here to give his office a makeover. She lifted her red-painted lips up into a smirk and winked at me, and all the while Lorenzo pounded into her over and over again.

Her chest bounced with each of his movements, and when he hit a spot she must have liked, her back bowed. She was fully naked, her small breasts pointed to the ceiling, but Lorenzo wasn't. I could barely see any of him, other than his hips pistoning forward.

"Lorenzo," she moaned, and he looked at her face, but she wasn't staring at him. She was looking at me, trying to prove some kind of point that I wasn't even aware of. Why would he do this? I didn't understand.

Lorenzo turned, and I took another step back. It was on the tip of my tongue to apologize, but that disappeared as soon as his gaze met mine. He didn't stop. He carried on pounding away at her.

My hand drifted to my mouth, my eyes welling up. We were married. Not in the traditional sense, but we'd made vows, and he was breaking those vows for everyone to hear. It wasn't a real relationship—that was being made crystal clear.

But this?

This was disrespectful on every level.

And I'd be damned if I was going to let him see it was affecting me. So, I pushed my shoulders back, moved my hand from over my mouth, took one final look at them, then spun around. My feet carried me to my bedroom, slow and steady, my heart thrumming so loud I could hear it pounding in my ears.

I just had to make it to my room, then I could let it all out. I could allow the tears to fall. I could mourn the loss of a fake relationship that was never there. I could make peace with the fact that this would be my life now.

My shaking hand turned the door handle, and slowly I stepped inside, too scared to make any sudden movements in fear I would fall apart. My life had been turned upside down in the last month. Everything had changed, and it was all because of him.

I'd let him control how I was feeling. I'd taken everything he'd given me and not questioned it. I'd been meek. I'd been the good Italian girl. But that wasn't who I was—or who I wanted to be. I didn't deserve this. I didn't deserve any of it.

The sight of my brand-new dress hanging on the back of my door had a lone tear streaming down my face. He expected me to be the good wife, attending functions with him and not having an opinion of my own. But he was mistaken.

I promised myself I wasn't going to take this. I

wasn't going to be the good girl he thought he was getting. I wasn't going to be silent. I wasn't going to take his bullshit anymore.

He'd drawn the battle lines. But he had no idea who he was messing with.

CHAPTER

9

LORENZO

I paced the foyer, cursing as I stared at my watch for the tenth time in the last minute. We were going to be late, and I didn't do well with being late when it wasn't my choice.

"Where is she?" I ground out at Ma, who was standing at the bottom of the stairs, watching me with caution.

"I don't know," she answered, concern evident on her face. "She knows it's tonight, right?"

I nodded. She did know it was tonight because I'd sent Mrs. Larson up to remind her after Veev had left. "Yes, she knows." My nostrils flared as I paced back and forth again. I was going to lose my damn patience with her. "If she's not down here in two minutes, I'm going without her."

"Give her time," Ma said, her tone soft and pleading. "She needs time to adjust."

I snorted, the sound so unlike me, but I was on edge, needing to get to this damn function so I could lay the groundwork for a deal in the city—a legitimate deal surrounded with illegal activity that I would carefully veil. But without attending this function, the deal would be off.

I stared at the stairs, and without thinking about it, I darted for them. Ma held her hand out, trying to stop me. "Let me go," she said, staring up at me. "Let me go, son."

I gritted my teeth. "Fine." I took one step back, watching as Ma shuffled up the stairs, but I couldn't stand here doing nothing, so I followed her.

My anger built the closer to her room we got, and I felt like I was going to blow by the time Ma stopped in front of Aida's door. She knocked twice with no answer, but when she called, "Aida, it's Ma," she finally got a response and opened up the door. "Lorenzo is waiting for you," she said softly, stepping into the room, and it took everything in me not to go closer and haul her ass out.

"I'm not feeling well," Aida groaned. "I don't think it's a good idea for me to go when I feel like I'm going to spew."

I pulled in a breath, trying to calm myself. She was fine. I knew that, and so did she. This was her protesting after what she'd seen. I'd put her back in her place, reminded her of who I was and what I did, and now she was throwing a tantrum.

"Oh, no." Ma walked farther into her room, but I wasn't going to stand here and listen to this bullshit.

I spun around, walking away from her and her lies. She was trying to save face, but she'd soon learn she couldn't do that with me. I wasn't going to stand for her insolence. I'd teach her the right way to behave as a Mafia boss's wife, but not right now. Right now, I had somewhere I needed to be.

I gripped my cell in the palm of my hand as I rushed out of the house and into the back of the SUV, then shot off a message to Veev, telling her to be at the house when I got home. If Aida wanted to play these games, I'd make sure she wouldn't win. She had no idea who she was up against. She may have won this battle, but I would always win the damn war.

———

AIDA

I shuffled from class to class, trying to put on a brave face, but it wasn't working. Nothing any of the professors said was going into my brain, and I knew I would have to read all of the extra notes they'd upload to the online platform we used, which meant extra work. But it didn't bother me. At least it would keep my mind off of the soundtrack inside the mansion.

Every night for the last three days, I'd heard Lorenzo stumble into his room opposite mine. Normally it wouldn't bother me, but since I'd witnessed what I did in his office, everything had changed—yet again. The female laughter and moans that rang out opposite my room had my stomach rolling, and my anger built higher and higher the longer it went on. It had taken all of my strength not to come out of my room last night and bang on his door. The only thing that stopped me was knowing it wouldn't make a bit of difference.

He was trying to teach me a lesson. A lesson he thought I didn't already know.

"Hey, Aida," said a voice I hadn't heard for nearly a month since our first date. "Wait up."

I closed my eyes, wishing he hadn't spotted me. I'd done a good job of avoiding Brad lately, but maybe this was what I needed now. Maybe having him as a distraction would help.

His hand landed on my shoulder, and I snapped my eyes open, firmly fitting a happy mask to my face. "Hey, Brad." I grinned up at him and slammed my hand into the pocket of my jacket—the hand that held the black wedding band Lorenzo had slipped onto my finger a month ago. I hadn't plucked up the courage to wear the engagement ring along with it. The size of it scared me, but more than that, I was afraid I'd lose it.

Had it really been that long?

"I haven't seen you around lately," he said, his deep voice not as captivating as Lorenzo's. I hated that I compared it to his, but I couldn't help it. I couldn't stop myself.

"I've been busy," I said, trying to not allow a single emotion slip onto my face.

"Gotcha," he said, holding the door to the building open for me. "Me too." He inhaled a breath as if to prepare himself. "Coach has us running drills every morning at five." He swiped his hand through his hair, causing it to flop forward. "And then there are all of the assignments and parties." He winked at me, and unlike before Lorenzo, I didn't have a reaction.

"Yeah," I murmured, not sure what else to say. My gaze drifted over campus, stopping on the black SUV sitting at the end of the pathway. I narrowed my eyes on it, realizing Christian was in the passenger seat.

Everything stopped.

My world tilted.

If Christian was in the front, then that meant Lorenzo was in the car too. For the first time that day, my body had a reaction other than somber. My stomach dropped, and my palms started to sweat. I was going to have to sit in an enclosed space with

Lorenzo when all I wanted was to be as far away from him as possible.

Mateo's head turned, his gaze meeting mine. He frowned and waved his hand, and I knew it was because I couldn't see Lorenzo through the tinted back windows. He was having to wait for me. And he hated waiting. I'd learned that the night of our wedding.

My lips curved up as I turned back to Brad and blinked up at him. Lorenzo thought he had all of the power, but I was about to show him that when it came to me, he had none. At least, that was what I wanted him to think. I'd never let him see how broken I felt inside because of what he'd done. I'd put my mask on in front of Brad, but maybe I needed to do it with Lorenzo too.

So, I reached up, placing my hand on Brad's chest, and listened as he talked about himself, but I wasn't really hearing anything he said because my heart pounded in my ears, threatening to deafen me.

"You should come to one sometime," Brad said, grinning down at me.

"Come to what?" I asked, putting on a show and stepping closer.

He inhaled a breath, his chest moving at the movement, and without warning, his hand landed on my hip. "To one of the parties," he said, his voice lower. "We never did get to a second date, did we?" *No, we didn't, because I got married.*

I shook my head, my brain screaming at me to abort, but it was too late. I'd committed to it now. Lorenzo had tried to teach me a lesson, but it was about time *he* was schooled.

"I'd love to." I lifted up onto my tiptoes and pressed a soft kiss to his lips. It was meant to be fleeting, just enough to show Lorenzo I wasn't who he thought I was. But Brad yanked me closer, pressing his mouth harder against mine, and slipped his tongue inside. Everything in me wanted to push him away, but I'd gotten myself into this now, so I let him kiss me.

I let him pull me against him.

I let him be the revenge I needed against my husband, the man who had more power than anyone thought possible.

I let myself get absorbed in the moment.

A car door slammed, and my pulse skipped as I heard my name being shouted. I pulled away, keeping my gaze attached to Brad's. "I'll call you," I whispered, putting my feet flat on the floor.

"Make sure you do," he said in a daze, watching me as I turned.

I kept the mask in place as I sauntered down the path, seeing Mateo standing next to the open back door. I could just make out Lorenzo's form from this far back, but the closer I got, the more I regretted what I'd done.

"Hey, Mateo," I greeted. He'd normally talk back, but he stayed carefully silent, just like the rest of the SUV did as I got inside.

Mateo slammed the door shut and slipped back into the front, then sped away from my college. The atmosphere was icy, threatening to render me incapable, but as I sat there in silence with Lorenzo next to me, I realized I didn't care.

I didn't care if he was angry.

I didn't care if I'd let Brad think we had something when we clearly didn't.

I didn't care if I'd just fucked up.

All I cared about was getting a reaction from Lorenzo. I needed something to keep me going. Something to explain why he blew hot and cold. Something to make me understand this entire fucked-up situation. But more than that, I just wanted him to feel even a little of what he made me feel when he fucked that woman in front of me.

The closer we got to the mansion, though, the more I wondered if I'd made the wrong move. Lorenzo hadn't said a single word—hadn't acknowledged me. Maybe he didn't care? Maybe seeing me with another man meant he didn't have to worry about me at all. Maybe I'd played right into his hands.

Mateo slowed down as we neared the gates. I

grabbed my backpack, ready to dart out of the car and away from Lorenzo. He hadn't even pulled to a full stop when I pushed open the door. And as soon as my feet hit the stones on the driveway, I ran inside the mansion as fast as I could.

I was hyperaware of the crunching stones behind me, but no one said a single word. I'd just put on a show and gained no reaction. I wasn't sure what was worse: me pretending to like Brad and kissing him or Lorenzo saying nothing about it. I'd fucked up. I'd tried to play a dirty game, and I'd failed.

Tears streamed down my face, unstoppable in their path of pain. I didn't make a move to swipe them away as I took the stairs two at a time. My breaths turned to gasps, my body threatening to close in on itself.

I was only a few feet away from my bedroom. Once I was inside, I could let it all go. I could scream and shout. I could hate on the people inside this house. I could—

A hand grabbed my wrist, halting me outside of my door. Long fingers tensed around my soft skin, promising to leave a bruise from their force.

I turned, meeting Lorenzo's gaze for the first time since I'd watched him fuck that woman in his office. But I wasn't prepared for what I would see reflected in his eyes. I wanted anger, but that wasn't what I got.

Staring back at me was a man who waged war inside his own head.

A man who didn't know what to do or what to say.

A man whose eyes lit with a roaring fire.

CHAPTER

10

LORENZO

I stared at her, trying to keep all of my emotions buried far down, but it was impossible as her big brown eyes stared up at me.

"You know what I do when someone takes something that's mine?" I asked, my voice rough. I was on the verge of losing my mind and tearing everything to pieces. *She'd* done that. She'd managed to make me feel like this with one single move.

"I…" Her throat bobbed as she swallowed. "I…"

I stepped closer to her, pressing her back against the wall. Her backpack hit the floor with a clang, but neither of us acknowledged it. "I take something away from them," I growled, bending my knees so our faces were level. I saw the recognition in her eyes. She was thinking about our wedding night—remembering what she'd seen. "He took what's mine," I gritted out, the words so low only she and I could hear them.

"I'm not yours," she snapped back, her feisty side making an appearance. "I'll never be yours."

My lips quirked. "Wanna bet on that, baby?"

"Fuck. You." She tried to push her body off the wall, but all she managed to do was press against me. Her breath caught as I thrust my hips against her, letting her know exactly what she was doing to me.

"Is that what you want?" I asked, lifting her arm I held in my vise-like grip and planting it above her head. "You want me to fuck you?"

A muscle in her jaw twitched, her anger making an appearance. Maybe I'd underestimated her.

"I hate you," she whispered. "I fucking hate you."

I shook my head, pushing even closer to her. Nearly every part of our bodies touched, and fuck if I didn't like the way she fit perfectly against me. "No, you don't." I skimmed my nose up her cheek, taking in a lungful of her scent. "If you hated me, you wouldn't have done what you did."

"What did I do?" she asked, her words a mere breath.

I placed my other hand on her hip, exactly where the college boy had, only I gripped her harder, showing her the difference between people like him and people like me.

My gaze clashed with hers, my lips so close it would only take one move to have them touching. "You let him kiss you." Her breath flowed over my face, and shivers rolled over my entire body. "You let him touch what's mine." I couldn't take another second of being this close to her, so I slammed my lips down onto hers.

Her hand pushed against my chest, but I didn't acknowledge it. I just kissed her harder, trapped her between me and the wall, and begged her to give in. To kiss me the way she'd kissed him.

I was jealous. Jealous of the way she'd looked up at him. Jealous of the way her body looked against his. He was the kind of man she should have ended up with, not someone like me, not someone who used violence as the answer. But I was damned if I was going to give this up. Not right then.

I swiped my tongue over her lips, hoping and praying that she'd let me in, and when her body finally softened, she opened up her mouth. She swiped her tongue against mine, driving me fuckin' crazy, and I couldn't hold back any longer. I'd fought with myself every step of the way, but now I was giving in to it—to her.

Aida was my wife. She couldn't escape me. She couldn't turn on me, not like they could. So, for the first time in my life, I let myself go. I let my body do exactly what it wanted to do.

My hands grabbed at her thighs, and I picked her up. She wrapped her legs around my waist, and I didn't hesitate to take her into my room. I'd fucked in many places in my lifetime, but never on any of my actual beds. That was my only sanctuary, but as I stepped inside my room and slammed the door closed behind us, I made a beeline for it. I'd brought Veev up here, but it was only ever on the sofa—her bent over it as I took what I wanted from her without a second thought.

But this was different. Aida was different.

She pulled her lips away from mine, her eyes half-open. "Lorenzo." Aida placed her hand on my face, her small fingers scratching against the scruff I hadn't shaved this morning. She stared at me, her eyes holding so many questions, but she didn't ask a single one of them. Instead, she placed her lips back onto mine, soft and gentle.

I didn't do soft and gentle, but at that moment, I allowed her to have it. I allowed her to take a piece of me, knowing that what we had in this room right now wouldn't last. It'd be a blip in my life. A blip I wouldn't forget.

I turned and sat on the bed, keeping her body pressed against mine as I trailed my hand to her waist, lifting up her T-shirt and groaning at the feel of her naked skin against my fingers. Her hips rocked against me, her body knowing exactly what it wanted.

"Fuck," I murmured as our lips disconnected. I yanked her T-shirt over her head, revealing her pink lace bra. Her nipples peeked through the material, enticing me. I leaned forward, closing my mouth over her nipple and the bra, sucking on it and cursing that I hadn't just ripped the damn thing off.

Her hand pushed through my hair, holding me in place as her hips continued to move against my cock. I was so hard, but I didn't want inside her, not yet. I never did foreplay, not with the other women, but something in me wanted to do it with Aida. I wanted to watch her squirm as I made her orgasm. I wanted to stare at her as she writhed beneath me. I wanted to commit the image of her naked body to my mind so I'd never forget.

I popped her nipple out of my mouth as I darted my hands behind her and pulled at the back of her bra, not having the patience to undo it properly. Her breasts sprung free, a handful that I grasped immediately. I rolled my thumbs over her nipples, staring at her and demanding, "Take my shirt off."

She bit down on her bottom lip, her shaky hands reaching for me. Slowly she undid the first button, then the second, revealing part of my tan chest. She shuffled back a little on my thighs, her body leaning forward so she could get to all the buttons.

"Your pants?" she asked, moaning as I pinched her nipple. I smirked, loving the way she sounded. It wasn't fake, wasn't put on to make me think she was enjoying it. No. This was real. *She* was real.

"Undo them." She flicked the clasp and undid the zipper, letting my shirt free. Her gaze lifted, connecting with mine as she slowly pushed my shirt off my shoulders, letting it land in a heap on the bed. I wrapped my arms around her, slamming her chest against mine as I twirled us so that her back was on the bed. I needed to be inside her. I needed to know what it felt like to have her pussy wrapped around my cock.

My hands slid down her waist and to her jeans, where I popped her button and undid her zipper. Her lightly tanned skin glistened as I pulled the denim off of her. We were a frenzy of hands and lips, neither one of us able to hold back.

"You drive me fuckin' insane," I told her, yanking at the material of her panties. They tore, the sound like a cannonball blasting through the air. She was bared to me, lying naked on my bed, and it was the most glorious damn sight I'd ever seen.

"You drive me fuckin' crazy," she replied, squirming as I stared down at her. "I never know where I stand with you."

I trailed my palm down the center of her chest,

over her stomach, then cupped her pussy. "Good." I breathed, trying to stay in control as I slipped my finger over her clit, finding the bundle of nerves that I knew would drive her even crazier.

"You blow hot and cold," she stammered out, jerking her hips in response to me pushing a finger inside her. She bit down on her bottom lip, not breaking my stare for a second as I pressed my thumb to her clit. I grinned down at her, unfastening my zipper the rest of the way and pulling my slacks down. My cock sprung free, the glistening head begging to be inside her.

"Lorenzo," she gasped as I pulled my finger out and spread more of her wetness over her clit.

I stroked her with one hand and my cock with the other, wondering what the fuck I did to deserve her. *Nothing*, I told myself. I'd done nothing to deserve her, but I was going to take her anyway. I was going to steal what shouldn't have been mine. I was going to ruin her for anybody else. Because with the ring on her finger and the look in her eyes, I knew I had her where I wanted her.

Leaning closer to her, I lined my cock up with her entrance, my hand rubbing her at lightning speed, and as soon as her back bowed with her impending orgasm, I pummeled inside her. She screamed, not expecting it, her pussy clamping down on my cock so hard I was afraid she'd cut off the blood supply.

She was tight, tighter than I thought she would be. "Fuck," I gritted out, watching her as the pain from me intruding her mixed in with the pleasure of her orgasm. My hips thrust forward, then back, my eyes squeezing shut at the intensity from being inside of her.

It was too much for me to handle. And I was beginning to think *she* was too much for me to handle. Had I taken on a task I wasn't ready for? Had I made the wrong move in choosing her?

It was too late now.

Too late, now I knew what her lips against mine felt like.

Too late, now I knew the feel of her pussy.

I thrust inside her again, picking up speed as her muscles loosened, and when I finally felt like I wouldn't snap, I opened my eyes back up, shocked at seeing her staring right at my face. She didn't say a word, not when I pumped in and out of her, not when she reached up and placed her hand on my chest over my heart, and not when I lost control, coming inside her.

"Fuck." I yanked my cock out, wide-eyed. "Fuck!" I clenched my hands, backing away from her. "I didn't use a condom."

"You didn't…" Aida laughed and sat up, grabbing the nearest thing to her—my shirt—and wrapping it around her body. "You didn't wear a condom?"

"No." I shook my head. "I made a mistake." I always wore protection. Always. But I'd been so wrapped up in her that I hadn't even thought about it. She'd made me forget. She'd made me forget my own rules.

———

AIDA

"I made a mistake."

His words spun around and around in my mind. Someone had clicked the repeat button because I couldn't get them out of my head as I stared at him. He was an Adonis who stood in front of me naked, his abs tensing as he backed away another step, his hands outstretched as if he was trying to find his way.

I stood, my stomach rolling and threatening to bring up everything I'd eaten that day.

He'd made a mistake.

Shaking my head, I stepped toward his bedroom door, noticing how he was still staring at the bed as if he could change what just happened.

He'd made a mistake.

My chest heaved as I walked away from him and across the hall, hearing his murmurings as I went. My backpack sat in a heap next to my door, but I didn't have the energy to pick it up. Instead, I quietly opened my door and stepped inside my room.

He'd made a mistake.

No.

I had made a mistake.

I'd made a mistake thinking he was anything but an asshole. I'd made a mistake in saying I would marry him. I'd made the mistake when I'd let him slip the ring on my finger.

I swallowed, trying to make the lump in my throat disappear, but it was no use. I'd let him have a part of me. I'd given myself over like I was worth nothing. I hated it. I hated him. But more than that, I hated myself.

My feet carried me to my bathroom, my body working on automatic as I walked toward the shower. I didn't bother taking off the shirt I was wearing. I just stepped inside, turned the water on, and relished in the cold blasting against me. It quickly warmed up, soothing me. But it wasn't enough to get his words out of my head or the feel of him inside me.

I could feel his cum running down my inner thigh, a reminder of what I'd done. What he'd done. What I'd let him do.

Why did I let him? I choked on a sob. Why did I let him do that? I wasn't anything more than a lay to him—an easy lay at that. All it had taken was the prospect of me being with another man, and he'd jumped on it, used it to his advantage. And I'd been the fool to not see it. I'd been the dumbass to take him at face value.

My head dropped down, my gaze focusing on the water as it rinsed down the drain, taking all of my sins with it, and for a moment, I wished it would take me too. I wasn't sure how long I stood there, staring at the bottom of the shower, but at some point, I stepped out in a daze complete with wrinkly fingers.

I tried to tell myself to snap out of it, to pretend like it never happened, but I couldn't, not when I was still wrapped up in his shirt. I growled, trying to pull it off of my wet skin, but it wouldn't budge, fusing to me like it never wanted to let go.

"Get off!" I screamed. "Get off, get off, get off!" I shouted over and over again, not stopping until the white material was gone and I stood naked in the middle of my bedroom. "Get off," I croaked out again. "Get off." My words turned to whispers, my fight leaving me feeling like an empty shell.

"Aida?" I gasped at the voice on the other side of the door. "Dinner is ready." I pulled in a sharp breath, trying to find relief that it was Mrs. Larson and not Lorenzo.

"I..." My hand skimmed to my neck. "I'm not coming down for dinner today."

Silence, and then, "Shall I tell Mr. Beretta?"

I gritted my teeth. He wouldn't care anyway.

He'd used me yet again, and I'd been stupid enough to not see it coming. "Tell him whatever you want, Mrs. Larson." I stepped toward my bed, then dove under the covers, wrapping myself up in a protective cocoon.

"Okay," she said, her voice sounding farther away now. "I'll let Mr. Beretta know."

"You do that," I whispered, closing my eyes and hoping that everything I'd done was just a bad dream.

CHAPTER

11

AIDA

Aida: I never thought I'd say this, but I need a night out and to get wasted.

I stared down at the message, biting down on my bottom lip as I stared at myself in the mirror. I'd been cooped up in my bedroom for two days, not willing to go outside the safety of the walls and see Lorenzo. I couldn't face him, not when I felt as fragile as I did. I was afraid if he looked at me with his dark eyes and broody stare, I would break apart. It was a risk I wasn't going to take, not then. But now...now my sadness had been fully replaced with anger. I needed out of here and as far away from Lorenzo as possible.

Noemi: Yes! When and where? Because I am there 100%

I'd held my breath as I typed the message, scared that she'd turn me down. Noemi was the only person I trusted, the only one who would try to understand and have advice I could actually follow. I hoped. If that failed, at least I'd have drowned my sorrows.

Aida: Tonight?

Noemi: Let me see if Ma will watch Vida.

I didn't move an inch as I waited for another message to come through, and as soon as it did, I sighed in relief.

Noemi: It's on like Donkey Kong! Get ready, I'll be at the "palace" in an hour.

I rolled my eyes at her calling the mansion a palace. Vida had called it that after the wedding, and the name had stuck.

"Dinner will be ready in ten minutes, Aida," Mrs. Larson shouted through my bedroom door, and I grinned. It was time to do what *I* wanted to— time to have some fun and not care about what anybody thought. I was taking a leaf out of Lorenzo's book, and I was going to have a damn good time doing it.

I darted into my walk-in closet and stared at the lack of clothes inside it. It was mainly jeans and T-shirts, along with a few church outfits. Nothing suitable for a night out, so I grabbed my cell and shot off another message to Noemi.

Aida: Bring me something to wear?

Noemi: Sure ;)

Pushing my shoulders back, I tried to put on a brave face as I left my bedroom. Voices traveled from downstairs, getting louder as I made it to the door that led into the dining room. Lorenzo's ma's distinctive tone mixed in with Dante's voice had me relaxing a little, but as soon as Lorenzo asked, "Where is she?" I gasped.

I'd managed to avoid him, but now it was time to put on a brave face. Time to show him what happened between us didn't matter to me anymore because I was done playing his games. Done adhering to all of his commands. It was time for me to do what was best for *me*, and that involved lining my stomach with food so I could drink as much alcohol as possible.

"She didn't answer me this time, Mr. Beretta," I heard Mrs. Larson say, and while they were all distracted, I decided now would be the perfect entrance.

I pushed open the door, pulled my lips up into a smile, and entered. I felt the burn of all of their stares on me, but I didn't look at anyone in particular. I kept my gaze focused on my seat, and once I was sitting, I stared at the table like my life depended on it.

"Aida," Ma said. "You look pale."

Slowly, I lifted my head. "I haven't been feeling well," I said softly, hyperaware of Lorenzo sitting next to me.

"Again?" she asked, her eyes drifting over to Lorenzo, then back to me. I could see she knew I was lying and that it was because of him, but she wouldn't say anything, especially in front of everyone else. He was her son first, but he was also the head of the family, and not just any family, but a *Mafia* family. No one spoke out against the boss, least of all his mother.

"Yeah." I swiped my hand through the air, trying to act as carefree as I could. "It must have just been one of those twenty-four-hour bugs." I inhaled a deep breath as Mrs. Larson placed my plate in front of me. "This looks delicious." I had no idea what it was on the plate, but right then, I didn't care. All I needed was to fill my stomach for alcohol purposes, so I chowed down on it, trying not to pay attention to anything around me.

I was on a mission, a singular vision of eating enough to satisfy me but not too much so I wouldn't fit into whatever Noemi brought with her for me to wear.

"Aida." Lorenzo's low voice pinged in my ears, causing the hairs on the back of my neck to stand up. "Look at me." I put another forkful of food in my mouth, not looking away from the edge of my plate. "Aida."

"What?" I growled, snapping my head toward him. Everyone else may have had to stay silent, but I was totally done with playing nice. "What do you want?"

"We need to talk—"

The sound of the doorbell ringing had me sagging with relief, and when I heard Noemi's loud voice, I jumped out of my seat. "Sorry," I said to Ma, trying my hardest not to be disrespectful while also needing to get away as fast as I could. "I made plans with my sister."

The dining room door swung open, and in the doorway stood my big sister, dressed to impress. She held up a bag, a huge grin on her face. "I brought you the perfect outfit." I had no doubt whatever it was would be slutty, but I didn't care. I was getting out of this house, and that was all that mattered right then.

"Thanks." I snapped it out of her grip and practically ran out of the dining room and back to my bedroom. I got changed in record time, slipped a pair of black strappy heels on, then walked into the bathroom.

The tight black velour dress had the tiniest straps attached to a sweetheart neckline. It was something I never would have worn. It pushed my boobs up, hugged my curves, and stopped just above my knees. It was perfect for my night out.

I let my hair out of the braid I'd kept it in for the last couple of days and smoothed it out so it looked like I'd styled it in beach waves. One slick of lip gloss and a brush of mascara, and I was ready.

My small purse held everything I needed for my night out, so I grabbed it, then sauntered back down the stairs where everyone was now gathered in the foyer.

"Dayum, sis." Noemi lunged forward, grabbing me at the waist and twirling me around. "You look hot."

My cheeks burned at her words. "Thanks." Noemi was never shy with her compliments, so I should have been used to it, but not in front of everyone else. I may have been trying to push everything to the back of my mind, but that didn't mean I wasn't aware of all the gazes pointed our way.

"Let's go," I said, hooking my arm through hers and stepping forward.

"We gotta wait," Noemi said, pulling me to a stop. "Sofia is coming with us." She paused, her attention focusing on me. "That's okay, right?"

It was on the tip of my tongue to say no. I was trying to get away from the Beretta family, not spend the night with one of them. But I didn't have a choice—like always—so I nodded. "Yeah, sure." I shuffled on the spot. "Where is she?"

"She's gone to get changed," Noemi whispered, looking at something over my shoulder. "I—"

"Aida," a deep voice said from behind me, but I ignored it. I wasn't going to give him my attention. I was done with him and with this entire messed-up agreement. "Aida," he repeated, this time louder so everyone could hear him.

I blew out a breath, my shoulders slumping at the move. "Yes?" I asked, blinking as I turned just enough to see him out of the corner of my eye.

"We need to talk."

"No, thanks." I smiled that sweet smile that I knew he'd hate, but I didn't care. Everything had been about him from the moment I'd met him in the kitchen when I was helping Dad with deliveries. He hadn't thought about anyone else around him. He hadn't cared how his actions affected other people. All he cared about was getting what he wanted.

"Aida," he growled, snatching my wrist. His movement was in complete contrast to how softly he held it, and I cursed when my body came alight with his touch. Apparently, my brain hadn't sent a memo to the rest of me. "I'm not letting you leave until we talk."

I raised a brow, feeling my anger bubbling up to the surface. "You won't let me leave?" I laughed, turning so that I was facing him fully. "You don't get a say, Lorenzo." I stepped toward him, hearing his sharp intake of breath. "You don't get a goddamn say in anything I do."

"Yeah, I fuckin' do," he growled out, lowering his face so it was only inches from mine. "I'm head of this family. Boss of the Beretta family—"

"And a pain in my ass," I interrupted, yanking my wrist from his grip. I wobbled a little but righted myself just as Sofia ran down the stairs. "I'm leaving."

The silence in the foyer echoed around us, and it was only then I realized everyone was listening to us. Part of me hated that I was coming across like a bitch, but the innermost part of me was rejoicing for standing up to him. No one ever told him no, but he was about to learn really fast that I was done taking any of his shit.

"No, you're not," Lorenzo ground out. I tilted my head at him, my eyes shooting laser beams, then he finally said, "Not without bodyguards."

"Bodyguards?" Sofia groaned.

I shook my head. There was no way I was going to the club with bodyguards. I opened my mouth to tell him as much, but he held his hand in the air. "You're the wife of the head of the Beretta family. You need protection." Lorenzo took a step back. "This is non-negotiable, Aida." He narrowed his eyes on me. "Christian and Mateo will take you and keep you safe." As if by magic, they appeared at the mansion doors, their faces stern and their attention on Lorenzo and me. He nodded at them in some kind of silent communication, then spun around, leaving all of us standing in the foyer.

"Well, shit." Noemi hooked her arm through mine, fanning herself with her other hand. "That was H.O.T. *Hot.*"

I rolled my eyes. "Shut up." Sofia sidled up on the other side of me, her gaze flicking from side to side. "Let's get out of here."

Sofia grasped on to my arm the closer to the doors we got. I frowned at how hard she gripped me and turned to look at her, but her gaze wasn't on me. It was on Christian.

I slowed down, my head whipping back and forth between the two of them. Christian's eyes narrowed, his gaze tracking down her, and not even I could miss the way his eyes heated when he got to her legs.

"Sofia," he greeted, his voice deeper than usual.

"Christian," she answered back, her grip so hard on my arm now that I was sure she was going to leave a bruise.

Mateo stepped to the side, but Christian didn't move as we walked through the open doors. Sofia's shoulder scraped against his chest, and for a second, I was captivated by the way they looked at each other. If I would have blinked, I'd have missed it. But I didn't. I'd seen the silent conversation happening between them.

"Sofia," I whispered, and at the sound of my voice, they both snapped their attention away from each other. "Ow." I wriggled my arm in her grip.

"Crap. Sorry." Her cheeks burned red. She'd been caught, but there was no way I was going to say anything, especially when I had my own things going on. I groaned at myself. For a few blissful seconds, I was thinking about something other than what Lorenzo and I had done, but now it was over. Now I was back to reality—a reality I didn't want any part in anymore.

The usual SUV Mateo drove was in the driveway, so I slid in. Noemi followed me, and then Sofia. We all stayed silent as Mateo and Christian got in the car and drove away from the mansion. I wasn't sure where we were going, but as long as there was alcohol and music, I didn't care.

I wasn't sure how long we all sat in the back of the SUV, squeezed together like sardines, but I found myself blurting out, "I slept with him." My hand slammed over my mouth, my eyes widening to the size of saucers. Crap. Why did I say that in front of everyone?

"You...what?" Noemi's hand gripped my knee, her nails digging into me. "You slept with who?"

"Lorenzo," I whispered, letting my head drop back. Now that it was out there for everyone to know, I felt a sense of relief. "I slept with him, and now I hate myself."

Noemi laughed, unable to contain herself. "You hate yourself because you slept with your husband?" She slapped my leg and turned back to face the front. "You, little sister, are insane."

"I'm not!" I threw my hands up in the air, narrowly missing Sofia's face. "You don't get it. He's...he's..."

"An asshole?" Sofia supplied.

"Yes!" I pointed at her. "That."

"An asshole *you* slept with," Noemi quipped.

"I'm not the only one he's slept with," I ground out, staring at the back of Christian's and Mateo's heads. They knew exactly what would have taken place behind my back. They knew everything that went on around Lorenzo. "He fucked that woman who redid his office." I waited, seeing if either of them would say anything, but they didn't.

"Veev," Sofia groaned out. "Her name is Veev."

I curled my lip up at the name. What kind of

person was called *Veev* anyway? "Veev," I said, seeing how the name sounded on my lips. "Yeah. I hate her too."

"You hate a lot of people," Noemi said.

"And?" I pursed my lips at her. "If I want to hate on people, I can, okay?"

She held her hands up in the air, surrendering. "Okay. Jeez. I can see why you wanted to get drunk."

I moaned. "I need to get so drunk that I forget my name."

"I'm down for that," Sofia sang, reaching for my hand. Her lips pulled up into a small smile, understanding shining in her eyes. She'd been part of this family from the moment she was born, which meant she knew the men inside it better than anyone. "And if that doesn't work, we can TP Veev's house."

I laughed, trying to keep the burning tears at bay. Tonight wasn't about anything other than spending time with my sister and drinking as much alcohol as possible, but somehow, I'd managed to gain another ally—an ally I hadn't seen coming. I hadn't even tried to get to know Sofia. I'd been so trapped inside my own head and what was happening with Lorenzo, that I'd forgotten about the other people in the house.

So as Sofia stared at me and we pulled up to the club, I promised myself that I'd get to know her. I'd stop being so consumed by Lorenzo and start living my life, whether he liked it or not.

———

LORENZO

I stared at the screen of my laptop, trying to make sense of the numbers on the spreadsheet, but my focus wasn't there. Every time I tried to do some work, all I could think about was a certain curvy, dark-haired woman who had flipped everything on its head.

Fuck.

I hated how she'd wormed her way inside. Hated how every time I heard her laugh, I wished it was me who had caused her to have that reaction. Despised how I looked forward to dinner so I could sit next to her.

Why? Why couldn't she have been a one-time thing that I could have gotten over right away? Why did she have to drive me nuts but also make everything so clear?

I let out a frustrated breath and slammed my laptop closed. There was no use in me even trying to work because nothing was going in. Nothing was making sense anymore. And it was all because of *her*. Aida. Fuckin' Aida.

Pulling out my cell, I checked if she'd replied to

my message this morning. She hadn't. She was ignoring me, but politely, which was even worse. I wanted her to shout at me, to call me an asshole, to tell me she hated me, but the pleasant silence was killing me. Every time I saw her, I wanted to shake her. I wanted to touch her. I wanted to fuckin' kiss her again.

I slammed my hand down on my desk, growling. It wasn't meant to be like this. She was meant to be my wife for show. She was supposed to go to college, live her own life, and not make an inch of difference to me. So how the hell had she managed to get under my skin so quickly? It had been six weeks since I'd put the ring on her finger, but it felt like I'd known her my entire life.

Soft laughter floated through the house, foot-steps ricocheted across the foyer, and I leaped up, not wanting to miss her again. It had been three days since she'd gone out with her sister and mine, and since then, I'd been coming up with a plan, one where she wouldn't shut me down and shut me out.

I halted at my office door, catching sight of Aida's smiling face as she talked animatedly to Sofia. I couldn't help but like the fact they got along so well. Sofia had always been a loner, trying to find her way through life and the people who had exploited her to get close to the family. Time and time again, her friends had used her to get to Dante or me.

"Aida," I called, my voice rougher than I intended it to be. Both of their heads whipped around as they got to the bottom of the stairs. "I need to see you in my office." I turned, not giving her the chance to tell me no. I was done with her defying me. She was going to listen to what I had to say whether she wanted to or not.

I walked across my office and to the bar cart, poured myself a whisky, then leaned against the front of my desk. I was calm, calmer than I had been for weeks. Maybe it was because I'd come to a decision? Maybe it was because I knew I couldn't pretend I didn't feel something for her. Or maybe it was because I was done listening to her silence.

My stomach rolled as her footsteps neared, and when she paused in the doorway, it took all of my strength not to stand and go to her. I was trying to act like this was just a normal conversation, but it wasn't.

"Yes?"

Silence spread out, permeating the air with tension.

"How was your day?" I asked, lifting my glass to my lips and cursing. Why the hell did I just ask her that?

"It was fine." She shrugged, her gaze moving to the desk I was leaning against. "I hope you cleaned that."

I frowned. "What?" I stood, looking behind me. "Cleaned what?"

"Your desk." I turned back to her, seeing her lips lift at the corners, but I knew it was one of her fake smiles, the ones she used when she was trying to put on a facade. But I saw through it. I always saw through it.

"Aida." I let out a breath and placed my glass on the desk, trying not to remember fucking Veev on it. It had been an asshole move, I knew that, but nothing could change it. I was who I was, but maybe...maybe I didn't want to be an asshole anymore, not to Aida anyway.

"Come with me to the gallery opening tomorrow night." I stepped toward her. "We can go for dinner afterward."

She snorted. "Hell to the no." She planted her hand on her hip. "I'm sure Veev would like to go." She winked, a move that I both hated and admired. "She'd never turn *you* down."

"I don't want to ask Veev," I rushed out and stepped toward her. "I'm asking you."

Aida stared at me, her light-brown eyes filling with fire. That was what I wanted. I wanted her to fight. I wanted her to have a reaction. Hope built in my chest. Hope that I hadn't fucked things up completely. It was ironic. I'd spent over a month pushing her away and pulling her in just enough to keep her sated, but all it had taken was one moment in time to change everything. To change the way I saw her, to change the way I'd been taught to feel.

I advanced toward her again, getting so close that if I reached my arm out, I could just about touch her. But the move had her stepping back into the hallway, her eyes shutting down everything they'd displayed.

"I think I'll pass." She tilted her head and lifted one shoulder in a shrug. "Have fun, though."

"Aida." She spun around, her feet carrying her as fast as they could to the stairs. "Aida," I ground out, frustrated beyond belief. "I swear to God, Aida."

"You shouldn't take the Lord's name in vain," she sang, climbing the stairs and looking back down at me. "Even Mafia bosses don't have sway over the big guy up there." She pointed at the ceiling and hiked her backpack higher on her shoulder, her gaze stuck to mine. I prayed that the fire and fight would come back, but it didn't. She was blank, not giving a single thing away, and for the first time, I wondered if I'd gone too far.

Had I blown my chance? Had I pushed her too far away? I scraped my hand down my face, not knowing what to do. I'd tried to talk to her. I'd tried to ask her out nicely. I'd tried. *Fuck, I'd tried.* What else did she want me to do? What else *could* I do?

"Be yourself," a voice said, and I spun on my heels, cursing myself for not being totally aware of my surroundings. I never let my guard down, but because of Aida, I had. This wasn't good. None of this was good. But I couldn't stop it.

"What?" I asked Sofia.

"Just be yourself." She said it like it was so easy —like it would solve all of my problems. "You're so used to having to prove yourself. You did it with Dad since you were a kid, and now that you're the boss, you think you have to prove it to everyone else." She shook her head. "You have nothing to prove, Lorenzo. Nothing at all."

"You don't get it," I gritted out, trying to keep my patience, but it was wearing thin.

"Maybe I don't." She shrugged. "But I know you slept together." She raised her brows. "And I know she deserves to see the real you. Not the you that you're trying to portray. She needs to see the Lorenzo we know. The one who is kind. The one who would go to war for the people he loves." She stepped closer to me, her hand resting over my chest. "The one who thinks with his heart and not his warped mind."

"Sofia," I murmured, not sure what else to say.

"Think about it," she said, her voice low. "Think about letting her see the side of you that you keep so well hidden." She stepped back, her focus not leaving my face. "If there's anyone who deserves that, it's her, big brother."

She left just as quickly as she appeared, leaving

me standing outside my office, wondering if I could do it. Could I let Aida in? Could I risk letting her see the part of me I kept locked away? Was she even worth it?

I closed my eyes, my breath stuttering inside my chest.

She was worth it. She'd always be worth it.

CHAPTER

12

AIDA

"And I told him, Auntie Aida, that palaces weren't *just* for princesses." Vida fluttered her lashes up at me, her hands waving in the air. "But he didn't believe me." She pursed her lips and shook her head. "Boys are the worst."

I chuckled, agreeing with her. "Well, you're *my* princess, and you're staying in the palace tonight, so he can just…" I cut myself off, reminding myself I was talking to a five-year-old.

"He can just, what?" she asked, her attention focused solely on me.

Mateo chuckled from the front the SUV, knowing I'd put my foot in it. "Vida," he called, pulling to a stop outside of the gates. "Would you like to press the button to open the gates?"

She gasped. "The gates open with a *button*?"

"Yep." He grinned back at her and handed her the device that he kept in the center console. "Click the button once, and they'll open." He paused, waving his hands in the air. "It's magic."

I squeezed my lips together to hold in my laughter as her little eyes got so wide, I thought they were going to pop out of her head. "Wow." She unplugged her belt and stood in the back. I placed my hand on her waist, keeping her steady as she took the device and pressed the button, her little face in awe as the gates opened. "That's so cool!" she shouted, placing the device back into Mateo's palm.

She planted herself right next to me, and I held her close as Mateo drove us through the gates that automatically closed behind us.

"Are there other magic things in the palace, Auntie Aida?"

I grinned down at her. "Of course, there are." Mateo opened the door for me, and I slipped out, holding my hand out for Vida.

"I'll get her bag, Aida," Mateo said as Vida jumped out, her bright pink dress lifting up as she did.

"Thanks, Mateo."

"This is amazing!" Vida shouted, letting go of my hand and running toward the water feature. She'd been here the night of the wedding, but she hadn't gotten to explore, not in the way I knew she wanted. She was inquisitive, but more than that, she was nosey.

Her little hands gripped on to the edge of the fountain as she looked down into it. "There's money in here!" She stared up at me. "Is it a wish fountain?"

"I…" I looked down, seeing the coins at the bottom of it. I'd never noticed it, not until she'd pointed it out. "I don't know." I frowned. "Maybe?"

"I bet Uncle Lorenzo knows!" She grinned up at me. "Is he here? I can ask him, and maybe I can make a wish and it'll come true."

My stomach rolled at the mention of Lorenzo's name. I knew it was coming, especially with Vida staying here for the night, but I'd tried not to focus on it too much. Vida asking to sleep over had been a welcome distraction, the buffer I'd needed after a week of not knowing if I was coming or going. I didn't realize how draining it was being mad at someone and how much effort it took to act blasé about things when it wasn't in your nature. But it was what I had to do to survive this place. To survive *him*.

I opened my mouth, about to give some kind of excuse as to why we couldn't go and see if Lorenzo was here, but before I could say anything, Mrs. Larson opened the mansion doors, and Vida went running through them. "Is my uncle Lorenzo here?" she asked Mrs. Larson.

"He is." She crouched down in front of her, and the air left me in a whoosh. "You must be Miss Vida." Mrs. Larson held her hand out for Vida. "I'm Mrs. Larson."

"Hi, Mrs. Larson." Vida shook it, her manners outshining everyone else I knew. She was such an amazing little girl. I sometimes wondered where she got it from. "Can you take me to Uncle Lorenzo?"

"I sure can." Mrs. Larson stood, her gaze floating over to me momentarily. She offered me a small smile, one that told me she knew there had been tension in the house for the last couple of weeks. "This way, Miss Vida." She led the way through the foyer, and Vida followed closely behind her, her head swiveling around, taking everything in.

"Shall I put this in your room?" Mateo asked from next to me, holding Vida's backpack in his hand.

"Please." I cleared my throat and pushed my shoulders back, preparing for Lorenzo's reaction. He had no idea Vida was coming to stay. At least, I didn't think he did. I rolled my eyes as I stepped into the foyer. Who was I kidding? Of course, he knew. He knew everything.

I spotted Mrs. Larson standing outside Lorenzo's office door with Vida beside her, my stomach flipping as she lifted her hand to knock. I couldn't hear what was said from this far away, but when she turned the door handle, I sped up, unwilling to let Vida enter the room without me.

"Sorry to disturb you, Mr. Beretta," Mrs. Larson started, her tone tentative. "I have someone here to see you."

"Who is——"

"Hi, Uncle Lorenzo!" Vida exclaimed, bounding into the room. I stood at the threshold, unwilling to enter the office, not after what I'd witnessed happening inside it.

"Vida." Lorenzo greeted from behind his desk, blinking at her as she came running toward him. His reflexes were lightning quick as she jumped at him. He caught her without a second thought and set her on his lap. "I love your dress."

"Thanks." She flashed her toothy grin at him, and I couldn't help but smile in response. "I wore it special for tonight." She dipped her head to the side, her two braids moving with the motion. "Did you know I'm sleeping here?"

Lorenzo smiled down at her, and I swore my heart skipped a beat at the action. I'd never seen him look at anyone like that before. I tried to block it from my brain, refusing to keep the memory, but it was near impossible. "I did know." He glanced over at me, his dark eyes fixating on me. I wasn't sure what was shining in them, but whatever it was had me backing away a step. "I have Mrs. Larson cooking pizza especially for you," he told Vida, looking back down at her. "You like pizza, right?"

"Yes! Pizza is my absolute favorite." She rubbed her stomach and licked her lips. "And garlic bread. I looooove garlic bread."

"Me too," Lorenzo said, leaning back on his seat. "Want to know what my favorite is?"

Vida nodded her head so quickly that I winced. "Yeah!"

"Auntie Aida's pasta." He rubbed his stomach in the same way Vida had. "It's the most yummiest pasta ever."

"I don't like pasta," Vida said, screwing up her face. "Pizza is way better."

Lorenzo chuckled, the sound so carefree it took me by surprise. In fact, the entire conversation was taking me by surprise. Why was he being so nice to Vida? Was it an act? Or was it real? All I knew was that I needed to get as far away from him as possible because I could feel my anger waning.

Anger I needed.

Anger that fueled me.

Anger that meant I made it through each day.

"Come on, Vida," I said, my voice small. It was only then that I realized there were other people in the office. Mrs. Larson had disappeared at some point and left me alone to face the room full of men. "Uncle Lorenzo is busy, and we have lots of plans." I tried to make my voice sound excited, but it was hard when everyone's attention was on me.

"Awww." Vida pushed out her bottom lip but perked up quickly. "Is the fountain a magic fountain like the gates?" she asked Lorenzo. "There's money inside it."

Lorenzo's gaze met mine, a question in his eyes. I nodded, trying to silently tell him to tell her that it was. He winked at me, and my stomach dipped like I was on a roller coaster. "It is." He stood, placed Vida's feet on the floor, then bent down so their faces were at the same level. "Take this." He pulled a coin out of his pocket and held it out to her. "Make a wish." She went to take it from him, but he pulled back at the last second. "You can't tell anyone what you wished for, though."

"I promise." She made a cross over her heart.

"Okay." He let her take it from his hold and leaned forward, whispering something to her, then pulled back. "Have fun."

She spun around and ran over to me, but I didn't look at her. I was too preoccupied, staring at Lorenzo. He was showing a different side of himself. A side I hadn't seen.

"Come on, Auntie Aida." Vida grabbed my hand, pulling me away. "Let's go make our wishes."

"Our wishes?" I asked, letting her pull me back through the foyer and outside to the fountain.

"Here." She handed me a coin, grinning up at me. "Uncle Lorenzo gave me one for you too."

I turned back to face the mansion at her words, spotting Lorenzo standing in his office doorway, his dark eyes focused on us. He nodded, silently trying to tell me something, but I had no idea what it was. I could feel him breaking me down, and it didn't matter how quickly I was replacing the bricks, building the walls around my heart, because he was tearing them down twice as fast.

"Done!" Vida shouted, clapping her hands. "Now, you."

I squeezed my eyes shut, said my wish silently in my head, then dropped the coin into the fountain. The only time I'd made a wish was when I blew the candles out on my birthday cake, but there was something about this wish that had me hoping it would come true. Maybe it was magic, or maybe it was hope, but part of me believed in a higher purpose. Everything happened for a reason, right? I clung to that thought as I gripped Vida's hand and led her back into the mansion.

———

LORENZO

"Confirm the meeting," I told Christian as I stood. It had been hours since Vida had come into my office with her toothy grin flashed my way. I hadn't known Vida was staying overnight, not until Mateo had called me from outside her family's store. I'd told Mrs. Larson to come straight to my office when they arrived, but I hadn't expected the whirlwind that was Vida to be with her.

I was trying to take Sofia's advice and show Aida who I really was. I didn't want to admit that it was hard, but it was. How was I meant to show her a side of me that I wasn't even sure was there anymore? How was I meant to do a one-eighty and get her to believe it was me?

"For Thursday?" he asked, typing away on his cell. I made a sound of agreement in the back of my throat as we walked to the door. The sound of laughter filled the air as soon as I opened it. Part of me wanted to stay hidden in my office. At least in here, I could be who I wanted to be. I could be the violent Mafia boss, the man who didn't take any shit from anyone. But out there, I'd have to be the man Aida deserved. The man she should have been able to marry.

I stood in my office doorway as Christian left, stopping to say bye to Aida and Vida as he went. But I couldn't move. I was stuck to the spot, wondering if it would have been easier to let things be what they were. Part of me said to let her go. To set her up in her own apartment like I'd planned to do originally. But deep down, I knew I couldn't. I couldn't watch her live her life without me in it.

Taking her to my room that day had changed everything. I hadn't been prepared for it—hadn't seen it coming—but now it was here, and I couldn't back down.

I needed her.

In more ways than one.

I pushed my shoulders back, giving myself a pep talk as I headed toward the living room—a room we never used. Vida ran around the sofa, her giggles taking over her entire body and slowing her down. But it was the way Aida chased after her, her hair whipping around her face and her lips spread into the biggest damn smile I'd ever seen, that had me wishing I was part of what they were doing.

"Save me!" Vida shouted, her face turning toward me. She pointed toward me, and I didn't think as I grabbed her around the waist and hoisted her in the air. Aida paused, hesitation flashing over her features. "You can't catch me now!" Vida shouted, and at the sound of her voice, Aida sprung back into action, running toward us.

I spun us around, boosting Vida onto my shoulders as I went, and made a dash for the stairs. "You can't get away from me," Aida cackled. I heard her footsteps behind us as I took the stairs two at a time, Vida's little hands grasping on to my hair as her giggles rang in my ears.

"Faster!" Vida shouted, and just as I got to the top of the stairs, I felt Aida's body collide with the back of mine, her arms coming around me to grab Vida's feet.

"Gotcha." Aida laughed, the sound so captivating, all I could do was stare at her.

"No fair," Vida whined. "You cheated."

"Did not."

"Did too," Vida quipped back. Aida raised her brow at her, pursing her lips, and whatever that facial expression meant, it had Vida changing her tune. "I'm hungry." Her stomach rumbled loudly in my ear, and I couldn't help but laugh.

"Let's see if Mrs. Larson has finished cooking dinner." I didn't acknowledge Aida as I spun us around and jogged down the stairs. As we got to the bottom, Mrs. Larson was walking down the hallway with several plates in her hands.

"Did you want it in the living room?" Mrs. Larson asked, glancing at Aida, and then at me.

"Yeah," I answered, already making my way back in there. "We can watch TV as we eat."

"We?" Aida asked. "You're eating with us?"

"If that's okay?" I asked, but it wasn't really a question. I *was* going to spend the night with them both because I had a feeling I wouldn't get the opportunity again. Maybe it was wrong that I was using Vida as a buffer, but at this stage, I was willing to do anything to get Aida to listen to me, even if it was only for a couple of minutes.

So, I made myself comfortable on the sofa. Vida sat in the middle of us, and I bought a princess film for us all to watch. I made conversation with Vida and found myself fascinated with the way she thought. By the time she settled down after a belly full of pizza and garlic bread, I understood why Aida loved her so much.

It wasn't long until Vida's soft snores filled the room. Her head was on Aida's lap, and her feet were in mine. I wasn't used to this type of thing, but the longer I sat there, my gaze focused on the movie playing, the more I knew I could get used to it. It was something that had never been in the cards for me—having kids—but now the possibility of it had me turning to look at Aida, wondering what kind of mother she would be.

Her hand stroked Vida's hair, her attention fully on her. I didn't look away as her eyes started to close, her body tired from running around with Vida for most of the day.

I slowly moved to the edge of the sofa, bringing Vida's legs with me. Aida's head snapped up, her gaze meeting mine. And for a brief second, all that stared back at me was a woman who wasn't angry anymore. A woman who could have been everything I ever needed.

"I'll carry her up," I whispered, trying not to wake Vida.

"No." Aida shook her head, blinking rapidly. "I'll take her." I didn't listen to her as I hooked my arm under Vida's back and behind her legs, bringing her with me as I stood. "Lorenzo," she whisper-shouted.

"What?" I walked out of the living room and up the stairs, hearing her footsteps padding behind me.

"I said I'd take her."

I shrugged, not saying a word as I turned at the top of the stairs and walked toward Aida's room. Vida stirred, her snores stopping for a second and then starting back up again. Aida growled, the sound causing a grin to spread across my lips. She was frustrated, but I had no doubt that wasn't the only reason she'd growled. I'd caught her looking at me several times throughout the night, and although I hadn't said anything, I knew I'd finally be able to talk to her without her walls erected between us.

Turning at the last second, I met Aida's gaze and pushed her door open with my back. She narrowed her eyes at me, her hands on her hips, and damn if she didn't look cute. It was on the tip of my tongue to tell her that, but I had a feeling it wouldn't go down well.

Aida rushed ahead of me, pulling her covers back just in time for me to place Vida down gently. She fussed over her, making sure she was settled, but

I didn't make a move to leave. I wasn't done with her, not yet. I didn't think I ever would be.

"Aida," I called, keeping my voice low so I wouldn't wake Vida up. "Aida." She didn't answer me, acting like I hadn't spoken. She'd done that time and time again over the last couple of weeks, but I was done taking her silent treatment. I was done with her ignoring me. "Aida," I said a final time, stepping toward her.

She let out a low breath. "What, Lorenzo?"

"Look at me." She shook her head, moving farther around the bed and away from me. But I wasn't giving up this time. I'd let her have her space. I'd taken a step back so that she could have space, but I was done waiting.

I grasped her arm, halting her as she tried to get to her bathroom. Her muscles tensed, her body frozen to the spot. "Don't," she whispered, her voice cracking.

"Don't what?" I asked, stepping closer to her, so close I could feel the heat coming off of her body.

"I don't have the energy." Her eyes opened, and her body turned. "I'm too tired for this. Just let me go."

"No." I pressed forward, our chests meeting, and her breaths stuttered, her body telling me that she wanted this—wanted me. And that was all I needed. She may have given up, but I had enough fight for the both of us. "I'm sorry," I croaked out.

I'd never apologized for anything, but for her, I'd say sorry a thousand times if it meant she'd look at me just one more time the way she had when she was spread out on my bed beneath me.

She blinked, probably in disbelief. "You're sorry?"

"I'm sorry," I repeated, this time firmly. "I'm sorry I put you here. I'm sorry for being an asshole." I pulled in a deep breath, and placed my palm on the side of her neck, willing her to take what I was saying at face value. "I'm sorry for everything, baby." I paused. "I'm sorry for everything but the day I had you in my arms. The day you let me kiss you. The day you looked at me like the world started and ended with me."

Her eyes welled up as she processed what I was saying. "I don't know whether to believe you or not." She shook her head, her body leaning toward me. She was at war in her own head, not sure which way to turn. I knew the feeling well because I'd battled with it too, but the thought of losing her altogether was too much to bear. I kept my gaze on her, trying to push my point home. "I think it's too late," she said softly, a tear slipping from the corner of her eye.

"No," I ground out, pressing my forehead to hers. "It's never too late." I heaved in a breath, my nerves on edge. I wasn't sure what else to say to her, what else I *could* say. So, I blurted out, "One chance." Her stare met mine. "Give me one chance to make it all right. One chance at a real shot."

My breaths turned heavier as if I'd just run a marathon. "Take a leap of faith," I begged her. "Take it with me."

Her silence was deafening, her face not giving anything away for such a long time that I was sure I'd lost her. I'd lost her before I even had the chance to find her.

"Okay," she said, the one word barely audible. "One shot." She held her finger in the air. "That's all you get."

I closed my eyes, a relief I'd never felt before washing over me. I wasn't sure what was happening between us, but I needed to find out.

"Stay with me tonight?" I asked, my stomach dipping with nerves. I'd never been nervous, but it was different with her.

Aida glanced back over at Vida, who lay cocooned in the sheets. "I…" She bit down on her bottom lip, a move that had me nudging my face closer to hers. I pressed my thumb on her chin, pulling her lip from between her teeth. "Just sleep-ing," I told her. "Nothing else." I paused as she turned back to me. "Nothing else once I've done this." I pressed my lips against hers, unable to hold back any longer. She tensed, her body unsure, but she soon softened, her hand reaching out to rest on my chest.

It was soft, gentle, cautious, but I knew it was what she needed at that moment. She needed to know this wasn't about sex. No. This was about me realizing she was becoming so much more than my wife in name alone. This was about me listening to my gut, just like I'd told her to do when I asked her to marry me.

I was taking my own advice. I just hoped she was too.

CHAPTER

13

AIDA

Warmth covered my entire back, a hand on my stomach, and for the briefest of moments, I forgot where I was. I forgot who I was lying next to. Forgot what had happened last night. But as I slowly opened my eyes and stared at the gray walls, it all came flooding back.

Lorenzo eating pizza with me and Vida on the sofa, ordering her the latest Disney movie to watch and then settling in with us. He'd made himself a fixture in our evening, and however much I wanted to deny it, I liked it. I liked that he made an effort with her. I liked that he didn't blink twice at watching a princess movie.

But none of that compared to him apologizing.

Out of everything that had happened last night, that was the most shocking. Even more so was the fact that I believed him. Every word he said had so much conviction behind it that it couldn't be anything but the truth.

He groaned from behind me, his hand tensing on my stomach for a second before he pulled me closer to him. My back met his front, my body fusing with his, and it took me right back to that night—the night I'd given him a piece of me, and he'd taken it without a second thought.

What had changed between then and now? What had made him apologize?

"You said I was a mistake," I whispered, feeling all the hope in me tumble to the ground. Had I been a fool to come into his room with him last night? Had I let the way he'd treated Vida impact my decision-making?

"When did I say that?" his deep, groggy voice asked.

I jumped, not expecting him to be awake. "I…" I pulled in a breath, regretting saying anything when I'd only just opened my eyes. But I couldn't help it. I couldn't keep everything locked up inside, not now I was here. Not when he was this close to me.

"The day we were in here," I started, staring at a picture on the wall and using it to center me. "You said you'd made a mistake."

He stilled, and I started to regret saying anything. Maybe I *should* have kept my mouth shut. "Wait…" He gripped me harder, then rolled me so that I was facing him. "That's not what I said."

My stare met his. "You did. You said you didn't wear a condom and that what we did was a mistake."

"No." He frowned down at me. "I said I'd made a mistake by not wearing a condom." He glanced away, his throat bobbing as he stared behind me. "I always use protection. *Always*." He looked back down at me. "But with you…I forgot." He pressed closer, his bare chest meeting my front and his legs intertwining with mine. "You made me forget. You make me forget a lot of things."

I pulled in a breath, my hand making its way to his arm and gripping it. "But…"

"But what?"

"The other woman?"

"Is done with. I don't make promises, Aida. I never commit to something I know I won't see through, so the second you agreed to give me a chance, I was all in." He blinked. "All in with you."

I bit down on my bottom lip, trying to process everything he was saying. In some ways, it sounded too good to be true. Only time would tell, but I knew I couldn't go forward, not until I'd said, "Change your desk." His brow rose at my words, but it only took him a second to register what I was saying.

"Done." His gaze drifted behind me again. "The sofa too."

"The sofa?" I asked, turning so I could see it on the wall beside the door. "Why the sofa?"

"That's where I fucked all the women I brought in here." I turned back to face him, realizing that if we were going to give this a real chance, we needed to be brutally honest with each other. And it looked like Lorenzo was on the same wavelength. "Never in my bed, though." He pulled me so close our lips were only a hairsbreadth away from each other. "Only you in my bed."

"Only me."

"Only you."

I smiled, the first real smile I'd ever given him, and dipped forward, placing my lips against his, sealing our deal with a kiss. He yanked me closer, his half-naked body covering mine as he slipped his tongue inside my mouth.

I got lost in the moment, lost in him, until a small knock sounded at his door.

"Auntie Aida? Are you in there?" My eyes widened, and I pushed at Lorenzo's chest with such force he groaned.

"I'm coming, V!" I leaped out of bed, cursing myself. She was in a new house, and I'd left her in the bed all alone, not even thinking about what she would think when she opened her little eyes and saw that I wasn't there with her.

I pulled open the door, spotting her standing there still half asleep in her purple *Dora the Explorer* pj's. "I woke up, and you were gone," she said, dipping her head back to look up at me.

"I'm sorry." I scooped her up and held her to my chest. "I was just checking on Uncle Lorenzo." I spun us around so she could see him.

"Morning, Uncle Lorenzo," she said softly, resting her head on my shoulder.

"Morning, princess." He sat up and pulled the covers over his lap. "Did you come for morning cuddles from Auntie Aida?"

"Mmm-hmm," she whispered, and I had no doubt she was falling back to sleep on me.

"Come on, then." Lorenzo pulled the covers back, and I didn't hesitate to get back into bed with him. I placed Vida between us and hugged her just like I used to back home, but within minutes she was back asleep, snoring her little head off. "She's all pooped out," Lorenzo said, staring down at her. He grasped my hand and brought it to his lips. "I've got to get to a meeting." His gaze locked with mine. "Stay in here with her. Go back to sleep." He pulled up a little and planted a second kiss on my lips. "I'll see you at dinner."

I sighed happily. "I'll see you at dinner," I replied, watching as he got out of bed and headed toward one of the doors in his bedroom. I heard the shower click on, and I closed my eyes for just a second, but that was all I needed to fall back to sleep, cuddling Vida and feeling like I was finally in the place I was meant to be.

———

LORENZO

"How many crates a week?" he asked, shuffling on the spot. He was nervous, the first sign that he wasn't the right person to make a deal with.

"How many crates can you load?" Christian asked the question he knew I was thinking. I wasn't going to talk, not when we were this new into a deal. I didn't know this guy from Adam, and my gut was already telling me he was undercover. I'd seen many undercover FBI agents try to infiltrate our ranks unsuccessfully, although one of them had been close a couple of years ago. Dad had made a deal with him, and just as they were about to exchange money, I caught him out, spotting the listening device he'd placed in a button on his shirt.

It wasn't like in the movies where they'd have a wire taped to their chest that you could feel when you patted them down. These days, all it took was a click on a link someone sent you, and they could get into your cell whenever they wanted, gaining all the information they'd ever need. They were high tech, but I was onto them.

"As many as you need," the guy said, pulling his confidence back, but it was too late. My gut had told me what I needed to know.

Christian glanced over at me, a question in his eyes, and with only a small shake of my head, he knew my answer. "We'll be in touch," he said, leaning back in his seat.

Neither of us moved as he exited. I never left a meeting first, especially one with a new contact. I flicked my wrist in the air as I ground out, "Follow him. See where he goes." I may not have been going into business with him, but that didn't mean I wasn't going to find out exactly who he was. I was always suspicious when someone new flashed on my radar, especially when my gut told me something wasn't right.

I pushed forward in my seat, planting my arms on my thighs and trying to make sense of it. I'd been boss for two months now, and I knew it would cause people to come out of the woodwork and try to take us down. But they'd made a mistake. I wasn't some fresh-faced guy who didn't know what he was doing. I'd been part of this business for two decades, learning the ins and outs and watching from afar. My dad always said being able to read people was a skill and a necessity in our way of life. Which was why I turned to Dante, narrowing my eyes on him. "What do you think?"

"He's undercover." His gaze met mine, not a single doubt displayed. "He was too fidgety. *And* he was recording us."

My lips quirked on one side, just enough to show him I knew it too. "Good." I stood, glancing down at my watch. "I'm taking Aida to the new bar." I turned to face Mateo. "Let's go."

No one said a word as Mateo and I left the building we'd used for this meeting. In fact, no one had said anything about the fact there was no tension between Aida and me—there hadn't been for five days, not since we took Vida home together. They knew better than to comment on my private life.

Mateo opened the back door for me, and I slipped into the SUV. I couldn't deny that I missed driving my sports cars, but I knew when I was driving, I wasn't protected, not in the way I needed to be. And there was no way in hell that I'd put Aida at risk by taking her in one, not when I could feel something brewing. Call it instinct, call it a gut feeling, but the tide was turning, promising a dark storm coming my way.

I was stuck inside my own head, trying to make sense of everything and analyzing every movement the suspected undercover agent had made. I'd watched him closely, but that didn't mean I caught everything he did.

"Did you record the meeting?" I asked Mateo as we pulled up outside the college.

"I did." He pulled his cell out. "Want me to send it to you?"

"Yeah. On the encrypted cell."

A couple of seconds went by, and then he announced, "Done."

I nodded, not saying another word as I turned to face the college, spotting Aida pushing through the doors. She kept her head down, her focus on something in her hands. She looked like every other student on campus wearing jeans and a T-shirt, but there was something else about her. It was the way she carried herself. The way she'd push her hair behind her ear, the way she smiled at strangers walking by.

My hand reached for the handle just as she halted in the middle of the pathway. I frowned, wondering why she'd stopped, then ground my teeth together as I saw the guy she'd kissed walk closer to her.

"Boss?" Mateo asked, but I didn't respond to him. All I could think about was the way he'd looked at her, the way he'd touched her, and I knew if he laid his hands on her just one more time, I'd not only chop them off, but I'd put a bullet in his head to boot. Maybe it was extreme, but when it came to Aida, I was irrational—I knew that, which was why I told myself to stay in the SUV and wait.

Aida said something to him, her gaze flicking to the SUV. I narrowed my eyes as she put her hand behind her back and held three fingers up. "What is she doing?"

I didn't expect Mateo to answer, so when he said, "She's giving a signal," I pulled on the door handle. I had no idea what the signal meant, but she wouldn't have done it if she didn't need help.

I cracked my neck from side to side as I got out of the SUV, and without thinking, I headed straight toward her, my attention on the college asshole who thought he could touch what was mine. I was two feet away when Aida turned to look at me. Her eyes widened, flicking behind me where I had no doubt Mateo was waiting at the SUV.

"Lorenzo?" Her voice was small, the shock evident, but so was the relief. "What are you doing here?" She sidestepped the college guy and moved toward me, her hand going straight to my chest.

"I thought I'd come pick you up," I said, staring down at her but hyperaware of our surroundings. "It's not a crime to pick my wife up, is it?"

"Wife?" the asshole asked. "You're his wife?"

I wrapped my arm around Aida's waist, bringing her close to me, then turned to face him. "She is." I held my hand out to him. "Name's

Lorenzo." He took my hand, frowning as he did. "Lorenzo Beretta."

"B-b-beretta?" he stammered, his face paling. I didn't let go of his hand, squeezing it just enough for him to know that what he was thinking was true. My name preceded me, even with college assholes who came here from out of town.

"That's me." I smiled at him, the kind of smile that said, *if you touch what's mine again, I will end you.* His eyes flashed, understanding the silent warning I was giving him, and then I let go, turning back to Aida and pretending like he wasn't there any longer. "Let's go. I have something to show you."

"You do?" she asked, her light-brown eyes focusing on me. She lifted up onto her tiptoes, and I instinctively bent at my knees to meet her halfway. Our lips connected for the briefest of moments, but that was all I needed to know that it wasn't the college asshat she wanted. No, it was me.

"I do," I said, grinning down at her. "Come on."

I didn't take my arm from around her waist as I maneuvered us toward the SUV. Mateo stood at the open door, his eyes narrowed on something behind us. "He's watching you," he ground out.

Aida went to turn around, but I stopped her. "Don't." I snapped my attention down at her. "Ignore him."

"But…" She bit down on her bottom lip.

"But what?" I tilted my head toward the SUV as

she stayed silent. "Get in. I really do have something to show you."

She rolled her eyes. "Fine."

I gritted my teeth at her move, still getting used to her defiance, but I couldn't deny that I enjoyed it. I liked the fact that she wasn't willing to take my shit, but it made me want to piss her off all the more.

I slid in beside her, turning back to face the pathway at the last second and lifting two fingers in a salute at the college asshole. He may have thought he knew who he was messing with, but he had no idea the lengths I would go to. And if I were honest, neither did I. This was all new territory for me with Aida, but I knew I would kill for her without blinking an eye.

Mateo pulled away from the college, revving the engine, a sure sign that he was pissed off too. But there was no need—I'd handle the situation if it got out of hand. Until then, I was going to forget all about him. He may have kissed her one time, but there wouldn't be a second. I'd make sure of that.

"So, you have a secret signal, huh?" I raised a brow, meeting Mateo's stare in the rearview mirror, then turned to face Aida.

She shrugged, placing her bag on the floor between her feet. "Mateo said we needed one just in case." She raised her brows. "I never thought I'd actually have to use it."

"Why did you need to use it?" What I really wanted to ask her was what the hell did he want.

Her lashes fluttered as she blinked at me. "He wanted to know when we were going on a second date."

I nodded, already thinking about all the ways to let—

"What's his name?"

"Brad."

"Right."

—I was thinking about all the ways I could let Brad know that Aida was mine.

"Why?" Aida asked, her eyes widening. "Lorenzo." She pushed closer to me. "I can see your brain working overtime." She placed her hand on my cheek, her fingertips pushing through the scruff covering my jaw. "You don't need to worry about him."

I wasn't worried about him, not when it came to Aida. She was mine whether she liked it or not.

"Lorenzo." She pulled my face closer to hers, making me look directly in her eyes. "I said I was giving this a chance, didn't I?"

I covered her hand with mine and gripped it. "You did."

"Exactly." She smiled. "You have nothing to worry about. I promise." It was on the tip of my tongue to tell her I wasn't worried, but instead of saying that, I simply planted my lips against hers, needing to feel her against me.

We'd slept in the same bed together every night since Vida had stayed over, and although I didn't want to push too quickly, my body begged to be as close to her as possible.

The SUV pulled to a stop, and we both moved with it, our lips separating at the impact. "Fuck." I leaned my head back and growled in frustration at how hard my cock was. Never in my life had I gotten this hard just from a kiss.

"We're here," Mateo announced like a goddamn tour guide.

"Where is *here?*" Aida asked, and when I lifted my head, I saw her staring out of the window, her face practically smushed against the glass.

"*Here* is the surprise." I pressed my hand against her back and leaned around her to open her door, then slid out behind her. She stared up at the front of the bar, but I'd already had the sign taken down. The new one wasn't being put in for another week, but I couldn't wait that long to show her. I needed her to see that I listened when she spoke but that I also heard what she did when she said nothing at all.

I grasped her hand and led her toward the bar, not saying a single word until we were inside. Construction was underway to refit it exactly how I wanted it, but there was something already finished, waiting for me to show her.

"What is this place?" she asked, her gaze roving around the space. On one side was a new bar top being put in, and in the middle, a new floor was being fitted, but just beyond that was the finished stage. A stage that held a grand piano.

"Holy fuck."

I grinned at her cursing.

"Is that a…" She spun to face me, then turned back, not waiting for me to answer as she darted across the floor and up onto the stage. "It's so beautiful," she murmured, trailing her hand over the shiny black surface.

"It's yours," I told her, halting at the edge of the stage.

"It's…what?" She frowned, causing two lines to etch into the skin between her eyes. "What do you mean it's mine?"

I shrugged, trying to act like this was an everyday occurrence, but in reality, I was nervous that she wouldn't like it. The guy who I'd bought the piano from said it was one of the best, but what if she didn't like it? What if she hated it? "Ma said you're doing music at college." She stared at me, her mouth hanging open. "So, I called your dad and asked what kind of music."

I stepped closer to the stage that came up to waist height. "I didn't know you played piano."

"You never asked," she whispered.

"I know." I nodded, taking a deep breath. There

were a lot of things I never asked, but I'd make up for it, even if it took the rest of my life. "So, I thought I'd buy you one."

"The piano is mine?" She blinked in confusion, her gaze veering from the piano to me.

"No." I shook my head, hating how the hope in her eyes diminished at my one word. "It's all yours." I stepped back and raised my arms. "The entire bar is yours."

She choked out a laugh. "What?" Her head snapped left and right. "What are you talking about."

"I bought you a piano bar." My words were low, my confidence waning. I'd never second-guessed myself, but I felt like I was constantly doing that with Aida.

"You bought me a piano bar?" I nodded, wincing as she stared at me like I'd lost my mind. "You're insane." She stepped forward, her stomach at the same level as my head with her standing on the stage. "You're totally, completely insane." Her hands gripped either side of my face. "But damn if I don't like it."

I grinned, my muscles finally relaxing now that I could see the smile on her face. "You like it, then?"

"Like it?" She sighed. "I love it." Her stare met mine, her light-brown eyes capturing me and promising to never let me go. "I suppose I should play you a song now, huh?"

"I wouldn't say no to that." She bent at the waist, placed a barely there kiss on my head, and spun around. I couldn't look away from her as she stroked the piano and pressed a couple of the keys, but it was when she started playing a haunting tune, getting lost in each of the notes, that I realized how much music meant to her. She was in a world of her own—just her and the music—and I knew then that I would do anything to protect her, even if it was from me.

CHAPTER

14

AIDA

"This is the way my ma taught me how to make cannoli," Lorenzo's ma said, putting some ingredients into a bowl. I listened intently, not wanting to miss a single word she said. "First, you add all of the dry ingredients." She glanced up at me. "Then the butter." She placed the butter in the bowl and started to mix it with her hands. "You mix it until all of the lumps are gone." She lifted her hands out of the bowl and pushed it toward me. "You try, cara."

I grinned at the term of endearment she'd started using as I pushed my fingers into the bowl. I'd never made cannoli before. My ma always made savory things because it meant she could batch cook them. I was excited not only to be spending time with Lorenzo's ma but also learning how to make them the traditional way that she'd been taught.

Ma cracked an egg into a bowl and added something else, whisking it up. "Is it lump-free?"

"I think so." I wasn't really sure, but one quick look over my shoulder had her nodding.

"Mix this into a dough," she said, placing the wet ingredients in and watching as I tried to mix it all together. It mostly stuck to my fingers, and I panicked, thinking I was messing it up. "Here." Ma reached into the bowl, pulling the mixture off my fingers and then taking over. She was a pro at it, and in no time had made it into the glossiest-looking dough I'd ever seen.

"What do we do now?" I asked Ma.

"We rest and chill it overnight." She wagged her finger in the air. "Too many times, people try to rush the process, but you need to let all the ingredients merge together to permeate into a tasty dough." She wrapped the dough in some plastic wrap and moved across the kitchen to the huge fridge. "Perfection takes time, cara."

I nodded, understanding what she was saying. Sometimes it would take all day to make the perfect pasta sauce, but everyone wanted everything right away. We lived in a fast-paced world, one where we could place an order for food on our phones and it would be at our door thirty minutes later. Traditions were being lost, and I wanted to make sure I was doing everything I could to uphold them.

"Did I not say you weren't allowed in here again?" Lorenzo's deep voice came from the doorway.

I raised a brow and turned to face him, holding my sticky dough-covered fingers in the air. "You did."

He stared at me, tilting his head to the side. "Then why are you in here with Ma?"

"I'm learning how to make cannoli." I turned to wash my hands and then leaned back against the counter to give him my full attention. "You have a problem with that?"

"Yeah." He stepped toward me, his eyes flashing, but I didn't take any notice of his facial expressions. I was too focused on the way his shirt sleeves were rolled up to his elbows and the way his chest moved with each of his breaths. "You're defying me again."

"I am," I breathed out, biting down on my bottom lip the closer he came. The top two buttons of his shirt were undone, and I couldn't look away from his tan skin, remembering what was beneath the rest of the material. "What are you going to do about it?"

I knew there was nothing he could do, not right then anyway, because it was the middle of the day. Uncle Alonzo and Antonio had only arrived twenty minutes ago, and whenever they came to the house, they'd be holed up in his office for hours at a time.

"Don't tempt me into something you're not prepared to finish, Aida."

I blinked up at him, having no intention of not following through. Weeks had gone by since I'd told him I would give us a proper chance, and since then, we'd done nothing but kiss.

I wanted more.

I needed more.

"Who said I wasn't going to finish it?"

Ma's footsteps echoed as she walked across the kitchen, and one quick look her way had me witnessing the smile on her face. She was seeing a side to Lorenzo I had no doubt she'd never seen before, but I didn't have time to overthink it as she exited the kitchen, leaving Lorenzo and me all alone.

"Aida," he warned, halting in front of me and placing both of his hands on the counter behind me.

"What?" I asked, meeting his stare and seeing the roaring fire in his eyes. He wanted this just as much as I did, so I didn't hesitate. I didn't wait for him to plant his lips on me. I dived for him, our lips connecting like magnets.

His hands came to my waist, yanking me closer to him, and I went without question. His cock pressed against me, and I reached down, pressing my palm along it over his pants.

"Fuck," he ground out, pulling his face away from mine. His nostrils flared as he breathed heavily, his eyes turning so dark they were nearly black. Neither of us said a word, the only sounds in the room our gasps for air.

And then he was on me, picking me up like I weighed the same as a feather. I wrapped my legs around his waist, tilting my hips so I could rock my core against his cock. He faltered at the move, pausing in the foyer, and I spotted his office door wide open. Voices came from inside, and for a second, I wondered if he was going to realize he was busy.

But he didn't. He simply took the stairs two at a time and headed right for his bedroom. The door swung open and slammed closed behind us. I registered that the sofa that used to be pressed up against the wall was gone, and in its place was a dresser.

I opened my mouth to ask him about it, but I didn't get the chance because I was flying in the air, my back hitting the bed. "Umph." I blinked, trying to get my bearings, but Lorenzo was already back on me, yanking down my leggings and panties in one smooth movement.

He slithered up to me, grasping the bottom of my top with both hands, then yanking at it. The material ripped, exposing my bare chest to him.

241

"Fuck," he groaned out. "Had I known you were wearing nothing underneath that, I would have come in here sooner."

"I never wear a bra at home." I gasped, trying to keep up with him as he slid back down my body and to the floor. "What are you doing?"

His lips lifted up into his telltale smirk, his hands pressed against my thighs, and then he parted them. "I'm taking what's mine." He dove between my legs, dragging his tongue up my slit, and it took all of my strength not to squeeze my legs together from the onslaught.

I moaned, gripping on to the sheets. "Lorenzo." I lifted my hips higher, needing… "More."

His fingers dug into my thighs, yanking me closer and lifting my ass off the bed. He took my clit into his mouth, sucking on it so hard I was scared I'd combust right there and then. The tip of his tongue flicked the bundle of nerves over and over again, and I reached my hand out to grab his hair. I pushed my fingers through it, jerking my hips into his face, not having a care in the world what I sounded or looked like.

Only Lorenzo managed to have me losing all of my inhibitions.

He slipped one finger inside me, swirling his tongue around and lapping me up like he couldn't get enough of me. His second finger had me squirming even more, and when I looked down, I groaned. His gaze met mine, the dark and broody stare mixed with him sucking on my clit one last time making me shoot off like a firework.

One hand gripped on to his hair, the other to the sheets. I didn't look away from him as my clit pulsated, relishing in the best damn feeling washing through my body.

"I could watch that all day long," he gritted out, his voice deeper than usual. Slowly, I let go of his hair, my fingers numb. I was sated, more than I ever had been. His long fingers undid the buttons on his shirt, his tongue licking his lips and lapping up the leftover juices. "Tastes like heaven," he murmured, yanking his shirt off and throwing it to the floor. His slacks were next; his cock springing free. My breaths turned to pants at the sight of him, his tan skin glistening.

He crawled over me like a lion stalking its prey, each of his muscles pulsating at his movements. My legs opened automatically, calling him to me silently. I gasped as his cock lined up at my entrance, but he didn't push any farther. He just stayed there, staring down at me.

"You're so goddamn beautiful," he murmured, placing his hand on the side of my face. I felt my cheeks heat at his attention, but I soaked it in, needing this side of him just as much as I wanted his asshole side. There were so many versions of Lorenzo, and I wanted to get to know them all. I wanted to see parts of him that he kept hidden from everyone else. And I knew that was what this was— a side he kept secret, just for me.

His hips moved forward, his cock pushing through my entrance. I tried to keep my eyes open, wanting to watch each of his reactions, and when his eyes closed, a moan vibrating from his throat, I let mine close too.

Slowly, he pushed in and out, relishing in it, in me, and I was doing the same. It was so different from the first time we'd been on this bed. We knew each other better. We were starting to understand each other.

I couldn't take his slow rhythm, though. I needed more. More of this. More of him. So, I slammed my hands on his chest, causing his eyes to pop open. A frown appeared on his face, but I didn't explain as I pushed him off me. I knelt at the side of him, threw one leg over him, then lined his cock back up at my entrance.

"Fuck," he groaned out as I lowered onto him. His hands grasped my hips, his body lifting so our faces were level, and for the first time, I took control. I rocked my hips, planting my hands on his shoulders for traction as I slipped him out and back in again.

His cock pinched the sides of my walls. I savored the slight pain mixed with the pleasure, but I lost my rhythm when his head dipped, his mouth taking my nipple into his mouth. He stood, banding his arms around my entire body, and popped my nipple out.

"My turn." He grinned, moving us away from the bed. My back hit a wall, his forehead pressed against mine, but he didn't let me go as he pounded into me.

"Yes," I gritted out, letting my head fall back. He didn't stop his relentless pounding, not when my second orgasm slammed through me, and not when my body sagged, not sure it was able to take anymore.

I rested my face on his shoulder, moaning as he pumped in and out of me. I tensed around him, felt him pulsate, and then he stilled, a growl escaping his throat as he emptied inside me.

And I knew right there, at that moment, that there was no turning back. Not now that I knew what it was like to be the center of his universe.

———

LORENZO

"Favorite day of the week?" I asked, staring up at the ceiling in the living room.

I sensed Aida turn her head, so I did the same, meeting her stare. "Tuesday."

My lips quirked at the corner. "Why Tuesday?"

She rolled to her side and leaned her head on her hand. "Monday is the start of the week, so that's out. Wednesday is the midway point, so that's neither here nor there." I blinked as she explained it to me. "Thursdays are meh."

I chuckled. "Obviously."

"And Fridays always get all of the attention." She smiled, pleased with herself. "So, there you have it. Tuesday."

"What about Saturday or Sunday?"

"They don't count." She winked. "They're week*ends*." She had a point. "What about you?"

I tilted my head to the side, glancing around the empty room. We'd been spending more and more time in the living room, so I decided that we should redecorate. The furniture and decor were the same from when I was a kid, but the mansion was mine now. I stared back at Aida—*ours*. It was ours.

The hardwood floors were cold and hard on our backs, but I didn't care. Any opportunity I had to spend time with Aida, I took it without a second thought.

"Mondays," I said, watching as her eyes widened. She opened her mouth, but I knew she was going to ask why, so I continued, "It's a new week. A fresh start." I leaned forward and planted a kiss on her lips. "I like fresh starts." I pressed my palms to the floor, lifting myself up. I hated leaving her, but there was no way I could bring her with me, not where I was about to go.

"You're leaving?" she asked as I stood.

"Yeah." I stepped back, grabbing my suit jacket off one of the new furniture boxes. "I have a meeting in the city." I didn't need to explain what meeting it was because she already knew it was Mafia business, and that was all I wanted her to know. The fewer details she had, the better. For the both of us.

She nodded and stood, staring around the room. "Is Mateo going with you?"

"Yeah." I pushed my arms through my jacket just as my cell pinged. A quick glance at it told me he was outside, ready to leave. "Why?"

"I was going to ask him to help put some of this furniture together with me."

I sauntered toward Aida, grabbing her by the waist and yanking her to me. "I'll do it when I get home." I pulled in a breath, unable to get enough of her rose scent. "Relax. Take a bath. Spend some time with Sofia." Her eyes flashed, and I knew I'd hit the perfect spot with my last words. "I'll be back soon."

She wrapped her arms around me, her head finding the place on my chest where she slept every night. In a matter of three months, I'd gone from hating the fact I had to find a wife to not wanting to leave her side. I wanted to spend every second next to her, listening to her talk about nothing and every-thing. But I couldn't. I had a business to run—a business that depended on me being the violent asshole I'd grown into.

As soon as I stepped away from her, I slipped my perfected mask back on and left the house, ready to do business. I pushed her to the back of my mind as Mateo drove us into the city. I was familiar with all of the streets, having spent days on them when I was younger. There was no better way to under-stand the way people were than to become one of them.

And that was what I'd done.

I'd made friends in low places as well as high. I'd committed crimes. I'd made allies as well as enemies. These city streets had molded me into the man I was today. A man who took no shit. A man who gave people second chances.

One chance. That was what I'd begged Aida for. It was what I gave everyone who crossed me. But that was all they got. You should learn from your mistakes, but as Mateo pulled to a stop at the ware-house, I knew this person hadn't.

Darkness covered the night, seeping into my bones and bringing my inner demon to the fore-front. The sounds of the city created the back-ground noise to what would be a long night, one I'd relish at every turn.

Drops of rain fell onto my face as I walked

toward the warehouse door, entered the code, then stepped inside. I could already hear pained moans. They'd started without me, but I'd be the one to finish it. I'd be the one to send a final message to everyone who thought they could cross me.

"Lorenzo," Dante greeted from the edge of the space they'd created between the crates of guns and ammunition. At the sound of my name, everyone stilled. My dress shoes clacked against the concrete floor, each step taking me closer to the man tied to a chair in the middle.

Blood ran down the side of his face and from his arm—the arm that had no hand on it. I'd already taught him one lesson, but apparently, that hadn't been enough for him. I moved past Uncle Antonio, his shirt splattered with blood. He was the person who'd taught me the best way to torture someone to inflict the maximum amount of pain.

Another chair sat to the side—a chair saved especially for me. I may have wanted to get my hands dirty, but not until Uncle Antonio has had his fun. I nodded at the man strapped to the chair—the man who I'd seen the night of my wedding. He hadn't begged to keep his hand, and he hadn't wanted forgiveness. No, he'd wanted another excuse to try and fuck me over.

I undid the button on my suit jacket, lowered into my seat, and waved my hand in the air, signaling for Uncle Antonio to continue.

He stepped forward, a pair of pliers gripped in his hand. "Hold his head, Dante," Uncle Antonio gritted out. Dante grabbed the man's head, and Antonio went to work, pulling out his teeth one at a time. He was methodical as he went, first the bottom teeth and then the top.

I leaned back in my seat, trying to have some patience as I let Antonio sate his desires. He needed to inflict torture. He needed it so he could be the man my auntie Vivianna needed. And with stark clarity, I understood that I wasn't so different from him. It was all about balance. A balance you only found when the time was right.

And that time for me was now.

Uncle Antonio turned and grabbed his favorite knife, plunging it into the man's chest and stomach. He flicked his wrist, cutting up and into his kidneys. He knew the human form better than most doctors. He knew what to hit when and what to miss. It was all about keeping them alive as long as possible and in as much pain as you could cause.

I blinked as Uncle Antonio held a Taser in his hand. When he'd first taught me all of those years ago, we hadn't used that. Instead, we'd used a live wire. But a Taser was easier…and harsher. I grinned. This was always my favorite part.

He lunged forward, slamming the Taser inside the cut he'd made on his stomach, frying his insides just enough to have the man howling in pain.

His head lulled to the side, his eyes trying to focus on one single thing, and when he caught sight of me, he laughed, blood spurting from his mouth. "You have no idea what's coming for you." I narrowed my eyes on him. "You're done." Red poured like a river down his chest, the open wounds not slowing down as the blood drained from him.

"I'm done?" I stood, my chest heaving.

"Yeah." He gurgled, his eyes closing. I stepped forward, and he snapped them back open. "You and your new wife."

I saw red, the demon inside roaring to life and taking over as I reached for my gun. He hadn't said a word, but now he wouldn't shut up, just as his heart was giving out I extended my arm, pressing the gun to his head as Uncle Antonio stood with the bloody Taser, ready to give him another round of shocks.

"Speak," I barked out at him.

"They're..." He coughed, more blood than before splattering from him. "Coming for you."

"Who?" I pressed the gun to his temple, needing an answer. I'd made enemies because of my name alone. There was always someone coming for me, but as he raised his head, his gaze meeting mine, he managed to croak out, "I'm FBI."

My attention snapped to the men in the room, seeing all of their shocked faces. Even Uncle

Antonio was confused. "Who fuckin' vetted him?" I shouted.

"I told Dante to do it," Christian said, his voice small. He knew he'd fucked up, but so had my brother. I tried to stay calm, but it was really goddamn hard when I had an FBI agent sitting in front of me, at least seventy percent dead.

"That true?" I asked Dante, cracking my neck side to side. His eyes widened. He knew he'd fucked up. The man who was meant to become my second-in-command hadn't even done a background check on someone who had tried to break in.

"I…"

"End him," I said, so calmly I shocked myself. Slowly, I stowed my gun away. "You fucked up. Now you fix it." I waved to the man in front of me. "End him, then chop him up and get rid of him in the four corners of the state." I stepped toward Dante. "I don't want to see your goddamn face in my house until you learn how to be a real fuckin' soldier."

I'd just drawn the lines between Mafia family and blood. Blood was always meant to come first, but he'd fucked up, and it was my job to teach him a lesson. To show him how you acted when you were a soldier. You did the shitty jobs. You earned your stripes. I had to, and now he would too.

I spun around, not turning back to the shit show as the sound of a gun going off vibrated through the warehouse. He was right. They would come for me. The feds never left a man behind. They wouldn't let this go, not now, not ever.

Dante had fucked up, but so had I. I'd let my guard down. I'd taken my eyes off the prize. But I wouldn't again. I wouldn't allow anyone to put my family at risk—to put Aida at risk.

CHAPTER

15

AIDA

"What do you mean I can't come inside?" The shrill shout had me wincing as I walked through the foyer and to the living room. We'd finished redecorating a week ago. All of the furniture had been put together, and the walls had been painted a crisp off-white. Indoor plants and little trinkets I'd found around the house were scattered around, but my favorite thing was the hanging chair I'd found on the internet. I spent hours sitting in that chair every night, staring out of the window at the lit-up water feature. Memories, both good and bad, hung around it, but that was what I loved. Nothing in this world was perfect. The room was becoming my own little sanctuary, and the more I added to it, the more everyone in the mansion seemed to drift toward it.

"I'm sorry, Miss Veev. I've been instructed that no visitors are allowed past the gates," I heard Mrs. Larson say through a speaker box near the front door.

I halted, frowning at it. I'd never seen that before. "Everything okay, Mrs. Larson?" I asked.

She jumped out of her skin, her hand flying to her chest. She panted, her face turning pale as she turned to face me. "You scared me!"

I made an "oops" face and headed toward her. "Sorry." I chuckled. "I didn't mean to sneak up on you."

She pulled in a deep breath, trying to calm herself. "It's okay, Aida." She swiped her hand over her forehead. "I've been on edge since Mr. Beretta put us on lockdown."

My lips spread into a grim line. "Me too." My stomach rolled as I remembered him coming home and calling a family meeting. There was no negotiation. He was putting us on lockdown until whatever was happening was over. I didn't want to admit that I kind of liked the fact none of us could leave. We were forced to be together. Ma was losing her mind being cooped up, but she'd found solace in cooking and baking. I was sure I'd put on ten pounds from her cannoli alone.

"Hello!" the shrill voice shouted through the speaker. "I demand you get Lorenzo."

"Who's that?" I asked Mrs. Larson, but when

she just stared at me with wide eyes, I remembered what she'd called the woman. *Veev.* My anger mixed with apprehension, and for a second, I wondered if Lorenzo had asked her to come here. But that idea flew out of my head as fast as it appeared. There was no way he would have told her to go to the mansion, not after everything we'd promised each other. "I'll handle it," I told Mrs. Larson, pulling open the front door.

I sauntered down the drive and to the gate where she stood. Her eyes widened, shock slamming over her features, but it was gone in a flash, replaced with a smirk—the same one she'd worn the day she'd been laid out on Lorenzo's desk as naked as the day she was born.

"Hi there," I greeted, keeping at least five meters between us. "Can I help you with something?"

Her nostrils flared, her perfectly red-painted lips lifting into a sneer. "Be a good girl and fetch Lorenzo." She flipped her hair behind her shoulder, her long fingernails painted to match her lips.

I looked her up and down, taking in the tight, dark-blue dress that was stuck to her like a second skin. Her long legs were on display, and the straps for her heels wrapped around her ankles. "Can I ask what it's regarding?" I tried to keep my rage tamped down—for now anyway.

"None of your business." She raised her brow at

me, making a shoo motion with her hand. "Run along."

I laughed so hard that I threw my head back, my stomach cramping at the force. I bent forward, holding my waist, knowing I looked crazy, but not giving a single fuck.

"What's so funny?" Veev asked, her shrill voice coming back in full force.

My laughter waned to chuckles as I tried to get ahold of myself. "You." I wiped the tears falling from my eyes and met her stare. "You are."

"What—"

I lunged forward, wrapping my hands around the bars on the gates, my emotions flipping so fast I made myself dizzy. "It's goddamn hilarious that you would turn up at *my* home, demanding that *I* get *my* husband for you." I narrowed my eyes, showing her I wasn't fucking around now. This wasn't her territory. It never had been.

Her fake lashes fluttered as she blinked, and I knew if this gate wasn't between us, I would have ripped them off her eyes. "You don't belong here." I slowly loosened the bars from my grip, counting to ten in my head so I could gain my control back. "Leave."

She snorted. "I doubt your husband would agree with that."

"*My husband* is being taken care of by *his wife.* Your whoring skills are no longer of use." I winked at her, pulling my lips up into a sweet smile. "Come here again, and I'll shoot you myself." I stepped back, lifting my hand in a wave. "Bye now."

I spun around, pushed my shoulders back, and sauntered up the driveway. Lorenzo stood in the doorway, his face a mixture of anger and appreciation. "You shouldn't have gone down there."

I shrugged, grabbing his shirt and yanking him inside. "I don't care." I stared up at him, giving him the same stare I gave her. "If I catch her here again, not only will I shoot her, I'll also chop your cock off." His eyes flared with anger. "Am I understood?"

He stared at me, his expression filtering from frustration to—

"I wanna fuck you so hard right now," he ground out, stepping toward me and not stopping until my back was pressed against the wall.

I bit down on my bottom lip as I trailed my hand down his chest and to his erection. "What are you waiting for?"

He slammed his hands on the wall above my head, caging me in. I gripped his cock, watching as his head tipped back, and a groan vibrated from the back of his throat. "You'll be the goddamn death of me."

"I'm okay with that." I lifted up onto my tiptoes, whispering against his lips, "Now fuck me." I paused. "Hard."

LORENZO

My focus was split, half listening to Aida as she spoke to Ma at the dining table, and half listening to Christian, who sat next to Sofia. From the moment I'd walked out of the warehouse two weeks ago, I'd put the entire house on lockdown. Those closest to me had to stay in the house, only going out if absolutely necessary, and only when they were surrounded by protection. I wasn't taking any chances, not when it came to my inner circle.

Uncle Alonzo and Uncle Antonio had taken their wives away on what they thought were vacations, and Dante was trying to make amends for the mess he'd created by staying in the city in my old apartment. I'd demanded Christian and Mateo move into the mansion, at least until I felt the dust had settled.

Nothing had outwardly happened—unless you counted Veev turning up out of the blue. Aida had schooled her in minutes, and even though I was mad as hell at her for going down to the gates without telling anyone, I couldn't deny it was hot as fuck watching her take charge of Veev. She'd warned her to stay away, but she'd also warned me, too. I didn't take people telling me what to do lightly, but when it came from Aida, I knew to fuckin' listen.

Happy wife, happy life, right?

"How is your brother?" Ma asked, bringing me out of my thoughts and crash-landing back into the here and now. Ma's gaze fixed on me. She knew better than anyone at this table that I wouldn't tell her what had caused me to close ranks, but she also understood it was bad enough for me to do it. My gut told me to be on guard even if people thought I shouldn't be.

"He's fine." All conversation stopped as I spoke, everyone listening intently for a tidbit of information. They wouldn't get it, though. I hadn't even told The Enterprise what had happened. It was none of their business. I kept things in-house because I had the tools to fix whatever came my way. I didn't need people involved, telling me how to handle my own goddamn business.

"He'll be home soon," I said, leaning back in my seat. I'd barely eaten anything the last couple of days, my appetite fading away, and it frustrated the hell out of me. I never reacted like this, but something was different this time.

My gaze slid to Aida, who was frowning at me. He'd mentioned her. He'd threatened that they were coming for her. And I wondered what she would do, how she would react. I honestly had no idea. All I had was hope. Hope that she wouldn't turn her back on me. Hope that she wouldn't force me to do something I didn't want to do.

I blew out a frustrated breath, hating that my mind went there. I couldn't think about it, not now, not after we'd come this far. I wanted her here with me, at my side, fighting my battles with me, not against me. But I couldn't quiet the small voice in my head that told me she was too good for me—too good for this life.

Her hand reached out, her gaze not moving from mine for even the briefest of seconds. "You okay?" she asked.

The question took me by surprise. No one had ever asked me that, and as I met her stare, searching her eyes for *something*, I found myself shaking my head no. I wasn't okay. I wouldn't be okay until I got my house in order. I wouldn't be okay until I knew she was safe.

"Lorenzo." She stood, ignoring everyone at the table as she moved toward me. She was within arm's reach, just centimeters from me, when a blast outside shook the house. I flew out of my seat, grabbing her around the waist and shoving her behind me.

Christian did the same, pushing Sofia toward Aida, and Mateo flung himself in front of Ma. Then together, we moved toward the dining-room door, but we weren't fast enough. Hordes of uniformed agents barreled inside, their guns raised, shouting for us to put our hands in the air.

Ma started shouting in Italian, and Sofia cried out as one of the officers pushed her to the ground and onto her knees. My hands were raised, just like Christian's and Mateo's. We knew how to handle raids like this, but more importantly, we knew they'd never find anything, so we cooperated because the sooner we did, the quicker they would be gone.

"Get off of me!" Aida shouted, and I turned just in time to see her pushing back against a woman wearing a bulletproof vest with the letters FBI written in white on the front.

"Get down, Lorenzo Beretta," a male agent barked at me. This wasn't anything new to me, and because I knew there was no way they had anything against me, I got down to my knees, keeping my attention focused on Aida. *Look at me,* I silently told her, but she was too busy staring the female agent down. Her hands were in the air, but she refused to get down on her knees. I smirked, thinking back to two nights ago when she'd done just that for me.

The butt of a gun slammed into the side of my face, and my world spun for a fraction of a second before my head dropped down. "Fuck," I gritted out, trying to hold my anger in.

"You were resisting," the agent said, and when I looked up at him, he winked at me. "That'll leave a bruise."

"You piece of shit!" Aida shouted, diving for me, but the woman caught her, shoving her to the ground on her stomach and slapping a pair of cuffs on her. Only then did Aida look at me, eyes wide, her face pale.

"You're under arrest," the female agent told her, reading her rights. I cursed silently, both at the throbbing pain in my face and the fact that Aida hadn't done what they told her to do. I should have explained what to do when being faced with any kind of law enforcement, but I doubt it would have made a difference. She was sweet, kind, sexy, but my favorite was feisty as fuck.

"We have a warrant to search the premises," the agent who'd jammed the butt of his gun into my face said, throwing a piece of paper on the floor in front of me.

I didn't even acknowledge it as I stared up at him. "Go right ahead." I paused, my lips lifting into a smirk. "You won't find anything."

"I'll be the judge of that." He looked at the agent who held Aida pinned to the ground. "Take her down to headquarters."

"No," I growled, starting to stand. "You're not taking her anywhere."

"Yeah?" the male agent asked, stepping closer to me. His vest was the same as the woman's, but it had an extra name badge. Agent Morgan. I stowed that name away, knowing I'd be finding out exactly who he was when they were done here.

"Go ahead, asshole. Resist her arrest and see where it lands you."

The sound of clattering came from the kitchen, and I pulled in a deep breath, knowing they would go through every inch of the house with a fine-tooth comb—the places they could see anyway.

I turned my head, just enough to spot the agent lifting Aida from the floor, and silently tried to tell her it would be okay. However much I'd tried to keep business away from her, she knew things that could go against me. Time would tell whose side she'd be on, but deep down, I already knew she wouldn't betray me. She was in this with me. Right?

CHAPTER

16

AIDA

The farther away from the house we drove, the more my fight drained away. The buzzing in my ears got louder, my breaths coming faster, and my hands started to tingle—the latter because of the cuffs.

The blacked-out SUV—not too dissimilar to the one Mateo drove—whizzed through the streets and toward the city. I had no idea where they were taking me, but I was relieved it was somewhere I knew. At least then I'd be able to find my way back if they ever let me go. I groaned as I looked down at my lap. I was only dressed in a pair of leggings, some slides, and one of Lorenzo's T-shirts, sans my bra. I knew that not wearing a bra inside the house would bite me in the ass.

Tires screeched to a halt as we took a turn too fast, and the SUV wobbled. Whoever was driving was acting as though they were being chased, and maybe they were. Lorenzo said he had eyes everywhere, but somehow, deep down, I knew he'd have no idea where they were taking me either.

Part of me wished I would have done as the rest of the family had—stayed relatively quiet and did what the FBI told us to do—but my instincts when I'd seen that asshole slam his gun into Lorenzo's face had kicked in. And now, here I was, in the back of an SUV with my wrists cuffed.

The car slammed to a stop, and my body flung forward, my face colliding with the back of the passenger seat. I felt the trickle of blood on my lip a second before I tasted it. I winced, howling as I snapped my mouth open, causing the tooth that had gone into my bottom lip to tear the sensitive skin. The trickle turned into a burst of blood, but neither of the agents said anything as they got out of the car and hauled me with them.

I could feel the warmth of it running down my neck, and each small tic of my muscles felt like it was tearing it apart even more. "I need a tissue," I groaned out. I was ignored, yet again, and dragged into a building that looked like a tower of offices. Was this where the headquarters was? Hiding in plain sight. Or was this somewhere different, somewhere that no one knew about?

Several people stood around, earpieces in their ears, their faces forward, not making a single move as we walked by them. The female agent who had tackled me to the floor back at the mansion gripped my arm harder, veering me to the left and into an open elevator.

The doors pinged shut, and then we were going up, the numbers above the doors flashing by at lightning speed. Everything was a blur as the doors opened back up. We traveled through several hallways, into a room, and then another hallway. Finally, I was pushed into a room, and they slammed the door behind me.

"Fuck you very much," I groaned, wishing I hadn't spoken as my lip burned and more blood trickled out of the cut.

I spun around in a circle, taking stock of the room. Three concrete walls surrounded me along with one mirrored one. I rolled my eyes. They couldn't have been more predictable if they tried. A lone table sat in the middle of the room, bolted to the floor. I moved toward it, sitting on one of the two chairs. I was debating going to the mirror and seeing how bad my lip was, but there was no way I was going to give them the satisfaction. They were probably watching me.

I smirked. What would Lorenzo do in this situation? I'd been asking myself that a lot lately. I was who I was, and there was no changing that. I hated hard, but I loved harder. I stood up for what I believed in, and I surrendered when I knew it was the right time. And maybe back at the mansion should have been one of those times, but my gut told me it wasn't.

The door clicked open, and I snapped my head to face it. I wasn't prepared for a new agent to enter, so when a tall, good-looking man strode in, I raised a brow. He had that bad-boy vibe, the kind Lorenzo had, only Lorenzo's wasn't an act—it was just who he was. This guy...this guy was playing make-believe.

"Mrs. Beretta," he said, his tone silky smooth. He stared down at a folder in his hands as he made his way to the chair opposite mine. "I see here that you resisted arrest while we were executing a warrant at..."

He paused, glancing up at me, then searching whatever papers he was holding. He was acting like he didn't know, but both he and I knew this probably would have been their biggest operation all year. You didn't execute a search warrant on a Mafia boss's house on just any day of the week.

"The residence of the Beretta family. Mainly, Lorenzo Beretta."

I stared at him, waiting for him to ask me a real question. He leaned back in his seat, tilting his head to the side. "What is a nice young woman like you doing marrying a scumbag like him?" I stared, not giving anything away. I'd watched enough true crime documentaries to know staying silent was my best bet. "Is it the money?" He placed his arms on the table, leaning closer to me and trying to disarm me with a smile. "Or is it the power?"

I pursed my lips, glancing around the room, acting like everything he said was boring. And it was. People always assumed things, but no one really knew what happened behind closed doors. To everyone else, Lorenzo was a lion, prowling around and taking whatever he wanted. But when it was just him and me, I saw a different side. I saw the wolf who protected his pack, the wolf who did anything for the people he loved.

"Staying quiet won't get you anywhere," the agent said, and I realized I didn't know his name.

"What's your name?" I asked, my voice sickly sweet.

"None of your business," he said, narrowing his eyes on me and letting his fake facade slip.

I nodded. "Just like my life is none of yours." I leaned forward, my shoulders screaming at the move because I still had the cuffs on behind my back. "I know my rights. I want a lawyer."

"Are you sure about that, Mrs. Beretta?" the agent asked, his lip curling up in disgust. "If we get you a lawyer, then you forfeit the deal."

"Deal?" I asked, figuring I may as well play along.

He sighed like I was too much work and taking up his valuable time. While I was over here with blood still trickling from my lip and numb hands. "If you cooperate, then we won't charge you with murder after the fact."

I laughed. I couldn't help it. He was absurd. This entire thing was nuts. And then I realized they had every intention of bringing me here, whether I resisted or not.

"You think this is funny?" He slammed his hand on the desk, standing up. "A man is dead. Murdered. And not just any man, but an FBI agent."

"Oh." I fluttered my lashes at him. "I'm sorry. How did he die?" His nostrils flared, his hands clenching. "Is that a hard question?" I asked, feeling something bubbling up inside me. The longer he was in here with me, the easier it was to read him. "You have his body, right? So, it can't be that hard to tell what he died of. Sorry, what he was *murdered* of."

He backed away a step, his chest heaving with breaths, and for a second, I doubted myself. I didn't know who this person was. I wasn't in an official police station. I was here on my own, still cuffed, with no one to help me. But the fight in me didn't wane. I wasn't standing for this.

"You don't have the body, do you?" I waited for him to answer, but when he didn't, I leaned back.

"So, you want to offer me a deal for the murder of someone who you're not even sure is dead?" I paused. "Am I hearing that right?" When he still didn't answer me, I gritted out, "I'm not saying another word to you until I see my lawyer, or you let me go."

"You will say a word!" he shouted, causing me to jump from the way it bounced off the walls. "You'll tell me where the agent is, and you'll assist in the investigation. Otherwise, I'll see to it myself that you don't leave this room until you're about to be charged."

I raised my brows and shrugged. I was done talking. Not just because he was talking out of his ass, but also because my lip was throbbing so badly, I could barely stand it.

He paced the room in front of me, jabbering on like I was listening to what he was saying, but it went in one ear and then straight back out of the other. Finally, after what felt like hours, he left the room, slamming the door behind him, giving me a break from his incessant chatter. I was sure he thought the more he talked, the more likely I was to bite back, but I'd already found out what I wanted to know—the reason they'd turned up to the mansion. They were looking for one of their agents, and slowly as the time passed by, I started to piece the last couple of weeks together. Was this what Lorenzo had put us on lockdown for? I groaned. Of course, it was.

The door swung open, and I turned my head just enough to see another agent standing in the doorway. My back straightened as I recognized him from back at the mansion. He was the one who had pistol-whipped Lorenzo and grinned while he did it. "Let's go," he barked, holding the door open for me.

I stood, feeling my legs wobble from the position I'd been in for who knew how many hours, and stumbled toward him. If I was anywhere else, I would have spat my words and told him exactly what I thought of him. But right then, I felt like I couldn't. I was trapped, trying to do what I was told so I could get the hell out of here.

He gripped my bicep, pulling me along through the maze of hallways again, and then the elevators came into view. We waited for the doors to open, then walked inside, all the while I was trying to keep my bubbling emotions under control. Were they taking me somewhere else? Was the other agent being serious about charging me with murder after the fact? They couldn't do that, right? *Right?*

I couldn't get control of my thoughts as they whirled around my head, not when the elevator doors opened, not when the agent marched me past the other agents on the lower level, and not when he spun me around and undid my cuffs.

"You're free to go," he said, sounding bored.

"I'm…" I turned to look out of the windows,

where morning light was starting to shine through. "I can go?"

"Yeah." He stepped closer, towering over me. "You may have gotten away with it this time, but I'll be watching." He paused, his face turning red with his anger. "I'll be watching all of you. Waiting for the mistake that you *will* make." His lips curved on one side. "And I'll be right there, dishing out the punishment trash like you deserve."

I raised my brows, not sure what to say to that, so instead of opening my mouth, I spun around, not wasting a single second to get the hell out of here. I darted for the main doors, hearing the agent's laughter follow me out.

The cool morning air slapped me in the face when I made it outside. I'd been in there all night. They'd kept me in that room for at least ten hours, but it hadn't felt like it. It had felt like moments in time rather than hours shooting by.

I glanced down at my wrists, seeing the purple bruising banding around them, and stretched my fingers out. My arms felt like they weren't mine as I gained the feeling back in them. I took one look back at the building, then sprinted away from it, afraid they'd scoop me back up if I lingered. I wasn't sure where I was heading, but when a yellow taxi drove by with the light on the top, I held my arm out.

The car skidded to a stop, so I jumped in,

reeling the address of the mansion off. I didn't lean back; I didn't relax. I kept turning around, sure that someone would be following me. But the roads were empty at this time of the morning, a peacefulness drifting over the city that I'd never witnessed before.

We pulled into the street the mansion was on, and a breath of relief left me in a whoosh. The gates were hanging open, and it was only then I realized the loud bang before they'd all come barging in was them ramming the gates. "Pull into the driveway," I told the taxi driver, and he did, stopping just outside the wide-open mansion doors.

Lorenzo was pacing in the foyer, his cell to his ear, when he turned and spotted me. He said something, dropped his cell to the floor, and sprinted toward me.

———

LORENZO

"Where the hell have you been?" I growled out, wrapping my arms around her and lifting her up off the ground. I'd been calling everyone and anyone, trying to find out where she was, but I'd had no luck. No one knew of an FBI headquarters in the city, but I was certain that was what the agent had said just before they'd taken her away.

"Ow," she groaned, but it wasn't just any kind of groan. No, it was a painful one.

I yanked back from her, searching her face and feeling white-hot anger slam into me with so much force I stumbled back. "What the fuck did they do?" I growled. Her lip was twice the size and turning dark purple, but it was the dried blood leading down to her neck that had me wanting to pull my gun and find Agent fuckin' Morgan. Watching him bark orders at everyone as they tore the house apart told me that he was the one in charge.

"Can you pay the taxi driver?" Aida asked, closing her eyes and leaning her head on my shoulder. Her body was spent, getting heavier the longer she leaned against me.

I spun us around, blinking at Mateo and Christian, who stood a few feet away. "Pay him." I stepped toward them. "And give him a tip for bringing her home safe."

Aida sighed, the kind of sigh that told me she was happy to be home, but I couldn't feel any of that, not right then. My rage had gripped me so tightly that all I could think about was finding out what the hell was going on and getting some answers.

I held Aida tightly as I headed up the stairs and to our room. All of our things were strewn on the floor: her clothes and makeup, my suits, even the mattress had been yanked off the bed and left half on it and half on the floor.

They'd torn apart every inch of the house, not giving a fuck if they broke anything. It was what they did, what they'd always done, which was yet another reason why I wasn't going to let this lie. They'd invaded my home on a warrant signed by a judge I knew was on The Enterprise's payroll—specifically Piero. He was the one who had his fingers in with politicians and judges, yet he hadn't warned me something was coming. I'd known it in my gut, but that was different from having solid information.

I moved us into the bathroom, switching the shower on and heading straight under it, not caring that we were still fully clothed. She clung to me as the water hit her back, her chest heaving at the move.

"I'm gonna kill them," I told her. "I'll kill every single one of them for hurting you." It was a promise I knew I would see through, whether it took me months or years. I'd make sure they got retribution for touching what was mine.

"Okay," she whispered, and I froze. I didn't expect her to agree with me, but I shouldn't have been surprised, not after everything she'd done in the last day. She'd tried to get to an agent who pistol-whipped me, not having a single care in the world that she was surrounded by the FBI. She fought for what she thought was right, and damn if I didn't love that about her.

"Let me clean you up," I said, letting her down. Her feet hit the tiled floor, and she slipped her slides off, flinging them to the edge of the shower. I helped her take her T-shirt off, grinning at the fact that she wasn't wearing a bra. I honestly wondered if the only time she wore one was when she was in college.

My hands trailed down her arms and to her wrists, where she winced, and my anger slowly turned to torment. Purple bands covered her small wrists, and I couldn't help but blame myself. If I'd checked out the two soldiers who had tried to steal from me on my wedding night, then maybe I would have found out one of them was FBI. I'd allowed other people to do the job, but I realized now that I couldn't rely on anyone else, not yet anyway.

Dad had always handled things himself, and time and time again I asked why he didn't let the people under him handle things he didn't need to be involved in. *You'll understand when the time comes.* His words echoed in my head. I understood now. I understood that I was at the top for a reason. The buck started and ended with me.

I bent down, helping her out of her leggings, then stood, reaching for a washcloth to get the dried blood off her neck. I was methodical, not stopping until she was clean, any traces other than bruises gone. I shucked out of my own shirt and slacks, then switched the shower off.

Our wet bodies collided as I wrapped my arms around her again, carrying her to our bedroom. "Stay here," I said, planting her in the middle of the room. I grabbed two towels from the bathroom, then wrapping her in one of them.

Her eyes closed as I dried myself and threw on some sweatpants. It was the middle of the week, and I had work to do, especially now, but none of that was my priority. All that mattered was making sure Aida was okay. And as I pushed the mattress back onto the bed and placed the pillows back where they belonged, I saw another trickle of blood coming from her lip.

"I'm calling the doctor in," I told her, grinding my teeth together.

She nodded, her eyes still closed. She wasn't fighting me on it, and I was glad because I was already sending a message to the doctor I kept on call. Normally he was there to fix members of the business when they got injured, but I knew he could handle this too.

I placed my cell into my pocket and reached for her. "Come and get into bed." She groaned as I helped her into it, her eyes still not opening, and within seconds, soft snores were sounding out. She'd been kept up all night, and although I wanted to know every single thing that happened, I knew what she needed right then was rest and her lip fixed.

So, I waited at her side, not moving a single inch until the doctor came. "Lorenzo," he greeted, standing in the doorway to my bedroom with Christian by his side. "You requested my services."

I stood, narrowing my eyes on Doctor Dubeke. "She has a cut on her lip that won't stop bleeding and bruises on her wrists." I kept my stare on him. "Fix her up."

"Hello to you too." He rolled his eyes, a move that didn't suit a fifty-year-old doctor, but he was used to the way I talked because he'd known me since I was a kid. Not only was he the doctor for the family, but he was also a friend, one who we knew wouldn't say a word to anyone—primarily because of the generous paycheck we gave him.

I didn't answer him as I turned back to Aida and gently placed my hand on her shoulder. "Baby?" I murmured, shaking her a little. She groaned, her eyes fluttering open. "The doctor is here." She hummed in the back of her throat, and I couldn't help but smile down at her. I'd panicked when I couldn't find her. I'd felt like I was missing half of my body, not knowing where she was, but now that she was home, I could relax. At least momentarily.

"I'm gonna head down into my office while he

fixes you up." I flicked my gaze over to Christian, who was still standing in the doorway.

"Okay." She squeezed my hand and gripped the towel still wrapped around her body.

Doctor Dubeke slipped past me, sitting on the edge of the bed, but I didn't make a move. I couldn't get my feet to work, my instinct to stay with her too strong.

"Lorenzo," Christian called, and I snapped my head around to face him. "We have some intel."

I nodded, my gaze veering back to Aida one last time. She was okay here. She was safe. I inhaled a deep breath, grabbed a T-shirt that was lying on the floor, then followed Christian out of my bedroom. I headed toward the door at the end of the hall, the secret passage that would take us straight into my office.

Voices leaked from the office, but when I entered, they silenced. Mateo and Dante were at the edges of the room, and Uncle Antonio and Uncle Alonzo were in the middle, along with Romeo, Antonio's twenty-year-old son. He was new to the family business, not usually allowed in meetings like this, but as I turned to face Dante, I knew having Romeo here so young would help. He wouldn't end up making mistakes, not like Dante had.

"We've checked this room. Found three. All clear now," Christian said, and I knew what he was saying. The FBI had been in here, which meant they could have planted listening devices anywhere they liked.

I kept my expression neutral as I headed toward my bar cart, then poured myself a double whisky. It burned the back of my throat, the liquid bringing me to life as I turned back, ready to take in all of the information they had.

"How's she doing?" Uncle Antonio asked.

"Dubeke is with her." It was enough of an explanation as I leaned against the front of my new desk. The black marble one had been replaced with a steady walnut wood one, chosen by Aida. She hadn't been kidding about my desk, and I couldn't help but lift one side of my lips at the memory. She was part of this house—part of *me*.

"He'll fix her," Uncle Alonzo said, his dark gaze meeting mine. He was just as pissed as I was over the entire raid. "Piero got back to me," he continued. "Said he had no idea it was going to happen. He's making inquiries now."

I nodded, taking the information in but not believing it. There was no way he didn't know what was going down. He had his ear to the ground at all times. Maybe he'd been in on it. My nostrils flared at the thought. If a member of The Enterprise had known this and kept it to themselves, it could mean full-out war. A war I knew I would win. A war that would destroy the balance my father had spent decades creating.

"The agent?" I asked.

Dante stepped forward. "Which one?" I narrowed my eyes on him, not willing to answer his stupid fuckin' question.

"Agent Morgan," Mateo supplied. "I have some contacts that are filtering down information as they get it." I turned to face him, glad that someone around here was doing their damn job. "Romeo and I are heading to meet with them in an hour." He glanced at his cell. "What I know so far is that Morgan was the partner of Heiver, the agent——"

"That was killed," a new voice said, a voice that shouldn't have been in my office, not while we were discussing this.

All attention swung her way. Aida stood in the doorway to the office, her lip and chin dark purple, her shoulders slumped, her body clearly exhausted, but her eyes…her eyes were lit with roaring flames, threatening to burn everything down to the ground.

"Aida," I warned, but she held her hand up in the air, then stepped inside. She closed the door behind her, the click of the lock turning like a gunshot ricocheting around the room.

"I know what happened." She leaned her back to the door. "Well, I kind of know." Her brows lowered. "When they took me from here, we headed into the city."

"Where about in the city?" I asked, placing my glass on the desk. She shouldn't have been in here, but whether I liked it or not, she was involved, more than she should have been.

"I don't know." She shook her head. "It looked like an office building." Her hand drifted up to her mouth. "They braked so fast I went flying forward, and my tooth went through my lip." I could just about make out several stitches in her bottom lip now. "Then they hauled me inside and put me in a room." She gripped on to her wrists. "They kept my hands cuffed behind my back, and a new agent came in."

Her head tilted to the side, her gaze drifting over everyone until it landed on me. "He said he was going to charge me with murder after the fact if I didn't take a deal to turn on you."

I growled, standing at her words. "He did what?"

She winked, stepping forward. "Obviously, I didn't take the deal." She moved between Romeo and Mateo, heading for me. "I did manage to find out that they raided us because an FBI agent was killed." She halted a foot away, her head dipping back so she could keep her gaze connected to mine. She placed her hand on my chest and over my rapidly beating heart. "I also found out they don't actually have a body to prove that."

My gaze flicked to Dante, glad that he'd at least done that job properly. I looked back down at Aida. "Then what happened?"

She shrugged, trying to lift her lips into a smile but wincing as her mouth twinged against the stitches. "Then, the agent went on and on." She rolled her eyes. "He wouldn't shut up. But I stayed silent because I've watched all of those true crime documentaries." She raised her brow. "There was no way they were going to get me to confess." She puffed her chest out, and I couldn't help but grin down at her.

"I thought you should know what happened." She turned to face the rest of the men in the room, halting on Romeo, who she'd only met once before. He tilted his head in a nod at her, a sign of respect that I took note of.

I pressed the side of my face to the back of her head, whispering in her ear, "You did good." She leaned her back against my chest, her hand gripping on to my arm. "Head upstairs. I'll be up there in a bit."

She nodded, not moving for a second, soaking in my embrace, then she left just as quickly as she appeared, leaving us all in my office, having gained more information from her than anyone who was actually in the business.

I turned to Uncle Alonzo. "Fill The Enterprise in on what's happened." I crossed my arms over my chest. "Tell them only what they need to know." He nodded, understanding what I was saying. "Set up a meeting in three weeks. We should have solid intel by then." I turned to face Christian. "Find out who the agent was that threatened Aida." I turned to face Mateo and Romeo. "Get all the intel from your contacts. Don't let up on them." I pulled in a breath, exhaustion slamming through me. "Meet back here tomorrow."

They all left my office without another word... all but Dante. He stayed in his position against the wall, his features schooled into a neutral look. "What about me?" he asked, his voice deeper than usual. He was pissed, I knew that, but I couldn't bring myself to give a flying fuck. He'd put us in this position by not doing his job properly.

"Do whatever the hell you want," I ground out, not moving from my position. My body craved to go to Aida, but not until everyone was gone. My guard was well and truly up.

"This is bullshit," Dante growled. "I made a mistake—"

I lunged for him, grabbing him around the collar and slamming his back against the wall. The framed photos shuddered, nearly falling off their hooks at the impact. "Your *mistake* cost us." I gripped him harder, bringing my face within inches of his. "Your *mistake* caused the fat lip and bruised wrists my wife has." I pulled him off the wall and slammed him back against it. "Your *mistake* was one a Beretta son never should have made."

He shook his head, his palms flattening on my

chest. "I'm sorry," he ground out, pushing me away, but I didn't let go of him. He needed to know what consequences his actions had. "I'm sorry I wasn't Dad's favorite." A muscle in his jaw twitched, his brows lowering. "I'm sorry I was never good enough to learn the business. I'm sorry I was always the sensitive one. I'm sorry. I'm fuckin' sorry!"

"What the hell are you talking about?" I blinked at him, trying to hold on to my anger, but it was waning the longer I stared at him.

"I'm talking about *you*." He pushed against my chest again, but this time I let him go. "You got all of his attention. You were his golden boy." He pushed his hand through his hair, gripping it tightly. "I was always left out, never good enough, never as great as *Lorenzo*." He let his head drop back. "Fuck this." He let out a sinister chuckle. "Fuck you."

He barged out of my office, leaving me wondering what the hell had just happened.

CHAPTER

17

AIDA

I lifted my hand in a wave at Mateo and Romeo, who sat at the back of my psych class, clearly bored out of their damn minds. I thought it was comical the way they grunted and groaned as the lecturer spoke about how the mind worked in weird and mysterious ways.

It was my last class of the day, and I told them as much when everyone started to pack their things away and head out of the room. I always lingered because Mateo wanted the hallways to be almost empty so he could have a clear view of everything around us.

"You know you could actually learn something if you paid attention," I told them, raising my brows and smiling. Thank God I could smile again. The stitches Doctor Dubeke had put in were taken out yesterday, and although I'd be left with a small scar, I didn't care because now I could lift my lips without feeling like they were burning off my face.

"I already did psych," Romeo said. He didn't often talk, so this information was a shock, not just to me, but Mateo too. We both turned to face him. "What?" Romeo asked as if his tidbit of information was him talking about the weather.

"You did psych?" I asked, blinking up at him as I went to throw my backpack over my shoulder. Mateo snatched it from me before I got the chance, but I didn't comment on it. I was getting used to having these two around me any time I wasn't home.

It had only been nine days since the raid, but things were already starting to get back to normal. Lorenzo said he wasn't going to let the FBI change the way we lived our lives, but that hadn't stopped him from putting an extra detail on me. He said he was being cautious just for now, and I couldn't deny him that. I felt safer with both Mateo and Romeo. Deep down, I knew I needed to push my shoulders back and live my life outside of the mansion without them, but it was a process, one I knew I couldn't rush.

"Yeah. I did it two years ago." Romeo stepped toward the door to the classroom, looking left and right. "I finished college last year."

I spluttered as I followed him down the hallway, turning back to look at Mateo, who was just as wide-eyed as I was. "How old are you again?"

"Twenty," Romeo said. He flashed a grin at me over his shoulder. "I went to college when I was sixteen."

"Holy shit." I blew out a breath. "And here I was thinking I was the shit for even *going* to college." I chuckled, the sound uneasy. "If it wasn't for my scholarships, I wouldn't even be here."

The cool wind whipped at us as Romeo opened the main doors to the building. "You're here on scholarship?" Mateo asked, coming to walk beside me now that we were outside. I was smushed inside a Romeo and Mateo sandwich as we made our way to the parking lot.

"Yep. I managed to get three. One for my grades, one for coming from a disadvantaged family, and one because I was first-generation Italian-American." I winked up at Mateo. "I applied to hundreds back in my senior year at high school. I was determined to be the first person in my family to make it to college."

"That's kind of inspiring," Mateo said, his gaze veering off as we made it to the SUV. He blinked several times and opened up the back door for me, a move he'd always done. "I never got to finish high school."

"You didn't?" I frowned at him. "Why?"

He shrugged, shaking his head and wiping the expression off his face. "Ma needed me to get a job and look after my little brother and sister. So, I quit junior year."

I opened my mouth, unsure what to say, but his cell rang, taking him away from the conversation. My mind spun as I got into the car and stared out of the window, watching him talk on his cell before getting into the SUV. He turned the engine on and drove away from the college.

I thought I'd had it hard trying to get into college and having to share a room with my sister and niece, but something about the way Mateo spoke made me wonder what his life was like. He was always around, taking me places, and not once had I asked about him.

I opened my mouth to ask him something— anything—but it was too late because we were pulling through the gates and into the mansion. "Lorenzo needs us to run an errand," Mateo told Romeo. His gaze met mine in the rearview mirror. "He's in the house with Christian."

"Okay." I glanced down as I plucked my backpack off the floor and slipped out of the car. They stayed where they were as I walked inside the mansion, and when the doors closed behind me, I just stood there, unable to get Mateo's words out of my mind. He hadn't even finished high school. I knew there were many people who didn't, but he was part of the family—not in blood but in spirit—so why hadn't they made sure he finished high school?

My gaze snapped to Lorenzo's office door as it opened, and Christian exited. He was saying something to someone behind him, and as soon as I spotted Lorenzo, I made a beeline for him. "Did you know Mateo never finished high school?" I planted my hands on my hips, screwing my face up.

"I…" Lorenzo laughed, clearly confused by my question. "What are you talking about?"

"I'm talking about the fact that Mateo never got his high school diploma." I shook my head, feeling something bubbling up inside me. I had no idea what it was, but I was furious that, in this day and age, someone had to quit school to get a job so they could help provide for their siblings. "He had to quit to get a job. Did you know that?"

"Yeah." Lorenzo raised a brow at me and leaned against the doorframe of his office. "It was me who gave him the job. I was a captain at the time. What's the big deal?"

"Did *you* finish high school?" I asked. He nodded, so I turned to Christian. "What about you?"

"I…yeah."

I pursed my lips and paced in front of them. "So, someone made sure *you* finished school, but instead of helping Mateo and making sure that he did, you gave him a job?" I threw my hands up in the air. "You pulled him into the Mafia, not caring why he was doing it?"

"Baby," Lorenzo said, his voice smoother. "It's not like—"

"And here I was, bragging about the fact that I got three scholarships so I could attend college. All the while, he didn't even get to finish high school!"

"Aida," Lorenzo barked. I turned to face him, frowning up at him. "I offered to loan him the money so he could finish school, but he wouldn't take it." He pushed off the doorframe. "I told him to go and get his GED, but he said it'd distract him from work and making sure his ma and siblings were taken care of." He took two steps toward me, placing his hands on the side of my face. "He'll get his GED when he's ready."

"But why would his ma—"

"She's a drunk," Christian supplied. "His ma is a drunk and doesn't give a fuck." I faced him, listening intently. "He does all of this to give his brother and sister a better life. He's been doing it for five years now."

"It's sad," I whispered, leaning into Lorenzo, feeling all of my anger slip away. "I feel like I should help."

"No." He shook his head, raising one brow in warning. "If Mateo needs help, he'll ask for it. Don't go interfering in someone else's life." He didn't look away, pushing his point home. "The fact that he told you means he trusts you."

"He does?" I asked.

"Yeah, baby." He pressed his forehead to mine. "He'll come to you if he needs anything."

"Okay." I sighed, my body itching to do more. Maybe I could have met his siblings, or helped him study, or...

I closed my eyes. Lorenzo was right. I shouldn't interfere in his life, but that didn't mean I wouldn't slowly prod away at Mateo for more information. I wouldn't stand by while someone was struggling, especially now that I had the means to help.

———

LORENZO

I leaned back in the seat, watching the doors as each member of The Enterprise entered, their personal bodyguards and underbosses with them. They took up their usual places behind the bosses of each family, just like mine had. Christian stood behind me to the left and Mateo to the right. He'd become a permanent fixture since I'd taken over as boss—someone who I knew I could trust. I didn't doubt his ability to keep the people around him safe, and I knew his prospects in the family were high. I was already forming the way I wanted to shape the family in my head. It would take time and patience, but I knew we'd be stronger than we'd ever been.

Slowly, the table filled with heads of families, but I didn't say anything. I waited, watching them all, taking in their body language. I was preparing for a meeting, unlike any other. Everything was about to change. I was about to make my mark in a way that no other boss ever had. I was about to show The Enterprise what happened when you crossed me.

"You gonna sit there watching us all day?" Alessandro asked, leaning forward in his seat and planting his hands on the table in front of him. He was frustrated, I could see that, but I didn't care.

"I'm waiting," I said, my tone sounding easy, but I was anything but that. My rage was a living thing, building inside me and threatening to explode. I tracked each of the men at the table. First, Alessandro, then Neri and Stefano, finally landing on Piero. "Waiting for Piero."

All heads turned his way, frowns and confusion on their faces. The two men Piero had brought with him stepped forward as if they knew in their gut what was about to happen. They were his closest advisors, the ones who went everywhere with him.

Neri's stare met mine, trying to read what I wasn't saying, then he turned to Piero. "What did you do?"

"Nothing," Piero stuttered out, shuffling in his

seat, the first sign of his nervousness. "I didn't do anything."

I tilted my head to the side, a smirk pulling at my lips. "That's not quite true though, is it, Piero." I met his gaze, daring him to look away from me. "You knew." I clasped my hands in front of me, my body at ease with the weight of my gun on my lap. Christian and Mateo stood deathly still, not making a move until I did. "You knew about the raid on my house."

"I didn't," Piero rushed out, putting his hands out in front of him as if that would help his case. His eyes widened, begging me to believe him. "I didn't know a thing, not until afterward. The judge—"

"Signed the warrant that you demanded he sign." I slowly leaned back in my seat, the chair wood creaking at the move. "You were the one who okayed the raid." The cool metal of my gun slipped across my fingertips, and I gripped the handle, placing my finger on the trigger. "You've approved them every step of the way." I paused, finally lifting my mask off my face and showing him all of my rage. "You knew they had someone undercover." I pushed my chair back, my signal for Christian and Mateo, and they stepped forward. "It was *your* idea." I extended my arm, showing everyone at the table what I held in my hand. Not one of them said a word, knowing what Piero had done was the ultimate death wish. We had rules we lived by, both inside our own organizations and The Enterprise, and Piero had disregarded all of that.

"You're not the only one with friends in high places." I squeezed the trigger, one shot blasting out as the bullet ripped through Piero's head. Two more shots fired off behind me, taking out Piero's men in one fell swoop.

Their bodies slumped, bright red blood staining the table and the people closest to them. I glanced down, seeing several droplets of blood that had made their way to my shirt. I cursed. Aida would be pissed if I turned up to dinner with blood on me.

"Take that as a warning," I told the rest of the table. "The Enterprise was made to keep the peace, to share information, so we're all safe against the law." I stowed my gun away in its holster. "The new boss of the Pozzi family will be his nephew, Gio. He'll be at the next meeting." I grinned as the shock registered on their faces. I'd been working behind the scenes for days, putting things in place as I waited for final confirmation of what I already knew.

"We haven't taken a vote!" Alessandro shouted, swiping at the blood on his face.

I huffed out a breath. I'd had my fun, and now I wanted to leave. "All those in favor of Gio Pozzi becoming head of the Pozzi family, raise your hands." Stefano and Neri raised their hands just as I did. "Votes counted and verified." I stepped away from the table. "Until next month." I nodded, pleased as fuck with myself. I'd made it known that I wasn't to be messed with. I just hoped they actually listened because I was done with second chances. They worked when I was captain, but now that I was the boss, I couldn't take the risk.

Making mistakes was all well and good as long as you learned from them. And that was what I'd done from the moment I'd become boss. I'd made mistakes, but they were ones that I'd never repeat. They made me stronger, more capable of becoming the boss my family needed.

No one spoke as we exited the meeting place and got into the SUV. I'd already known someone had their hands in what happened with the FBI, and after Mateo's contact confirmed it today with the evidence I needed, I hadn't wasted a single second calling the impromptu meeting. The longer Piero was out there, the more damage he would have done. At least with Gio at the helm of their family, I'd have some sense of control over him.

My dad had built his legacy, but it was time for me to build mine. I wasn't walking in his shadow anymore. I wasn't only Luca Beretta's son. I was Lorenzo Beretta, the Mafia boss you didn't dare fuckin' cross.

I glanced down at the few red spots on my shirt as we pulled into the gates, cursing at the sight of

Aida's dad's delivery truck already being here. "Fuck." If she saw the evidence of what I'd just done on my shirt, she'd kill me. She'd spoken nonstop about the meal with both of our families, and now here I was, about to enter with another Mafia boss's blood on my shirt. I darted out of the SUV, ran across the stones, and straight through the front door, hoping I could make it by unseen.

"Uncle Lorenzo!"

My eyes widened, my body freezing at the bottom of the stairs. I should have known Vida would have caught me. "Hey, princess." I turned and smiled at her, trying to keep my body pointed toward the stairs. "I'll be back down in a minute. I just need to get changed."

She stepped forward, her head tilted to one side as Christian and Mateo walked in the front door with matching grins on their faces. "But you're already dressed." Her little face screwed up in confusion. "Why do you need to get dressed again?"

"Well…" I cleared my throat, feeling like I was being interrogated. Not even my Uncle Antonio had made me feel like that when I was a kid, and he grilled me on whether I'd understood how to electrocute someone or not. "I…erm…."

Noemi appeared behind Vida, planting her hand on her shoulder. "Hey, Lorenzo," she greeted, and I begged her to distract Vida, but instead, she asked, "Where you heading?"

What was with this family and asking questions?

"I'm going to——"

"Lorenzo?" I breathed a sigh of relief as Aida appeared. "What are you doing?" She walked toward me, meeting me at the bottom of the stairs. "Where——"

"Something smells amazing," I said, interrupting her and turning my body. "I wouldn't want to stain my white shirt with the pasta sauce." I had no idea if that was what we were having, but I hoped she'd read into what I was saying. "I'm going to go get changed." I hooked my thumb toward the stairs, widening my eyes at her.

"What?" She laughed and shook her head. "You..." Her gaze flicked down, her attention zooming in on the blood splatter. She glanced back up at me, lowering her voice so only I could hear her. "You couldn't leave it until after we'd had dinner?" she ground out.

"It couldn't wait." I tried to communicate with her silently. She knew we were looking into what had happened when we got raided, and she was there when I'd received the call to confirm my suspicions.

"Fine." She narrowed her eyes at me, then flicked her attention to Vida and Noemi. "Shall we go make wishes while we wait for Uncle Lorenzo?"

"Yes!" Vida jumped up and down, grasping Noemi's hand and pulling her toward the door.

"The fountain outside is magic," she told her. "Last time I made a wish that Auntie Aida would fall in love with Uncle Lorenzo." She turned back to face me, her huge grin flashing my way. "And it came true!"

My stomach dipped at her words, my attention snapping toward Aida, but she was walking away with her head down. I wasn't sure what to do, what to say, so I turned, heading upstairs and preparing for the first joint family meal since we'd married.

CHAPTER

18

AIDA

I rolled over as the sound of the shower drifted into the bedroom. A strip of sun shone through the curtains, hitting the partly open bathroom door. I stared at it, wondering whether I should roll back over and get more sleep or whether to get up.

We'd slipped into a routine the last couple of months with me going to college and Lorenzo making his mark in the city as boss. I'd accompanied him to countless events where he made friends with politicians and donated money to their campaigns. He walked a fine line, managing to sit on both sides of the track without falling. I wasn't sure how he managed it, but I was fascinated watching him achieve it as if it was nothing.

It wasn't, though. Normal people didn't do what he did, at least, not successfully anyway.

His soft humming rang out, and I smiled. He didn't realize he did it, but it was one of my favorite sounds, and that was what had me slipping out of our bed and walking toward the bathroom.

I wrapped my arms around my waist and Lorenzo's T-shirt that I was wearing, unable to take my gaze off him. He let his head dip back, the water washing over him and through his inky black hair. Each of his perfectly chiseled muscles moved as he tilted his head side to side.

Slowly, I dropped my arms from my waist, stepped forward, and pulled the T-shirt over my head. I didn't make a sound as I stepped into the shower with him, but from the way his body tensed and then relaxed, he knew I was there.

"Morning," I murmured, trailing my hands over his sides and around to his stomach. His abs jumped at my touch.

"Morning, baby." He turned, his wet body pressing against mine. "You're up early."

I couldn't get enough of his dark eyes and the way he leaned forward, caging me in. "I am." I felt his erection press against me and moaned. "I wanted to save water with you."

"That right?" he asked, his voice deeper.

I planted my hand on his chest, feeling his heart beating an erratic rhythm at my touch. "Yeah." I pushed closer, biting down on my bottom lip as my nipples scraped against his chest. "I also wanted to do this." I didn't think as I got down to my knees, my face coming level with his hard cock.

It jumped as I dragged the tip of my finger along the underside and up to the head, a drop of pre-cum escaping. My tongue flicked out, lapping up the salty liquid. His hand moved to the top of my head, his fingers pushing their way through my hair and holding me there.

My lips parted, and I dipped forward, taking all of him in my mouth. I twirled my tongue around him while at the same time, cupping his balls and humming, the vibrations causing his hand to grip my hair harder. He pulled, trying to set the pace, but I wasn't going to allow him. This wasn't just about him. It was about me too.

I halted as the head of his cock hit the back of my mouth, unable to get him all of the way in, then reached between my legs, finding my bundle of nerves and strumming. I moaned louder, pulling my head forward and backward harder and faster, knowing it would drive him crazy.

"Fuck," he gritted out, and when I glanced up at him, I saw that he was staring down at me, watching intently as I played with myself. He planted his feet wider apart, his hand resting on the side of the shower, and ordered, "Show me." He licked his lips. "Show me your pussy."

I wasn't sure what he meant, so I pulled my mouth back, letting his cock slide out. "Wha—"

"Open your pussy lips." My breath stalled in my chest at his words. Everything sounded so much dirtier when he said it with his deep, raspy voice. "Open them up and let me see your pretty clit, baby."

I leaned back, my knees and thighs burning at the position I was putting myself in, but I didn't care. I was so turned on by him watching me that I would have stayed like this for hours if it meant he didn't look away.

"That's it." His hand moved to his cock, his long fingers wrapping around his girth and slowly moving up and down. "Faster," he demanded, so I did as he said.

My arms burned at how fast I was going, my wrist threatening to give up, but I didn't stop—I couldn't stop. I let go of his balls, trailing my hand up my stomach and to my nipple. I groaned as my finger skimmed over it, but it wasn't enough, so I rolled it between my finger and thumb. The burn at the base of my stomach teased me, promising my orgasm, and it started, slow at first, building and building the faster I strummed my fingers over my clit. I felt it get bigger, and then everything hit me all at once, knocking me off-kilter.

I cried out, my body screaming with sweet relief, and before I knew it, I was in the air, my back slammed against the wet, tiled wall, and Lorenzo's cock was pounding into me.

"Fuck, yes," he gritted out, unrelenting in his rhythm. I held on to him, my nails digging into his shoulders, sure to leave marks, but I didn't care, and neither did he. "You're like a goddamn angel sent from heaven just for me," he croaked out, pushing his face between my neck and shoulder.

I closed my eyes, taking each of his bruising thrusts, and knowing that I wouldn't be able to spend another day on this earth if he wasn't by my side. I'd fallen for him, there was no doubt about it, but I couldn't bring myself to tell him. Not when I didn't know if he felt the same. So, I kept my mouth shut. I kept all of my bubbling feelings inside, hoping that he'd feel the same somewhere along the line.

His body stilled, his cum spilling inside of me, and then he halted, his breaths so heavy it was as if he'd just taken part in the Olympics. It was always the same when it came to us. We got lost in the moment, lost in each other. And before I knew what was happening, my mouth was opening, my body taking charge of my brain, and I blurted out, "I like you." I felt him still, his muscles tensed so hard it was like holding on to a block of ice.

I held my breath as he pulled his face away from my shoulder, his eyes telling me nothing as he stared at me. Had I said the wrong thing? Why couldn't I have just kept my mouth shut and basked in the after-sex moment? I just had to open my big mouth and tell him something, didn't I?

His lips parted, and I prepared myself for what he was going to say. This was it. This was going to be the moment where he'd tell me he didn't feel like that about me. That it was too soon—even though it had been nearly five months since we had what I'd dubbed *our fake wedding*.

"I…" He paused, his eyes misting over, and I blinked. There was something echoing back at me, something I'd never seen before. "I like you too, Aida."

LORENZO

I couldn't stop watching her as she glided around the room, talking to anyone and everyone. She stopped at our joint family table several times, making sure they were okay. She was in her element.

Soft music played from the stage, setting the tone of the night—opening night. The piano bar had finally been refurbished in its entirety, and now all that was left to do was open it to the public. This was a soft opening, though—something they called it in the business. I had no idea what it was until

Neri had explained it to me. He'd had plenty of "soft openings" over the years with his casinos, which was why he was here, celebrating the night with us.

None of the other heads of the families had come, although they did have an open invitation, as did Dante. I ground my teeth together as I looked down at my cell, clearly able to see that he had read my message but left it unanswered. I was starting to get worried because I'd only heard from him once since he'd stormed out of my office. He wanted to move across the state and start a new thread to the business. It was a good idea, but I didn't like the fact that he'd be so far away, though I'd given him the green light because I knew what it was like wanting to create something for yourself, to prove yourself. That had been three days ago, and I hadn't heard from him since. If it wasn't for Ma and Sofia having communication with him, I would have thought he'd been killed.

"Turn that frown upside down!" Aida shouted, bounding over to me. I leaned my elbow on the bar top and pushed my cell into my pocket. Tonight wasn't about business. It was all about Aida, the woman who had turned my world upside down.

I winked at her and pulled her closer, unable to stop myself from touching her. The dress she'd worn was a black, slinky number, one that showed most of her back and dipped down to her chest, giving everyone a small tease of her cleavage. She looked hot as fuck, and she was all mine.

"I think it's about time you got up there," I told her, tilting my head to the stage where the piano sat without a player.

"What?" Her eyes widened, her head swiveling around to look at the packed bar. The lights were dimmed, just enough to give off a sense of atmosphere, and the carefully placed tables with chairs and booths allowed for everyone to see the stage without the people in front blocking them. Aida had thought of everything when she'd helped draw the plans up a few weeks ago.

"I can't get up there, not tonight."

"You can." I grasped her waist and gave it a small squeeze. "They'll love it, I promise."

She groaned, her gaze slipping over all of the patrons again. "I don't know…" She bit down on her bottom lip, indecision on her face, so I made the choice for her.

I moved away from the bar, my hand trailing down her arm and to her hand, then pulled her with me to the stage. Cheers rang out, the loudest ones from her sister, knowing what was about to happen. No one else had heard her play, but I had. Every time she was here, the first thing she did was test out the keys and play a tune she loved.

Aida yanked back on my hand, trying to stop me, but I had the momentum. "Lorenzo, no."

I didn't turn back to face her. I kept going until we were at the piano. "Sit." She raised her brows at me, her hand planted firmly on her hip. She was mad, but it was sexy mad, not real mad. "Please," I tacked on, finally getting a response from her.

Her chest heaved as she took a breath, then she sat down, her fingers already finding the keys, like they'd just gotten home and knew where everything was. I turned to face everyone in the bar, unsure what I should say, and then I decided the ivory keys and her musical ability would say it all. So, with a tilt of my head, I walked off stage and stood at the edge, watching her from the side.

Her gaze bore into mine, her lips lifting just slightly on one side, and then she mouthed, "This one is for you."

My pulse thrummed, my heart feeling like it was stuck in my throat as she began to slide her fingertips over the keys. I couldn't take my eyes off her as she closed her eyes, causing everyone's attention to focus on her. There were no sounds but the soft tune she played and then gasps as she ramped it up, slamming her fingers down so hard I wondered if it hurt her. If it did, she didn't give any indication.

She was so entrancing, captivating like nothing else, that I barely registered when she stopped. Clapping and whooping and hollering were sent her way, but I couldn't move from the spot I was in. She bowed, raising her hand in the air, a blush rising on her cheeks, and that was when I knew. I knew it without a single doubt.

I was in love with her.

I was in love with Aida.

I stumbled back at the realization, my body impacted by my thoughts alone. But even it knew the truth. I couldn't live without her. Couldn't imagine my life without her in it. We'd already exchanged "I like yous," a prequel to what was destined to happen, but I'd never thought it would be like this, never understood this all-consuming kind of feeling.

She tilted her head as she turned to face me, a frown etched onto her features. But I wasn't going to tell her what I was thinking, not here, not with all of these people around. I knew it now, and part of me wanted to keep it to myself in fear she didn't feel the same. But I wouldn't. I'd tell her when the time was right. I'd tell her when I knew she needed to hear it most.

"You okay?" she asked.

I nodded, taking her hand and leading her down the side steps of the stage. "Yeah." I placed a soft kiss on her hand. "Go do your thing." I didn't want her to leave my side. In fact, if I would have had it my way, I'd have taken her home right then and there. It was her night, though—her night to bask in the opening of her very own bar. A bar she'd named after my father.

When she'd first come to me and asked if it was okay to name it *Luca's*, I didn't know what to think, but the more I thought about it, the more I understood. He was the reason we were here. He was the reason I'd fallen in love with her. If it wasn't for my dad dying, I never would have met Aida. I never would have looked at her twice.

"You'll be at the bar?"

"Yeah."

I stared at her as she made a beeline for the family's table, unwilling to move my attention from her. I watched her for hours, milling around, her head thrown back as someone made her laugh, and finally, when everyone was gone, and it was just us and the staff left, she sighed.

"My feet are killing me." She yanked the heels off her feet and leaned against me, her eyes half-closed. "I need my bed." I wrapped my arm around her waist and stood, taking her by surprise when I picked her up. She squealed, her soft laughter sweet music to my ears. "If I had known you'd do that, I would have come over to you sooner," she quipped, resting her head on my shoulder as I sauntered out of the club.

Mateo stood at the door with two other soldiers and darted toward us when he saw us exit. "I'll go get the SUV." He ran halfway down the street and to the lone car while we waited. He pulled up right in front of us, and I moved more of Aida's weight to one side so I could open the door. I bent down, placing her in the SUV so that her feet didn't touch the ground, then pushed in beside her.

Mateo jerked away from the sidewalk and onto the quiet road. I slid my hand to her thigh, itching to go higher up her leg and feel her bare skin on my hand. It was already 1 a.m., so I had no doubt we'd be home in no time, and I knew exactly what I was going to do to her as soon as we got inside. I couldn't get enough of her. Her body. Her mind. Her attitude. She was like an everlasting gobstopper —you never got tired of sucking on it. I snorted at my one thought, gaining her attention.

"What?" She grinned at me, her eyes the happiest I'd ever seen them.

"Nothing." I dipped my head so our faces were closer. "I was just thinking about all the things I'm gonna do to you once we're home."

"Lorenzo." She shook her head, but there was no denying the way her breaths picked up. "You're so bad."

"I'm bad?" I pointed at my chest and raised a brow. "You're far worse than me."

She gasped. "I am not."

"You are too! You're the one who keeps sneaking in the shower with me every morning."

"I already told you." She pushed some hair behind her ear, trying to look innocent, but I knew her way better than that. She may have been able to fool everyone else, but there was no fooling me. I knew her too damn well. "I'm saving water."

"Sure." I chuckled, whispering my hand up her arm and to the side of her face. "You're also—"

"Fuck!" Mateo shouted from the front of the SUV, swerving as a car came out of nowhere and nearly side-swiped us. "Sorry, boss." He looked frantic as he glanced out of the window and then to the mirrors. "He came from—"

The other car swerved, slamming into the side of us, and I held Aida closer. "What the fuck!" Another car came up the other side, only this one didn't swerve into us, it opened its windows, something glinting off the streetlights, and then I realized—

"Gun!"

I shoved Aida down into the floorboard, trying to cover as much of her body as possible as the other car hit us again. The SUV tilted, Mateo losing control of it, and then metal crunched, mixing with the blasting of bullets.

"Stay down!" I shouted at Aida, feeling the blood pumping through my body and adrenaline taking me over. Her hand gripped on to my thigh, her nails digging in, and then we were both shunted forward. My head smacked off the edge of the center console, but I'd managed to keep Aida safe.

I groaned as the car rolled to a stop. I tried to take stock of everything. My ears pinged, smoke filled the inside of the SUV, and when I looked up, a pair of eyes stared back at me. Eyes I knew well. I opened my mouth, about to say something, but something smacked me in the temple. I lost grip of Aida, lost all sense of where I was, and then everything went black.

CHAPTER

19

AIDA

I wasn't sure what hurt more: my aching body, or my thumping head. I didn't want to move, too afraid I'd make my head throb even more, but I rolled my head from side to side, wincing as the banging inside my brain intensified. What the hell had I done last night? I screwed my face up, smacking my lips together, and groaning at how dry my mouth was. I needed a drink, and definitely some painkillers.

I reached my arm out, my eyes still closed, but it wouldn't move. It took me way too long to realize I wasn't in bed next to Lorenzo. Instead, I was sitting up. Had I fallen asleep on the sofa last night? I frowned as I tried to open my eyes, but they felt like they were stuck together like I'd just slept for twenty-four hours straight.

My hands jerked to wipe at my eyes, but when they wouldn't move a second time, my eyes snapped open, blaring sunlight nearly blinding me. I slammed them close again, my heart racing in my chest as I slowly remembered what had happened last night.

Opening the piano bar.

Mateo driving.

Car swerving.

Lorenzo holding me down.

Bullets.

And then…

Nothing. I had nothing after that.

Oh my God, what had happened? Where was I? And where the hell was Lorenzo?

I kept my eyes closed as I listened for any sounds, trying my hardest to hear *something*. But it was silent except for my own breathing and…

I slowly opened my eyes, sagging in relief at the sight of Lorenzo in front of me. My gaze tracked his body, his legs tied to the chair, his arms tied to his thighs, and rope banding around his stomach. A quick glance at my own lap told me I was in the same position.

"Lorenzo," I whispered, wincing at the dryness in my throat. His body didn't twitch, his head hanging forward. I couldn't see his face—I needed to see his face. "Lorenzo," I said, a little louder but not too loud to alert anyone that I was awake. He still didn't move, and I could feel my panic rising. I had no idea where we were, no idea what was—

The sound of a ship horn blared out, so thunderous that it sounded like it was right beside me. I jumped, a gasp escaping and echoing around the warehouse we were in. I blinked. A ship? I pulled in a deep breath, feeling the burn of it against my chest, but it was all I needed to figure out that we were down at the docks. We weren't far from the city. This was good. This meant we could be found...right?

Footsteps echoed closer, and the sound of metal scraping against metal ricocheted around the otherwise empty space. Instinctively, I slammed my eyes closed and let my head drop forward in the same way Lorenzo's was. No one knew I was awake, so I'd play like I was still asleep, at least until I figured out where I was...or until Lorenzo woke up.

Heels clicked against the floor, a woman's voice made my ears perk up, and then a man's joined in with hers.

"He said he'd be here in an hour," the man said. "Once he arrives, we can make a plan moving forward."

"No." My breath stammered as I recognized the voice. Rage mixed with confusion slammed through me. *Veev.* What the hell was she doing here? "I get to have my fun before he gets here."

"He won't be happy," the man warned as the woman's footsteps got closer.

"I don't care," she snapped back, and I opened my eyes, just about able to see her legs in front of me. They weren't pointed my way, though. They were directed toward Lorenzo. They took another step, and then one went out of view.

"What are you doing?" the man asked, and I was wondering the exact same thing.

"Having fun." She laughed, the sound so much louder in the warehouse. "Loosen up, Pedro."

Her other leg lifted off the floor, and I knew in my gut what she was doing. I should have kept my head down and played like I had no idea what was going on, but as I lifted just enough to see that she had climbed onto Lorenzo's lap, I saw red.

"What the fuck do you think you're doing?" I ground out, keeping deathly still. I'd already tugged at the ropes wrapped around me and knew there was no way out of them, not yet anyway.

She turned her head, her long, wavy hair moving off her shoulder as her gaze met mine. "Oh, good, you're awake." She smirked, pushing her chest closer to Lorenzo's head. "I didn't want you to miss the show."

It was on the tip of my tongue to ask her what show, but I kept it in, not willing to entertain her.

That was what she wanted. She wanted my attention on her. I bared my teeth to her, the only part of my body I was able to move. I may have kept my gaze on her, but I wasn't going to give her the satisfaction of my voice. It was a small thing, one she probably didn't care about, but it was the only thing I could control.

"You're no fun," she moaned, pushing out her bottom lip in the exact same way Vida did when she wanted something from you. The difference was that Vida was a child, and Veev was a grown-ass woman. "Lorenzo used to be fun." She winked. "With me anyway." She licked her bottom lip, her hand trailing over his chest and down to his groin. I growled louder, trying to get out of these damn ropes, but it was no use. I wasn't going anywhere, and the smirk on her face told me she knew that.

"Veev," the guy who came in with her said, shuffling on the spot. I turned to face him, recognizing his face from somewhere. I couldn't place it though, he just looked...familiar. "He won't be happy."

Veev rolled her eyes at him, rocking her hips on Lorenzo's lap. "He's not here, so what do I care?"

"You'll care because you're disobeying orders," a new voice said, this one laced in an accent. Veev froze to the spot but didn't make a move to get off of Lorenzo. The longer she was touching him, the more my anger built. I'd threatened to kill her at the gates of the mansion when she'd tried to get inside, and there was no doubt I was going to follow through with that, especially now.

"Awww, come on, I should get to have some fun." Veev's head tilted to the side, her attention focusing on the new man, but I didn't look at him, too afraid of what I'd see. I was trying to tell myself that I was fine—that we were fine—but that wasn't the reality. We were tied up—I squirmed, testing the binds again—with no way out.

I kept my full attention on Lorenzo, silently begging him to wake up. He'd know what to do. He'd know how to get us out of this. And if all that failed, at least I wouldn't be alone.

"This isn't about fun," the new voice whipped out, his footsteps echoing across the concrete ground. Several more followed him, but still, I couldn't look over. I just kept staring at Lorenzo, narrowing my eyes on Veev as she stayed put in his lap. "This is about me taking what is rightfully mine."

"Ours," Veev tacked on. "Taking what is ours, Papa."

My eyes widened at her words. Papa? This man was her dad? What the hell was going on? And what did they think was rightfully theirs? I was in a vortex, aware of my surroundings but with a singular focus on Lorenzo.

"Yes, yes," he replied, and I imagined him waving his hand in the air, shooing the notion away, and I realized that she was just a pawn in his game —whoever he was. "I hope you haven't killed him—"

The footsteps paused, the atmosphere in the warehouse dropping to icy cold levels. "What is she doing here?"

"She was in the car with him," Veev said, pushing her chest forward into Lorenzo's head. I grunted, jerking forward, but it was no use. I was trapped. Trapped with no way out. Frustrated tears leaked from my eyes, my rage trying to break free in the only way that was possible.

"So, you brought her here instead of killing her?" The man tutted. "I thought I'd taught you better than that." Veev looked down, her lashes fluttering against her cheeks. She was ashamed, the first time I'd see her look anything but undignified. "Get rid of her." My eyes widened as footsteps neared, my breaths halting in my chest, too scared to move a single inch.

Lorenzo's head snapped up, his gaze clashing with mine right away. My heart skipped a beat, hope rising in my chest at the sight of him. Dried blood covered half of his face, a bruise forming on the side of his head and part of his eye. "Touch her." He paused, his head slowly turning to look at the man. "And I'll kill you." His lip curled up into a sneer. "Uncle Paolo."

My face dropped, my head spinning to look at

the man for the first time. I should have put the accented voice to the name, but I was too occupied with Veev, who was still planted firmly on Lorenzo's lap.

Uncle Paolo. Why was he doing this? I blinked. Wait…Veev had called him Papa. I snapped my attention back to Lorenzo. They were cousins.

Holy shit.

———

LORENZO

My attention was laser-focused on Paolo, not turning away from him for a single second. I needed to make sense of all of this, but it was really goddamn hard when my head was throbbing.

Paolo chuckled as he leaned on his cane, thinking over my threat. I didn't care that I was tied to a chair because there was no way in hell I was going to let him touch Aida.

"I'd like to see you try." He tilted his head, his gaze traveling to Aida. I jerked, my body snapping back at the binds. "This may actually work in my favor." He took a step forward, his eyes lighting up. "Tell me, nephew, did Antonio tell you where he learned his torturing techniques?" He reached out, his finger trailing over her bare shoulder. She was still in the black dress, but it had fallen down her arm, exposing her shoulder.

I ground my teeth together, trying to get out of the binds. "Don't fuckin' touch her," I sneered, trying to push Veev off of me, but she was stuck to me like glue. Her hand pressed against the side of my face, her nails digging into my cheek, but I refused to acknowledge her. I'd heard every word she'd said, every word Paolo had said.

I should have known she was up to something with the amount she'd been hanging around before I got married. She'd call me at all hours, and I'd call her when I needed to relieve some stress. Fuck. She'd been the one to redecorate my office. I'd given her access to the one place that was most sacred in the mansion. I'd been too focused on fighting against my bubbling feelings. I hadn't paid enough attention.

Paolo placed his hand on top of Aida's head, stroking her hair. I craned my neck to see around Veev, but she leaned over, obscuring my view. "Get the fuck off of me." I bucked, causing her to lose her balance, but she soon caught it and righted herself. "I mean it, Veev." My nostrils flared as I finally gave her my attention. "Get the fuck off. *Now.*"

She giggled like this was one big giant game. And maybe it was to her, but to me, it was life or death. I couldn't live without Aida, and I damn sure didn't want to die when we'd only just gotten started. I'd fight until my last dying breath for her. I'd give up everything—I'd do anything—if it meant she'd be okay.

"Do you remember the night we met?" Veev asked, fluttering her lashes at me.

"I don't give a fuck about the night we met." I jolted again, feeling the rope loosening on my arms.

"It was—"

A deafening bang rang out, and for a fraction of a second, I didn't know what to feel or think. Wetness spread over my chest, bright red blood seeping through the material of my shirt.

"No!" Aida screamed, the sound so haunting it hit me right in the pit of my stomach. "No, no, no."

I blinked, trying to see through the red liquid spatter on my face. Veev stared at me, confusion evident on her features. "What…" she gurgled, her body swaying to the left. "I…Lorenzo," she croaked out, her hand reaching for me. And even if I wasn't tied up, I wouldn't have helped her. She fell to the ground in a heap, blood spluttering from her mouth and a wound in her chest. She tried to place her hand on it, but the blood gushed out of her like a rapid river.

"Finally," Uncle Paolo groaned out. I turned to face him just in time to see him pushing his gun into the holster strapped to his chest. "She wouldn't shut up." He shook his head, disappointment flashing

over his features. "Such a shame." His eyes trans-
fixed on her for a second, and then he shook his
head, grinning over at me. "Now, where were we?"

"You...you killed her," Aida stammered out, her
face pale. "You killed her."

"I did," Paolo said, stroking her hair again.

"But she was your daughter."

I cringed at her words. I'd fucked her. I'd fucked
her, and she'd known all along that we were cousins.
A shiver rolled through me, my gut churning. Had
she known the entire time? I gritted my teeth. Of
course, she'd known.

Paolo frowned. "And?" He laughed. "What does
that matter?" He raised a brow at me and pointed
down at Aida. "She's a bit cuckoo, no?"

"Touch her again..." I warned, completely
ignoring Veev dying at my feet. She'd known what
she was getting into. This was her consequence for
trusting Paolo.

"And you'll what?" He winked at me and lifted
his other hand, playing with Aida's hair, and there
wasn't a thing I could do to stop him. *Fuck.* "As I was
saying." He cleared his throat, but I didn't lose sight
of his hands as one traveled down to her neck. His
tan fingers reached around, stroking her soft skin.
"Did Antonio ever tell you who taught him?" I
ground my teeth together so hard that I was sure I
heard one of them crack.

"No?" His body snapped upright, his hand

clamping around the front of Aida's neck. I jerked forward, the front chair legs smacking against Veev's body. "It was me." His face turned red at the force he was using. "I taught him everything he knows."

Aida gasped for breath, her eyes popping open so wide I was sure they'd fall from the sockets from the force he was using. She squirmed, her instincts kicking in to try and fight, but it was no use because she was just as tied up as I was.

"He probably taught you the power of a wife, huh?" His chest heaved, Aida's mouth opened on a silent plea, the life leaving her eyes, and then finally, he let go. I hadn't realized I'd been holding my breath until it whooshed out of me. "I'm talking to you, nephew!" he roared, making Aida jump. If it was only me here, I wouldn't have answered him. I would have played him at his own game. But it wasn't just me. Aida's life was at stake too. He was going to use her against me. That was what he meant about the power of a wife.

He clicked his fingers and pointed at me. "You get it now." He stepped back from Aida and slowly removed his suit jacket. It was the same one he'd been wearing when I told him to leave the country all those months ago. I stared at him, taking in all of him. Dark circles ringed his eyes, and there was a wild look in his eyes. A look that told me he was on the edge of something he'd never come back from.

My chest burned as I put everything together,

trying to make sense of it in my head. And I realized…

"You didn't leave." I clenched my jaw, narrowing my eyes on him, frustrated that I didn't know he hadn't left. Christian had watched him get on the plane, so how the hell did he get off it without me knowing? "You didn't leave the country, did you?"

Paolo tutted, slowly and methodically undoing his shirt cuffs and rolling them up to his elbows. "For someone who is boss, you're not very aware, are you?" He smirked. "But then again, I am good at what I do." He stepped to the side, pulling some material off a crate next to Aida. My breath stalled in my chest as he revealed a mixture of tools—tools I knew were only used for one reason: torture.

"No," I growled, knowing deep down that I didn't have a say. There was nothing I could do, no way I could get to her. I pushed against the binds again, the ropes burning my skin where they cut into me, but it was no use.

Paolo's gaze clashed with mine again. "When I was boss, I knew everything that happened in my territory. I ruled with an iron fist." His nostrils flared. "Some may say that I was too harsh, but when you're a Mafia boss, you don't have a choice." His eyes darkened. "I spent almost my entire life creating a legacy that my father would have been proud of, and they ripped it away like it meant nothing."

"What?" I stilled, soaking in his words. "What are you talking about?"

"Your father!" Paolo shouted, his rage over-taking him. If Uncle Antonio had taught me anything, it was never to torture when you were angry. You needed control to inflict the maximum amount of pain. "He conspired against me! Me!" He threw his hands up in the air. "His big bother." He paused. "He betrayed me."

I opened my mouth, but he beat me to it. "He took it all away from me." His voice lowered, his shoulders pushed back. "So, I did the same." He grinned, glee flashing in his eyes. "My daughter was already in place with you, she had been for years, so all it took was one little slip in dead daddy's drink and boom"—he flashed his hands in front of him —"heart attack." He blew out a breath.

"Then you got in the way of me taking over." He winked. "I'll resolve that now, though."

"You'll never be in charge," I gritted out, knowing deep down that without me, there wouldn't be anyone to take over. Dante was too young, and Christian wasn't blood, which would only leave Paolo. Fuck. He'd have it all in the palms of his hands, and there would be nothing I could do to stop it if I wasn't alive.

Paolo ignored me, his hand hovering over the

tools as he decided what to use first. "Hmmm." He tapped his finger on his chin. "Where to start."

He'd offered up more information than he'd probably meant to, but he'd made a mistake. His words had fueled me and made me even more determined to get out of here.

"Aida," I called, but her attention was focused on Paolo too, her face so pale I was sure she was going to pass out. "Baby," I said, softer this time. "Look at me." She blinked, a tear falling from the corner of her eye. It slid down her face and down to her chest, the material of her black dress soaking it up.

"Lorenzo," she whispered, her breath catching in her throat. I wasn't sure what to say to her, not when I couldn't get to her.

"Keep your eyes on me, baby," I told her, nodding to drill my point home. "Just keep looking at me."

"Okay," she croaked out, blinking rapidly and wincing as Paolo moved closer to her. I glanced at him, just long enough to see what he'd chosen, and wasn't sure whether to be relieved or not. He'd chosen a whip, one that had sharp teeth on each of the strands.

She hadn't seen what I had, so as he widened his stance behind her and brought his hand in the air, she didn't see it coming. I wasn't sure whether that was a good thing or not.

He slashed his arm out, the strands whipping through the air and whistling at how fast they moved. They hit her back in what felt like slow motion. The slap of the strands hitting her skin had me wincing, and she squealed so loudly that it hurt my ears. I fought even harder against the ropes. I needed to get to her. I needed to do something to help.

Fuck! Why did it have to be like this? Why did I have to fall in love with her? If I hadn't, then what Paolo was doing wouldn't have bothered me.

But I had.

I'd fallen head over heels in love with her, and there was nothing I could do about it. The train had left the platform with no way back. It was her and me now in our own world as she kept her eyes on me, screaming at each of his lashes. Blood sprayed over his crisp white shirt, and I knew then that he'd broken skin. I imagined all the ways I would hurt him for touching her. Imagined having him tied to the chair and giving him a taste of his own medicine. But it did nothing to take her pain away, nothing to relieve the ache I felt in my chest from watching her get hurt.

My breath stuck in the back of my throat. I was powerless.

CHAPTER

20

AIDA

My head lulled forward; all of my energy zapped. Blood trailed down my back, burning the cuts like someone was rubbing salt into an open wound. My skin was a weird mixture of numbness and pain, all mixed in together, my nerve endings not sure which one should have taken prevalence.

Paolo groaned from behind me, the whoosh of air giving a moment of sweet relief until he slapped the whip against my skin again. My throat burned from each of my shouts, so all that managed to come out was a broken cry, enough to tell him that he'd hurt me again. I'd lost count after twenty, the numbers all blurring together just as Lorenzo had. I tried to keep my focus on him, needing something to center me, but I could barely keep my eyes open.

I was falling…

Falling into something I wasn't sure I'd come out of.

———

AIDA

I wasn't sure what was happening around me, but the grunts of pain and threats of death slowly worked their way into my ringing ears. My body was cold, but my back burned so hot I was sure I was pressed against an open flame.

"I can see your mind working." I cringed at the sound of Paolo's voice. "It won't work, though. I have plans for you."

"And I have plans for you," Lorenzo gritted out. At the sound of his voice, I slowly lifted my head, gasping as the skin on my back stretched and expanded. I blinked, trying to stop the room from spinning, but it was no use. My body couldn't take it. It couldn't handle the pain.

The smell of burning skin wafted over to me, and I willed my head to stay upright, for my eyes to make sense of what was happening in front of me. I counted to ten in my head, determined to get a clear picture, but I hadn't even made it to five when my world went black once again.

———

AIDA

"Aida." Shuffling, a whoosh of air, and then. "Aida." I hauled in a deep breath as the sound of a chair scraping across the ground echoed around me. "Baby, wake up. Wake up." My body swayed to the side, my instincts to right myself kicking in.

And I howled.

Screamed.

Cried out.

I'd never been in so much pain in my life. The agony was too much to bear. It was all too much to bear.

"Just keep breathing, baby." His voice drifted toward me, offering solace when I needed it the most. "Hang in there. I'll get us out." Footsteps neared. "I promise. I'll get us out of here."

———

AIDA

"Motherfucker!"

My eyes snapped open, each of my senses trying to take everything in. A pained groan came from in front of me, the scent of burned skin mixing in with…was that bleach? I frowned, not trusting myself as I turned my shoulders, testing out the pain in my back. It stung like someone had pressed a white-hot poker against my skin. I tried to move as little as possible, only raising my head so that I could see what was happening around me.

Paolo stood to the side of Lorenzo, a sadistic grin on his face as he held a rod. "Hold still," he warned Lorenzo, but I knew it wasn't out of kindness and worry. He was saying it for his own amusement.

He smashed the bright orange tip of the rod against Lorenzo's stomach. I winced as the sizzling of his skin got louder. Every part of Lorenzo's body was tense, his jaw twitching as he clenched it, trying not to make a sound. My heart sped up, pounding in my chest so fast I was sure it would jump from my body.

I narrowed my eyes on them, willing Lorenzo to look my way. The warehouse had darkened, a signal that we'd been here at least an entire day. The hope of someone finding us was starting to dissipate. Surely Mateo would have—

I gasped, so loud it caused Paolo to pause inches from Lorenzo's stomach. And it was then that I realized they'd changed his binds. He wasn't tied up like I was anymore. His hands were behind his back, his legs still tied to the chair, but he was shirtless now, his bare skin on full display for Paolo to do whatever he wanted to.

"Ahhh, sleeping beauty is finally awake."

My breaths turned to pants as I darted my gaze over Lorenzo's chest and abs. His perfectly tanned skin had been painted with burns, some round, some lines, thin and thick. A few looked fresh, but a few looked like they were trying to heal.

Paolo took one step away from Lorenzo, his gaze meeting mine, and I hoped he'd come for me again because Lorenzo was barely holding his head up now. What had they done to him while I was passed out? And how long had it been? I'd assumed it had only been a day, but from the way the bruises on Lorenzo's face were changing colors, I was starting to realize we'd been here longer. All sense of time was lost.

"Watch this," Paolo said, his sweaty face grinning over at me a second before he whipped his arm out and slammed the metal pole into Lorenzo's stomach. It wasn't hot enough to burn the skin now, but whatever he'd hit had Lorenzo growling. "Fun, no?" Paolo dropped the pole to the ground, the pinging ringing in my ears, then took two steps away from Lorenzo. He crossed his arms over his chest, smiling in appreciation as he glanced at the both of us, proud of the work he'd done.

"Bastard," Lorenzo croaked out, not giving up his fight. I smiled at him, a warmth spreading through me at the sight of him trying to hold on to his strength. Paolo was trying to break him, trying to cause him as much pain as possible using both his and my body, but he wasn't successful. He'd never be successful.

"Name-calling isn't nice." Paolo tutted, a yawn breaking free as he did. "Rest is in order, I think." He nodded to himself. "Yes. Tiresome work this game is." I wasn't sure whether he was purposefully trying to sound weird or whether that was just the way he spoke. Either way, with him gone, it meant a reprieve for Lorenzo.

Paolo took slow steps toward Lorenzo, walking around him in a circle, then moved over to me, doing the same but halting behind me. "Wow." His finger trailed over my shoulder. I jumped from the impact of the soft touch, then yelled as he jammed his fingertip into one of the lashes. Wetness poured out of it, trickling down my back, the healing skin crying out. "It's even better than a great work of art." He whistled, then chuckled. "Now, all that's left is the front."

I felt his body come closer, his front smashing into my back. The burn intensified to such a point where the warehouse spun again, my body threatening to give up. But I couldn't. Not now. Not now that he was about to leave to rest. It was our only opportunity to get out. The only way I could talk to Lorenzo without him around.

Lorenzo tried to lift his head, his dark gaze meeting mine and then Paolo's. He'd heard what he'd said too, but unlike earlier when he barked threats at him, he stayed silent.

Paolo's hands landed on my shoulders, his fingers digging into my collarbone. I tried to move away from him, but the bindings and burning of my skin stopped me. "What do you think, nephew?" He waited for Lorenzo to answer him, but when he didn't, he continued, "Should I make her front match her back?"

He pushed into my back harder as he flattened his palm and shunted downward, grabbing my breast and squeezing. I wasn't sure what was worse, being whipped from behind or him touching a part of me that was reserved only for Lorenzo. Fear built the longer his hand stayed there. Fear that it wouldn't end there. I could take the physical punishment, but I wasn't sure I'd be able to take anything else.

Lorenzo's eyes fired to life, his body jerking forward. "Death," he growled out. "Death is coming for you, old man."

Paolo laughed, his whole body moving with the force and scraping against my back. "Promises, promises." He ripped his front from my back, purposely causing even more pain. I squealed, sobs bubbling up inside that I had no way to hold back. My ears rang as he said something else, but I couldn't make it out. I was falling again, falling into a darkness I couldn't afford to be consumed by. But there was nothing I could do to stop it.

———

LORENZO

Two days.

Three nights.

That was how long we'd been here, trapped inside Paolo's hell. He'd created a cycle I wasn't sure was going to end. For hours he'd hurt me in any way he wanted, then he'd leave, appearing again just as my body was starting to rest. The only positive was that he'd concentrated on me, leaving Aida out of it after he'd ripped her back to shreds.

Each time he disappeared for a few hours, I was sure it would be our chance to break free, to get away from him, but he knew what he was doing. He never left us alone, always placing guards on the two exits that I'd been tracking. There weren't any cameras that I could see, no cars coming and going. It was locked up tight, just like I'd expected.

Except…there was a fundamental flaw in his plan. He wasn't a native, but his guards were. I recognized each and every one of them as people who had crossed me before. All of them had a missing limb, and I wondered how Paolo had managed to find them. It had taken hours of watching Aida passed out for me to finally realize that this wasn't a quick, off-the-cuff thing.

Veev had been in my life for years, trying to get closer and closer to me, and if it hadn't been for Aida, she'd be in that position now. She'd been his inside person, the one who was able to relay all of the information back to him.

I glanced at Aida, my stomach churning at how at peace but also in pain she looked. Part of me was glad her body was passing out and protecting her because it meant she didn't have to witness what Paolo had been doing to me. He'd gotten bored of her and paid extra special attention to me, and that was exactly how I wanted it. The more his eyes were turned to me, the less she had to suffer.

The door squeaked open, and the bodyguard stood to attention. They were starting to tire of their jobs, a clear sign that they had no loyalty to Paolo. He paid them to do the work only true loyalty could take care of.

Paolo stepped inside the warehouse, the sunlight blaring in behind him, and I knew from the moment Paolo had landed in the States, this had been his plan. Aida hadn't, though. She'd just been a wrench thrown in the works.

A wrench he'd used against me.

A wrench he was going to regret.

He clapped his hands, causing Aida's head to snap up. Her face screwed up, a groan ripping from the back of her throat. I couldn't see her back from here, but I had no doubt the longer she sat there with it trying to heal, the worse it would get. It made getting out of here even more of a priority. I just had to work out how. I'd gone over and over scenarios in my head, tried to figure out if someone would find where we were, but I knew it was down to me. *I* had to get us out of this. *I* had to end Paolo's reign of terror before it was too late.

"Time for round…" He paused, halting in the middle of the warehouse and tilting his head up to the leaky roof. It had rained over the last few hours, leaving behind wet patches on the concrete. "Huh." He shrugged, then continued forward. "I've lost count." He halted next to Aida, winking down at her. "Shall we have some more fun?" He knelt down next to her, slipping his hand up her leg and to her knee. All I could think about was chopping it off. My mouth salivated at the thought, my brain working overtime on all of the ways I would destroy him for hurting her.

She narrowed her eyes on him, her feistiness pushing through, but she didn't answer. She stayed silent, having worked out that it didn't matter what you said to him, nothing made a difference to what he was going to do.

He reached up, lightning quick, and grabbed her face in his hand, squeezing so hard that her lips puckered at the force. "Answer me."

Her gaze flicked over to me, a question in her eyes. I shook my head, pulling at the binds on my wrists some more and feeling something tugging at them. I thought I'd had my opportunity to escape when he'd changed the way I'd been tied up, but he knew exactly what to do to keep me under control. A gun pressed to Aida's head had done the trick, but he'd made a mistake coming back into the room this time.

I was focused on the fact that he'd come back in here in only a shirt and slacks. His jacket was gone, and so was his holster he kept his gun in. He'd been too focused on getting back in here sooner than he should have, and now he'd opened everything up. Now he'd signed his own death warrant. Only one guard stood at the door, a guard who had been standing there for at least fifteen hours. He hadn't been there the first time Paolo had hurt Aida, and from the way the guard was slowly moving forward, he didn't like what Paolo was doing.

I slowly moved my attention to the guard who was halfway to us, and when his gaze met mine, I frowned. He'd been the soldier who'd tried to steal from me on our wedding day, the one who had been brought to me for punishment. He blinked, darting his gaze left and right, but there were only the four of us in here.

Paolo stood, and the soldier froze to the spot. I tried to keep my attention on him, silently asking what he was doing, but I couldn't focus on him when I needed to make sure Aida was okay.

"Disrespectful!" Paolo spat, raising his hand and slapping her across the face. Her head whipped to the side, a bright red handprint marking her skin. "I'll teach you how to respect a man." He grabbed her neck, squeezing her delicate skin, just as his other hand tore her dress, exposing her. The ropes binding her stomach kept the rest of the material in place, but it didn't stop him from accessing her naked chest.

Aida's gaze snapped to mine again, tears shining in her eyes, then she glanced next to me, her frown intensifying as she tried to breathe against Paolo's grip around her neck. I fought at the binds around my wrists. I straightened my back, the bindings stretching taut, then turned my wrist as far as I could, feeling to the end of the rope. It whispered over my fingertip, and I stretched as far as I could, grasping on to it and feeling a breath of relief wash through me. I tugged at it, but nothing happened. Nothing released. I was frantic, trying to get the fuckin' ropes off and to Aida before Paolo did something to her that I wasn't sure she'd be able to come back from. She was one of the strongest women I knew, but that didn't mean she could take his torture over and over again.

She gasped, her face turning purple. Paolo laughed, pawing at her chest and making her squirm. Each of her movements had her crying out in pain. I couldn't take it anymore. I couldn't take him touching her. I was going to combust if I didn't—

A hand landed on mine, and I jumped, about to ask what the fuck was going on, but a voice said, "Shhh." The guard. What was he doing? I turned just enough to see his face crouched behind me. His one hand pulled on the ropes, but it was no use. He couldn't get them undone either.

I glanced at Aida out of the corner of my eyes and saw Paolo move back a step. We both paused, waiting to see what he would do, and when the sound of his zipper ricocheted in the warehouse, panic set in.

"I can't get it," the guard grumbled, keeping his voice low enough so only I could hear him.

I whipped my head around, trying not to watch what Paolo was doing. He bent at the waist, his focus entirely on Aida. Her gaze veered to me, a small frown working its way between her brows. I shook my head, trying to silently tell her not to say a word. The longer he was preoccupied with her, the more time it would allow me to do what I needed to.

"Knife," I whispered, staring at the tools Paolo had laid out next to me days ago.

The guard slid over to it, not moving from behind me, and grabbed the knife. He pushed it between my hands, the sharp edge slicing at my skin. I gritted my teeth together, finally focusing on Aida again. I wasn't overthinking the fact that the man who had been with the undercover FBI agent and had begged for me not to hurt him was now trying to set me free. I didn't think about the way he rushed to saw through my bindings. He was helping me—helping us—and if we made it out of here alive, I'd make sure he was rewarded.

I shook my head, trying to keep my attention in the moment and not on the hope of being free from here—free to live our lives. Using all of my strength, I pulled my hands apart, giving resistance so the knife would go through quicker.

"I haven't had a pretty girl like you for a while," Paolo said, his tone turning predatory. His hips bucked forward, his slacks coming down just a little, and I knew then he'd pulled his cock out. His fingers jammed against her mouth, yanking her lips apart, and then *finally*, the binds snapped free. It was so loud I was sure he'd hear us, but he didn't. He was too occupied with what he was doing to my wife.

I leaned forward, holding in my groan at the way my burned skin on my stomach and chest pulled, threatening to knock me off-kilter, but I couldn't worry about that now. We were close, so close I could taste our freedom. My fingers fumbled at the ropes on my legs, unable to figure out how the hell to undo them until light glinted off the knife the guard had used. I took it from him, sawed at the ropes, and finally, I was free.

Paolo shuffled forward, lining himself up at Aida's mouth. I dropped the knife to the ground, the sound of it clanking, causing Paolo to pause.

I stood, my lips pulling into a sneer. This was it. This was my moment.

A hand touched my arm, and I flicked my gaze to the guard. He held a gun out to me, his throat bobbing as I stared at it. Everything was happening in slow motion, my brain taking in everything around me. It begged for me to hurt Paolo, to torture him in all the ways I'd imagined over and over again.

But that wasn't what my heart told me. I'd always listened to my head, but as I took the gun from the guard, I knew it was time to listen to my heart.

I extended my arm, stepping over Veev's decaying body, and growled, "Time's up, old man."

His body tensed, his arms moving as he slipped himself back into his slacks. Aida sat up straighter, the hope in her eyes shining as bright as the morning sun. He turned, slowly and carefully, as if he knew his fate had been sealed.

The guard shuffled next to me, not moving from my side. I'd taken from him, yet his loyalty had him standing with me.

Paolo's gaze met mine, his eyes shuttering all of

his emotions down in a millisecond. He opened his mouth, but I was done with him talking.

"I promised myself I would torture you." I paused, taking another step toward him. "But knowing you're no longer breathing is enough." I squeezed the trigger, the bullet flying through the air and ripping straight through his head. He stood, his body swaying to the side, his life draining from his eyes. His body was trying to fight, but it was too late. He was done.

His body slumped forward, crashing to the ground, right on top of Veev. I pointed the gun down at him, firing off another two rounds into his head to make sure I'd finished the job. I wasn't taking chances, not now.

"Lorenzo," Aida gasped out.

I snapped my attention her way and darted forward, diving for her. The guard picked up the knife and ran behind her. "It's okay, baby." I pressed my hand to her face, trying to smile at her. "I got you now." She nodded, wincing as the binds broke free. She inhaled a breath, pushing through the pain as I reached for her dress and held it up, covering her as much as I could. "I love you," I confessed, unable to keep it in a moment longer. I'd waited to tell her, trying to find the right time, but I knew that there never was a right time. I'd nearly missed my moment with her, but I'd spend the rest of my life making sure I'd never miss a single opportunity to tell her how I felt.

She choked out a sob, her legs now free, and reached for me. "I love you too, Lorenzo." Her arms wrapped around my neck. "So damn much."

CHAPTER

21

AIDA

I held on to him, too afraid to let go. We were finally free, but that didn't mean we were out of the woods yet. We were still in the warehouse, trapped inside, not knowing what was on the other side of the door.

"Don't let go," Lorenzo said, wrapping his arm around me and boosting me higher. He turned us so he could face the soldier who had helped us get free. A soldier who had watched Paolo torture us over and over again. "How many soldiers?" Lorenzo barked, his arms moving. Metal clinking told me he was checking how many bullets he had in his gun.

"Five," the soldier stammered. "Three in the hall and two outside."

I felt Lorenzo nod, and for a brief second, I closed my eyes. Hope built within me as he started to move across the warehouse, but when the door opened, and bullets flew our way, it diminished, a flame being snuffed out.

Lorenzo dipped us behind a corner, shots still coming our way, and grasped the side of my face. "Can you walk?"

I stared into his dark eyes, wincing as I moved, but knew that if he had to carry me, there was no way we'd both get out of here alive. It was time to be brave, time to put all of my pent-up anger at what we'd been through to use. "I'll try."

He nodded, planted a kiss on my lips, and took a breath. "Hold on to me. Don't let go." He paused. "Ever." He was talking about more than in this moment, and all I wanted was to tell him that I had no intention of letting go, but instead, I dropped my legs from around him, my bare feet touching the cool concrete floor. "Ready?"

"Ready." I grasped on to his pants, staying close but giving him enough room to make his shots. He fired off the gun three times, then smacked his back into the wall.

"Three down," he huffed out, bringing the gun higher and pulling the clip out. "Two bullets left."

My breaths came faster. There were still two soldiers left, and from the way he'd shot the three in here, I knew he had good aim, but that didn't mean he'd be able to use his last two shots just as well.

Lorenzo's chest heaved as he took a breath, and

with one last look at me, he grabbed my hand and ran across the warehouse. I wasn't sure where we were heading, and I didn't think Lorenzo knew either, but there was only one hallway with one door at the end. A stream of light cascaded from the edge of it; a beacon calling to us.

He didn't let go of me as he moved toward it, keeping his back to the wall, and I was right there next to him, not willing to be apart from him. He slammed his palm down on the door, then waited.

"What—"

The metal door flung open, and as soon as the first soldier stepped inside, Lorenzo let off one shot, hitting him right between the eyes.

"Fuck!" a deep voice shouted, but Lorenzo was lightning quick, twisting his body around the half-open door and letting off his final shot. The sound of a body hitting the ground had my shoulders slumping, and I knew then, we were free. We were *finally* free.

My head spun as I leaned my shoulder against the scratchy brick wall. All of the fight was leaving my body, my brain trying to shut down, but I couldn't let it, not yet, not until we were away from here. I blinked several times, trying to clear the blurriness from my eyes as Lorenzo dipped outside, then darted back in.

"Stay with me, baby." He bent, his one arm coming beneath my thighs and his other at the base of my back. He was trying not to touch the wounds on my back, but what he didn't know was that every single time I moved, they burned like a hot poker was thrusting inside of me. "We're nearly there," he whispered, running toward the door.

I gasped as the air slapped off my bare back. "It hurts," I groaned, finally feeling like I could tell him. I'd tried my hardest to keep up a front, but when it was just him and me, I could let the barriers down.

"Keys," Lorenzo barked, and I opened my eyes, seeing the soldier again. His gaze met mine, his pale face telling me that he wasn't sure whether he was going to live or die.

"I…"

"Keys. Now," Lorenzo gritted out, moving his hand off the base of my back.

The soldier placed them in his palm and took several steps back. "What…what happens now?" the soldier asked.

"Now, you run." Lorenzo straightened up, and I knew without looking at him that he meant business. "You get a one-time pass for helping us out of there." He paused, his chest heaving. "But if I see you in the city again, I won't hesitate to kill you for becoming *his* soldier."

"I…I…"

Lorenzo spun around, and I was glad we didn't have to stand and listen to him any longer. I was grateful he'd helped us, but he'd also stood in that warehouse and watched as Paolo tried to break us down and break us apart.

I gripped Lorenzo tighter as he ran across the yard, not knowing where he was going, but when he halted, I saw the edge of a car. "Lie on your front," he told me, yanking open the back door. I felt the tears building as he maneuvered me into the back of the car and bit down on my bottom lip to stop them from falling. The car smelled like raw meat, but I didn't care because this was our only way out of here.

He stroked my hair, his lips connecting with the side of my face as he said, "We're out now, baby. We're out."

———

LORENZO

I didn't care how many laws I broke driving from the other side of the city and back to the mansion. Every gasp and groan of pain coming from Aida had my foot pressing harder against the gas pedal. I'd left behind a bloodbath, but it still hadn't sated the rage inside me. I needed something more, I needed—I needed Aida to be okay.

"We're nearly there," I rushed out as I turned the corner to our street. The mansion gates were closed, with several soldiers standing outside of them. They were focused straight ahead, their guns in plain sight for everyone to see, and yet they hadn't even noticed me speeding up the street. It was time to get new soldiers, that much was clear.

I swerved to a stop, beeping my horn at them, but it took several seconds until they realized who I was. When they did, they spoke into their radios, and the gates whooshed open.

Slamming my foot down again, I sped through the gates and to the main doors. The engine stayed running as I pushed out and ran around to Aida, wincing as the wounds on her back had opened back up again, blood pouring out of them and staining her skin. I may have spent more time being physically tortured by Paolo, but she was the one who had taken the brunt of it. She was the one who had come off so much worse. Most importantly, she was the one who didn't deserve it.

"Lorenzo!" Ma screamed, but I didn't turn to look at her. I stayed focused on Aida, trying to help her out of the back of the car. "Lorenzo!" Ma shouted again.

"Call the doctor," I barked out, placing my hands under Aida's arms. "Get him here *now*!"

Footsteps rushed toward us, and several sets of hands reached for Aida, but my growl of warning was enough to get them to back off. I pulled her halfway out, enough so she could place her feet on

Lorenzo Beretta

the ground, and as soon as she was upright, I hauled her to me, needing to feel her against me.

Everything was a blur as we rushed into the mansion and into the living room—the closest room to the front doors. I didn't let go of her as I sat us down, keeping her front to my front. Eyes widened around us, gasps and curses flung around, but I didn't look at a single one of them.

My anger was building again, but this time for an entirely new reason. We'd been missing for nearly three days, and no one had found us. Had they even been fuckin' looking? Conversations around me started up, whispers about what they were witnessing, but I didn't need to hear any of it, not right then, not when Aida's soft cries were floating into my ears, threatening to destroy me.

I lifted my head, my narrowed eyes glancing around the room. Christian stood with Dante and Mateo, my two uncles behind them, and Ma and Sofia were on the other side, their faces pale. There were a thousand things I wanted to say, but I didn't voice a single one of them as we waited for the doctor to come.

I wasn't sure how long we all stared at each other, but as soon as Doctor Dubeke walked in the door, a sigh of relief washed through me. His gaze met mine, then swerved to Aida's back.

"Fuck," he whispered.

I heaved a breath as he came closer, flinching as

365

he reached out but didn't quite touch her back. "She's going to need stitches." He paused. "Lots of them."

"Stich her up, then," I demanded.

"I…" Doctor Dubeke glanced around the room, his face paling. "I'm not even going to ask how it happened."

"Good, because I wouldn't fuckin' tell you." I stared him down, silently telling him to fix the woman who meant most to me.

"I need her on a table."

I nodded, not hesitating as I stood, placing a soft kiss on the side of Aida's head as she sobbed from the movement. "It's okay, baby." I moved past everyone and into the dining room, slowly lowering her to the table. I set her on the edge, bent my knees so our faces were level, and told her, "You got this."

"I don't think I do," she whispered, her gaze flicking behind me.

"You do." I placed my hands on either side of her face and pressed my forehead to hers. "You do. You're so strong. So much stronger than anyone knows."

Her beautiful eyes welled up with more tears, but a deep breath was all it took for her to hold them in. "Okay." She paused, her eyes closing for the briefest of seconds until they opened back up. "I got this." She looked behind me again. "Ma and Sofia can stay with me."

"No. I'm stay—"

She placed her finger over my mouth, her own lips pulling up into the barest of smiles. "You need to handle business." She nodded. "Go be the Mafia boss I know and love." I shook my head, every bone in my body wanting me to stay. "I'm not going anywhere. I'm safe now."

She was right.

She was safe here.

Safe with me.

"Fine." I stepped back, hating that I wasn't touching her any longer. "I'll be as quick as I can."

"It's going to take me a couple of hours," Doctor Dubeke said, placing his kit on the table.

I pulled in another breath, needing to calm my racing heart, and turned, feeling like I was missing half of my body as I stepped back into the hallway. There was a time when I wanted nothing more than to *not* be around her, but it was all so different now. I was different. She was different. *We* were different.

I'd married her to become the Mafia boss, and now was the time to be that person. To find out what the fuck happened.

My gaze met Christian's, and I didn't have to say a single word as I darted into my office. I headed right for my whisky, pouring the biggest goddamn glass of the amber liquid, and waited for the sound of the door to close.

I told myself to take it steady, to be calm, but as

soon as I turned back around and saw the five men in my office, I couldn't keep my anger down. "What the fuck happened?"

No one spoke, all of their faces frozen as they stared at me until Mateo said, "I…" He blinked. "You were dead."

"Does it look like I'm dead?" I fumed. My skin burned hot, my rage bubbling over and threatening to ruin everything in its path.

"I…I watched them." Mateo shook his head, the dark purple bruises on his face telling me that he hadn't gotten away without any injuries either. "When I woke up, the SUV was burning and—"

"They found two bodies in there," Dante finished for him, stepping forward. "They thought it was you and Aida."

I chugged back the whisky, trying to make sense of what they were saying.

"What happened?" Uncle Antonio asked, his deep voice deceptively calm, but I knew it was an act.

"Paolo." I snapped my head up, looking at each of them in turn. "He never left the country. He wanted to take over the business." I laughed, leaning against the edge of my desk. Tiredness was setting in quickly. "He made it look like we were already dead, so you wouldn't come looking for us." I shook my head. "Clever. Real fuckin' clever."

"Where is he now?" Dante asked, his hands

clenched at his sides. I hadn't seen him since he'd stormed out of my office, but now he was here, his rage trying to match mine.

"Dead. And so is his daughter."

"Daughter?" Uncle Alonzo asked, frowning at me. "Paolo doesn't have a daughter."

I scrubbed my hands over my face, not wanting to relive this but knowing I didn't have a choice. "Yeah, he did." I paused. "Veev. Veev was his daughter."

"Was?" Dante asked, his lips pulling up into a smirk. "You killed her too?"

"Damn fuckin' straight I did." I pulled in a breath, wincing as Aida's cries thrashed through the mansion. I stood. I wasn't going to do this, not right now. There was nothing left to do but fill them in on what had happened, and it could wait. The threat was over. I'd made sure of that. "Meeting tomorrow morning," I stated, clearing my throat as I took a step away from the desk. "I'll fill you all in then, but right now...right now I need to be with my wife."

They all nodded in understanding, not that they had a choice anyway. I was the boss. I was the one in charge.

"I won't be here," Dante murmured. I halted halfway to the door, my gaze meeting his. "I'm leaving for the other side of the state. Remember?"

I frowned. I did remember. The only contact we'd had since he'd stormed out of my office was for him to have permission to move away for a while, to create his own soldiers. To find his own path.

"I'll call you." I placed my hand on his shoulder. "Be careful out there, brother."

"I will."

I took one final look at the men who were closest to me, the men who thought I was dead, and knew that if I lost it all, it wouldn't matter, not as long as Aida was at my side.

EPILOGUE

AIDA

I waited at the bottom of the aisle, nerves rolling around in my stomach as if this was the first time I was doing this. Twelve months ago, I'd been standing at the end of an aisle, not realizing how much my life would change. I thought I'd had an idea, but I hadn't, not really. Back then, I'd had no expectations, but now I did. Now I knew what waited for me, and I wanted nothing more than to run to him, kiss him, hold him, but more importantly, start the rest of our lives.

There was a thin line between love and hate. A line I'd traveled over the last year. A line that had been scrubbed out, leaving Lorenzo and me standing next to each other instead of on opposite sides. It had been a long, winding road to this point, but as soft music played, signaling it was time, I knew it had all been worth it.

The grass in our backyard whispered across my feet as I started walking, following the flower petals Vida had laid out, marking the path I needed to take. My gaze flicked around the small gathering, only people who mattered the most in attendance. Christian and Mateo were in the front row next to Lorenzo's ma and Sofia. Mateo smiled at me, and I lifted my lips in return. A small bump in his nose was the only indication that it had been broken that night, but I knew he was forever changed just the way Lorenzo and I were. Mateo had been left behind, an insignificant person to anyone else, but they'd never know how important he was to us. He was part of this family, a family that I'd go to battle for.

I frowned as I spotted the empty seat in the row. Dante had been invited, but we hadn't heard back from him, not since he'd moved to the other side of the state. Lorenzo had said he was giving him space, letting him find himself, but I didn't think that was what he needed. He needed to be with his family, not on the outskirts of it.

I shook my head, trying to get rid of my thoughts as I glanced at Vida, who stood on a chair in the front row on the left side along with my ma, dad, and Noemi. I stepped forward. Every moment that I'd spent with Lorenzo had been one I wouldn't change, not now, not ever. He was my destiny. A destiny I had no control over.

I tried to soak in every moment as I started walking past the chairs, but I couldn't stop the memories bubbling up. Memories that I'd spent what felt like a lifetime trying to get rid of, but the scars remained, both physical and mental. I halted in the middle of the aisle, needing something to ground me, and as soon as I met Lorenzo's stare, I knew that was all I needed. We silently relived everything that had happened in the warehouse all of those months ago, but we also acknowledged how far we'd come since then too.

My back was healed, leaving behind puckered skin, but deep down, I knew I wouldn't heal fully. I wasn't sure anyone could after an ordeal like that.

Lorenzo took a step toward me, moving away from the altar, and everything faded away. I got lost in his dark eyes, got lost in the smile on his face. He consumed every part of me, and there wasn't a single thing I'd do to change that. He was it for me. He'd always be it.

He didn't stop until he was only a few feet away, his hand extended for me. I took it without a single hesitation, knowing I couldn't live without him. "Hey, baby," he whispered. His white linen slacks and shirt danced on his body as the wind flowed around us, and he didn't waste a single second planting his lips onto mine. His arm wrapped around my back, and I winced. It didn't hurt, not anymore, but it was a knee-jerk reaction.

His palm flattened over the thin material of my flowy white dress. We'd both purposefully worn white to signal a fresh start. We'd said our vows a year ago to the date, but today would mark the beginning of the rest of our lives.

"That's meant to wait until after the ceremony!" Noemi shouted, and I couldn't help but grin at her words. She was right, but Lorenzo and I didn't follow the rules—we broke them.

I pulled away, just enough to look into his eyes, and breathed out, "Hey."

He grinned, his eyes showing me every emotion they could. He didn't keep anything shuttered away from me. He was open and honest, to a point where sometimes I wished he'd keep some things secret, but I knew he was doing it so that I was never caught off guard again. He'd promised he'd spend the rest of his life making it better, but what he didn't know was him simply standing beside me was all I needed.

"Ready to do this?" he asked.

"With you?" I paused. "Always."

Acknowledgments

My first *huge* thank you needs to go to Paige. You're the most awesomest Alpha Reader and PA. Thank you for loving my stories as much as I do, and generally just being you! But most of all, thank you for reading these on a time constraint. I'm not sure what I'd do without you!

Thank you to my husband and two awesome daughters who never fail to make me smile and continue to support the crazy road that is being an author. I love you all lots and lots like jelly tots!

My next thank you has to go to Jenn, my editor. I swear you saved my life and I appreciate so much you understanding everything that has been going on and *still* fitting me in. You're the best Canadian a girl could ask for!

Linda. I swear I'd be lost without you! Thank you soooo much for everything you do. You're always there no matter what, and I'm not sure what I'd do without you! You push me when I need to be pushed, and tell me to slow down when I need to stop. You save my ass more times than I can count, and I love you!

My proofreader, Judy. Thank you for putting up with me! Thank you for switching dates with me constantly. I swear, one of these days I'll be on time. Never leave me, because I'd be lost without you!

I'd liked to say a huge thank you to my BETAs readers: Nikki & Yvonne. You ladies are amazeballs and I couldn't do this without your continued support.

To my ARC team. You ladies are simply amazing and I love for each and every one of your messages! Thank you for taking the time to ready my stories, I appreciate so much.

To the bloggers who help share EVERY-THING. I love you so much, and I can't put into words how grateful I am! You are a special bunch of people who continue to put a smile on my face.

To all the authors in the community. You continue to support me and I can't thank you enough for that. I love our little slice of heaven, and wouldn't want to be anywhere else!

Lastly, I want to say thank you, to *you*. Thank you for taking a chance on this book. Thank you for reading. And thank you for being awesome!

MAC SECURITY SERIES (Alpha Security/Military)

Book 1: Fractured Lies

Book 2: Exposed

Book 2.5: Flying Free (Standalone Spin-off)

Book 3: The Distance Between Us

Book 4: ReBoot

Book 5: Catching Teardrops

Six Book Boxset

THE EASTON FAMILY SAGA

Fallen Duet (Forbidden Angst)

Book 1: Free Fall

Book 2: Down Fall

Fated Duet (Student/Teacher Angst)

Book 1: Defy Fate

Book 2: Obey Fate

Bonded Duet (Age gap/Forbidden Angst)

Book 1: Torn Bond

Book 2: Tied Bond

Burned Duet (Age Gap/Emotional Angst

Book 1: Fast Burn

Book 2: Deep Burn

———

CONFESSIONS SERIES (Romantic Comedies)

Book 1: Confessions Of A Klutz

Book 2: Confessions Of A Chatterbox

Book 3: Confessions Of A Fratgirl

———

BROKEN TRACKS SERIES,

(co-authored with Danielle Dickson)

Book 1: Etching Our Way

Book 2: Fighting Our Way

———

A. A. DAVIES (Darker, alter ego)

Inferno World Novella

Verboten (Extreme Taboo.)

Carnaval Series

————

About the Author

Abigail is the author of over twenty novels; her favorite to write being anything full of angst and drama. Her writing space is her safe haven where she can get lost—and tortured—in the world of her characters.

When not writing, Abi is mother to two beautiful daughters, a black cat, and a chocolate labrador.

Follow Abi on Facebook and Instagram to see all of her latest updates, and consider signing up to her newsletter to get a free novella!

Connect with Abigail

Reader group: Abi's Aces
Newsletter
www.abigaildaviesauthor.com

facebook.com/abigaildaviesauthor

twitter.com/abigailadavies

instagram.com/abigaildaviesauthor

goodreads.com/abigaildavies

bookbub.com/authors/abigail-davies

amazon.com/author/abigaildavies

pinterest.com/abigaildaviesauthor

Printed in Great Britain
by Amazon